'So? What

Richard looked

'That is what I wonder every day,' Meg
answered. 'Why am I here, Richard? Why are
you trying so hard to change me? What was
wrong with me before you brought me to this
place?'

'Nothing, Meg. I have no wish to change you.'
A husky note deepened his voice. The tone in
which he spoke, caressingly soft, affected her.
It weakened her, as if she had been struck by a
blow in the ribs, but there was no pain, only an
overwhelming joy.

For **Olga Daniels**, home is a sixteenth-century reed-thatched farmhouse in Norfolk. Her study overlooks the beautiful gardens created by her husband, Stan. History clings to the ancient ivy-clad flint walls, the nearby round-towered Saxon church and the waterways and marshes of Broadland. A lovely, lonely place, the inspiration for Olga's tales of romance and intrigue. 'Love is the most intangible of all human emotions,' she says, but she has no doubt of its existence, its strength and its power.

A ROYAL
ENGAGEMENT

Olga Daniels

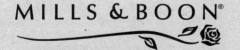

MILLS & BOON®

**To Luke,
wishing him all the good things in life.**

*First published in Great Britain 1999
Harlequin Mills & Boon Limited,
Eton House, 18-24 Paradise Road, Richmond, Surrey TW9 1SR*

© Olga Daniels 1999

ISBN 0 263 81948 5

*Set in Times Roman 10½ on 12 pt.
04-0002-75447*

*Printed and bound in Spain
by Litografia Rosés S.A., Barcelona*

Chapter One

1539

It was market day in Norwich, and the city was crowded. Not only had the countryfolk walked in from the villages and hamlets round about, but most of them had brought in livestock and produce to sell. Anything and everything that might be marketable was penned or tied up or offered in baskets or sacks. On that fine summer day most of the people who lived within the high flint walls of the city were also out, filling the narrow streets. They were haggling and bargain-hunting, drinking and eating, or just gathered together for a good old gossip.

Meg, or Lady Margaret Thurton to give her full name, was threading her way back towards the nunnery, with a rush basket hooked on one arm. She lifted her skirts in a hopeless attempt to prevent them from being muddied and messed by the muck and puddles left by passing animals, or the even more unpleasant rubbish tipped from the overhanging upper storeys of the houses that lined the street. She shouldered her way through the crowd, just as everyone else did, and she was dressed just as everyone else was, too, in rough homespun garments.

She hurried down Goat Lane and turned into Pottergate, aware that she had been out for longer than usual for she had found poor old Betsy Carter so ill she could no longer move from the straw mattress on which she lay, crippled with arthritis. Meg had administered a dose of physic she had made from herbs grown in the priory garden or gathered from the heath beyond the city walls.

'Bless you, my dear,' the old woman murmured as she settled back on the pillows and closed her eyes.

She was so weak and frail that Meg was reluctant to leave her, for there was no one to look after her other than her husband, Davy, and he was blind and rather soft in the head, and more often out of the house, as now, than at home. Meg sat on beside old Betsy, gently holding her thin, twisted hand.

'I was so sorry to hear that your dear mother had died,' Betsy said, and tears glistened in her eyes. 'I remember so clearly when she first brought you to see me. You were but a wee mite of a thing then.'

'That must be fourteen years ago—I was about three years old—' Meg broke off, too choked to continue.

Her mother, Lady Elizabeth Thurton, had then been newly widowed, and had been forced to flee when her villainous brother-in-law, Edmund, Earl Thurton, had seized all his older brother's property: the castle, its vast estates and his wealth. His heartbroken widow had had no strength to resist the Earl's claims. When she had protested, he had threatened physical violence, not only towards herself, but also to little Meg.

Knowing him to be utterly ruthless, Lady Elizabeth had fled to the nunnery on the outskirts of Norwich, where the Prioress was a distant relation. She had received them coolly, but as part of her religious duty had provided all that they needed, including the privacy of a small suite of rooms, befitting their noble status. There they had lived in modest comfort, frugally but in safety, and Meg had known no other life.

Now everything was to change. There was fear throughout the order. King Henry VIII had issued an edict for the dissolution of all religious houses, and that included the Benedictine nunnery. The future was uncertain for all the inmates, and Meg had nowhere to go, no one to whom she could turn. The one thing she knew for certain was that she had no calling for the religious life. A shiver of fear ran over her at the unknown future.

'You better go, my lady,' old Betsy said. 'Don't you worry about me—'

She would soon drift away into a sleep partly induced by the herbal sedatives.

'I'll come again tomorrow,' Meg promised, though even as she said it she wondered if Betsy would last another day. As always, she was saddened to realise how little she could do to ease the sufferings of the poor people.

Now, out in the narrow street, she struggled through the crowd, making her way back to the priory as quickly as she could.

'Clear the way.' An imperious voice was raised above the cries of vendors and the chatter of country voices.

The shout was reinforced by the clatter of horses' hooves.

'Make way for your betters, you scum.'

Meg looked behind her in amazement; there was scarcely space for pedestrians, let alone horses. Men and women pressed back under the eaves of the overhanging houses, pulling their children with them, lifting the smallest for safety. A narrow gap was opened, through which the horsemen were proceeding, three of them, their magnificent steeds walking, tossing their heads, blowing foam from wide nostrils, as if they had been ridden hard and disliked this slow pace.

Then Meg noticed old blind Davy. He was standing immediately in the path of the horses, gazing around him, bewildered and afraid, not knowing which way to go, unable to understand what was happening.

'Watch out, Davy,' shouted someone. 'Hosses a'comin'.'

One of the horsemen flicked a whip in the direction of the old man; it caught him on the shoulder of his ragged shirt. He tried to turn, to move, too quickly, and his feet slipped in the slime of the gutter. He fell in the path of the horseman.

'Out of the way, old man. Make way for Sir Richard.'

Meg dashed forward. She glared at the horseman. He sat high in the saddle, a dismissive sneer on his haughty face, lank blond hair hanging from beneath his blue velvet cap. His expression betrayed a callous disregard for the people around him.

'Move back,' she shouted.

'Tell him to get up—quick—or he'll be trampled under the horse,' the man growled impatiently.

'Give him time—and space,' Meg flung back at the horseman. 'Old Davy can't see—'

'Shouldn't be out in the street, then.' Sir Richard's man tried to push Meg aside, but she stepped forward and stood defiantly between the horses and old Davy.

'He has as much right as anyone to be out on the King's highway,' Meg said, loud and clear.

'Leave him, Gervase.' The voice was coolly authoritative.

She looked beyond the first rider and caught the eyes of the gentleman behind him, instantly assessing him to be the highest ranking of the three, the one referred to as Sir Richard. The third man remained a few paces behind. He might once have been handsome, but his face was disfigured by a scar that puckered his left cheek. Sir Richard, mounted on a powerful black charger, towered over all. Dark brown hair curled up the sides of his flat hat of crimson velvet, decorated with an ostrich plume. He was richly clad in a broadshouldered doublet, cut square, revealing a strong neck that proclaimed strength and masculinity, and he carried his head proudly.

He returned her gaze and she felt her heartbeat quicken. She was unaccustomed to such a searching look from a gentleman. It infuriated her, yet she gazed back at him, strangely mesmerised, for there was something arresting about his face, something that demanded respect. And though she did not find it handsome—it was too rugged for that—she could not help admiring the strength of his cleanshaven features.

His expression, however, showed only disdain, making her aware not only of the poverty of her costume, but also how dirty and dishevelled she had become from the muddy gutters and the animals' droppings. Still she stared back at him, determined not to allow herself to be cowed by this man, despite the curious effect he was having upon her.

'If he's your grandfather, you should take better care of him, young woman,' he said.

He spoke slowly, with an edge to his voice, as if he had chosen his words deliberately to annoy her, or

maybe just to test her reaction. All the while he continued to run his eyes over her, and, inexperienced though
she was, she knew that look was triggered by the male
in him. How dare he regard her like that? Yet she could
not deny that something deep in her being throbbed in
response—and that infuriated her.

'You should watch where you're going,' Meg replied,
with a sharp toss of her head.

She might at that moment look like the scum of the
earth, and was indeed virtually penniless, but she knew
her own standing. Through her mother she was descended from one of the ancient kings of England,
though she could never remember which. Her self-
esteem and the rightness of her attitude gave her assur-
ance and enabled her to stand her ground.

Sir Richard reined in his horse, bringing it to a standstill as the crowd gathered around, listening in awed
silence to Meg's boldness. They knew her as the young
lady from the priory who, as a child, had accompanied
her mother on errands of mercy to the poor. When the
sweet and kind Lady Elizabeth had become too ill to
carry on with her mission, Meg had continued to visit
those in greatest need. She was safe amongst them, even
though she walked alone, taking herbs and lotions to
those who were sick, loaves of bread to the starving.
They would have defended her if one of their own had
dared to molest her, but to challenge the powerful lords,
as she was doing now, was a different matter.

Her usually soft blue eyes flashed with fury, but she
controlled it and spoke with her normal cultured pre-
cision of tone, which was directed at Sir Richard.

'Kindly move back, sir.'

Careless of her own safety, she moved almost under
the nose of the great horse. She heard the intake of

breath from the crowd, followed by a tense silence. She stood absolutely rigid, staring up at Sir Richard. She had never been so frightened in her life. Time seemed to stand still. Then unexpectedly he lifted his elegant velvet hat in a flamboyant gesture, which could have been gallant had not a sardonic smile twisted one corner of his shapely lips. Then, to her relief, he drew his horse two steps back.

Immediately Meg put a hand under the blind man's arm. 'Are you all right, Davy?' she asked gently.

'My lady—help me. Please help me.' He recognised her voice.

'It's all right.' She spoke to him calmly. 'Try to stand.'

'You knows I doesn't mean no harm.'

'I know, Davy. I won't let them hurt you,' she said. 'Now, then, up on to your feet.'

A young man came forward out of the crowd and took hold of Davy's other arm. Everyone had been afraid to get involved until Meg had moved, but now several willing hands reached out and helped the old man back close against the walls of the houses.

Only Meg now prevented the horsemen from moving on again. She was very much aware of them. The breath from the horses' nostrils wafted over the thin linen of her cap and she kept a watchful eye on their strong sinewy legs. Their hooves pawed restively on the cobblestones; the animals were anxious to move on. She had to trust their riders to hold them back, yet forced herself to ignore them, hiding her fear. She didn't mean to look up, she didn't want to meet that disturbing gaze again, yet perversely she felt drawn to do that.

Her eyes clashed with his. 'What is your name, young woman?' he asked.

'What is that to you?' she countered.

Coolly she picked up the basket which she had set down on the cobbles when she'd gone to Davy's aid. One more glance towards the old man, to make sure he was safe, then, satisfied on that score, she turned sharply. For a few paces she marched along in front of the riders. The sound of their hooves told her they were moving slowly behind her. Nervous though she was, she would not increase her pace, until she reached an alley-way with a steep set of steps. She ran then, through the bystanders, who parted to make way for her, and darted down it, fleet, sure-footed, even in her wooden-soled shoes. It was in the wrong direction, and it would take her half an hour longer to get back to the nunnery and she had already been out longer than usual, but that couldn't be helped. Her one desire was to get away.

Her courage had been false. She was shaking and mightily relieved when she stopped, close to a high wall, and looked back to see the horsemen pass on along the street above. Breathing heavily, she leaned on the wall, glad of its support. Never before had she been so close to gentlemen of quality. It was that, more than the event, that had unnerved her. Until that morning she had spoken to very few men, other than the priests and poor labourers. They had been cringingly subservient, knowing that she was a relation of the formidable Prioress. Never before had she encountered anyone whose eyes had met and held hers with such a challenge. Sir Richard had seemed to be looking right into her inner being, as if he knew some of her secret thoughts— thoughts that she would never have spoken even at confession. She blushed at the very idea.

Thank goodness she was never likely to see him again!

* * *

Back at the priory, Meg slipped in through a small side door that led into the cloisters. She stood for a moment, savouring the cool, calm peace of the place. This was the only home she had ever known.

Her childhood had not been unhappy, for she'd had the love of her gentle mother. Lady Elizabeth had been intelligent and better-educated than most women of her age. She had passed on her knowledge to her daughter, instructing her in those social graces necessary to a lady of breeding as well as reading and writing. An elderly priest, who had been like a grandfather to Meg, had added to that by teaching her Classics and mathematics, as if she had been a boy.

At other times she'd had free run of a large part of the extensive buildings and the well-kept gardens of the nunnery, though there were some parts she was not permitted to enter. These were the magnificent rooms which the Prioress had built for her own private use. That lady was a being apart, aristocratic and wealthy, quite unlike most of the nuns, who came from all walks of life, some from very humble families. Most of them were kind and friendly, and, whenever they were free from their devotions and their work, the younger ones had enjoyed playing with the pretty little girl whose unfortunate mother had so often been unwell.

Slowly, at a pace befitting her surroundings, Meg made her way along the cloister to the suite of rooms that she had shared with her mother. Sarah Wilgress was sitting beside the empty chair which Lady Elizabeth had occupied for many hours in the last months of her life.

'Thank goodness you're back, my lady.' Sarah jumped up as Meg entered. 'You've to get changed into your good clothes and go to the Lady Prioress at once.' She began to pull Meg towards her bed-chamber.

'Why? What has happened, Sarah?'

'All I know is that Sister Obligata came to say the Prioress wanted to see you immediately, and that was half an hour ago. I said as how you was out visiting the sick, just as your dear mother did before she was took ill. Sister Obligata seemed upset about that—well, you know the Prioress never did approve of you goin' out on your own. Now come on through here, an' be quick about it, do; she'll be back a-clackin' on again.'

'I can't possibly visit the Prioress in this state—'

'That you can't, my lady. You gotta get washed and changed right away.' Sarah began to unfasten Meg's clothes even as she spoke. 'You know the Prioress don't like to be kep' waiting.'

'I know, but the town was crowded—and poor old Betsy was so poorly—'

'That I have no doubt, mistress. But do get changed double quick. I've got water in the kettle, an' I've kep' it a-simmering, so's you can get properly cleaned up. Sister Obligata's been back here twice already looking for you. I've put your best gown out—'

Sarah had been brought to the nunnery as a child, orphaned when her parents had died of a fever that had ravaged the countryside. Lady Elizabeth had taken the poor, sad and undernourished child into her motherly care, and she had grown healthy and strong.

Two years older than Meg, Sarah had played with her, and they had grown up like sisters. Sarah had been encouraged to take part in some of Meg's lessons, and had learned to read and write, but she had found little interest in other subjects. She had been happiest when she was sewing or cleaning, or looking after Lady Elizabeth, whom she had adored. When the elderly woman who had been Lady Elizabeth's servant had died, Sarah had insisted that she should be allowed to take her place. No one could have been more loyal and conscientious. She mourned the death of her mistress as deeply as did Meg.

For both of them, as for all the inhabitants of the priory, the King's threats to the monasteries made their future uncertain. But Sarah willingly tackled her daily tasks and sang the old songs of the countryside as she worked. If the Prioress was not about she'd dance too, clattering her wood-soled shoes on the stone floors.

Meg was not unwilling to get out of the muddied everyday clothes. It was good to get washed and feel pleasantly clean again. Sarah stood holding a clean kirtle, ready to drop it over Meg's head, and at once began lacing it up. Her best gown was of blue-green velvet, with a tight bodice, beautifully fitted, enhancing her small waist, decorously edged with narrow frilling and trimmed with pearls. The skirt, long and full, trailed on the ground.

The garments were old-fashioned, for there had never been money to buy anything new for Meg. The beautiful gown had been made for her mother, and she had worn it only once, on the occasion of a grand banquet at Bixholm Castle, shortly before her husband had left for France. He had been killed leading his troops into battle so had never returned.

Meg unfastened her plaits and Sarah brushed out her long fair hair, then covered it with a tight-fitting undercap. Over this went a French hood of black silk with front lappets decorated with a multi-coloured pattern of embroidery.

Even though the transformation was carried out with all possible speed, Sister Obligata came bustling in before they had quite finished. The tiny nun, one of the oldest in the nunnery, was wringing her hands anxiously.

'Wherever have you been, Meg? There's an important visitor waiting to see you.'

'A visitor? To see me?' said Meg. Such a thing had never happened in her life before.

'That's right. Are you ready now?'

'Wheesh, Sister,' admonished Sarah. 'You don't want her gown to be coming apart when she gets to the Prioress's room, now, do you? She'd have the shock of her life!' She pulled the lacing tighter as she spoke.

'Sarah,' admonished Sister Obligata. 'That is no way to speak of the Prioress.'

'I know.' Sarah hung her head, then glanced at Meg and whispered, 'But it's true, my lady, isn't it?'

Meg shook her head reprovingly, but could not keep the smile from her lips. She turned to the little nun.

'Sister, dear, why is there such a hurry? Who wants to see me?'

'You'll find out soon enough. No need for me to tell you,' said Sister Obligata. 'Come along now.'

Despite her age and small stature she set off at a pace that was almost undignified for one in holy orders. Realising it would be useless to ask any further questions, Meg followed in silence. They waited briefly outside the solar. The little nun cast a critical eye over Meg, tweaked at one of the lappets, then knocked on the door.

'Enter.'

Meg braced herself. Visits to the Prioress had never brought her any joy in the past. They had usually followed some small misdemeanour over which the Prioress had lashed out with her stinging tongue. She prepared herself for the encounter on this occasion, as she had done in the past, by holding herself very upright, her head high and an expression of defiance on her face.

Sister Obligata opened the door and indicated that Meg should pass through, whilst she remained outside and closed the door. Meg stepped into the sumptuous apartment of her distant relative—and almost cried out in surprise. Her heart began to thump violently and her mouth felt suddenly dry. She stood stock-still, stunned, taking in the scene.

The Prioress, as she had expected, was seated on one side of the stone fireplace—but opposite her was the horseman she had encountered in the street that morning. The one they had called Sir Richard. He sprang to his feet. She stared at him, lifted a hand to her mouth to stifle a gasp.

'An important visitor waiting to see you,' Sister Obligata had said. What did that mean? Who was he? Why did he want to see her? Was his presence in some way connected with the earlier episode in the street? Had he made a complaint about her behaviour to the Prioress?

Her eyes sought his—she remembered with shame and anger how scornfully he had looked at her then. Now his expression was quite different—for one thing he appeared to be just as surprised as she was. Their eyes met and clashed, yet lingered. He recovered his equilibrium quicker than she did. She saw his expression relax, though his eyes remained fixed on her. It was a searching contemplation, and this time he gave the impression of being pleased with what he saw.

Then he looked down, his gaze moving slowly, taking in the length and slenderness of her neck, which rose elegantly from the square line of her gown, dropping lower to move over the gentle swelling of her bosom to the smallness of her waist. Again that sardonic smile lifted a corner of his lip as his gaze swept back up to her face. She wished desperately that she was able to regard him coolly, but she felt flustered, was aware that she was blushing and unsure of herself. She was quite unable to think of any reason why he should be there, or why he had asked to see her.

'Sir Richard—this is the young lady you have come to fetch; Lady Margaret Thurton, the daughter of my second cousin, Lady Elizabeth Thurton.' The Prioress performed the introductions in her usual haughty manner. Turning to Margaret, she added, 'Sir Richard de Heigham has been sent by your uncle Edmund, Earl Thurton, to escort you to his castle at Bixholm.'

Meg could scarcely believe what she heard. She had no recollection of her uncle, had never even seen him, and everything she knew about him was disturbing. He had forced her mother to flee from Bixholm, even though it had been rightfully hers.

'Lady Margaret.' Sir Richard executed an elegant bow. His voice was smooth and friendly. 'It's a pleasure and an honour to make your acquaintance.'

With her mind in turmoil, Meg pulled herself together and lowered herself in a curtsey. She knew he did not mean those gallant words he uttered. She had no doubt that he had recognised her, and was grateful he made no reference to their encounter earlier in the day. It would have been difficult to explain to the Prioress, whose ideas on seemly behaviour were very different to her own.

'The honour is mine, Sir Richard,' Meg replied, managing at last to take control of herself and speak with studied politeness. Then, turning towards the Prioress, she asked, 'May I ask why I am to be taken to my uncle at Bixholm?'

'I sent a message to your uncle, informing him of the death of your mother, God rest her soul,' said the Prioress. 'Lord Thurton is now your next of kin, Margaret. He replied almost immediately, sending a messenger to enquire about you. I did not inform you before, for I was not sure of the outcome, but as you are now alone in the world he has most generously offered to give you his protection—until he can arrange a suitable marriage for you.'

'M-marriage?' Meg stammered.

'Of course. You are no longer a child, my dear.'

Meg did not recollect ever before such an endearment falling from the tight, thin lips of the Prioress. Far from reassuring her, it increased her alarm. 'Must I go?' she asked.

'It is undoubtedly in your best interest.' The Prioress wore an air of smug satisfaction. 'You should be grateful to your uncle for this beneficent gesture.'

'But I do not know him,' Meg protested. 'He never came here to see me or my mother—'

'Your uncle has a great deal to attend to,' snapped the Prioress. 'He moves in the highest of circles and is in constant attendance at Court. Besides, you must know there was ill feeling between him and your mother; that was the reason she brought you here. Now he is willing to overlook the past, and I deem it exceedingly generous of him to make you this offer.'

'But I have no wish to leave—please, dear Mother Prioress, will you not allow me to stay? I can make myself useful—'

'No, Margaret,' said the Prioress. 'It is all settled. You will go to Bixholm and behave in a manner befitting the training and tuition you have received here in the priory. I trust that you will obey your illustrious uncle and endeavour to please him in every way.'

Meg regarded the Prioress with growing horror. She had never heard a good word about Earl Thurton. She feared him, even more than she feared the Prioress.

'Please—' She was about to plead further but the Prioress silenced her with an up sweep of one long pale hand.

'It is no use arguing, Margaret. I know you have no calling for the religious life. You have told me so in the past.' She brought her lips together tightly, her eyes chilling in their disapproval. 'The priory is soon to be closed. Everyone has to go. Though I shall be permitted to stay on in my own apartments and keep my own staff. I have worried about what should become of you and it was for that reason I wrote to Lord Thurton.'

Meg's last hope faded. She had to accept that she was no more than a chattel, to be passed from one to another, and it was true she had no wish to become a nun. She stood in silence as the Prioress continued.

'This is the ideal solution for everyone. I shall pray that a suitable husband will be found for you, and that you may bear him many strong sons.' Again she clamped her thin lips together, making it absolutely clear she was not prepared to discuss the matter further.

Meg turned to Sir Richard and looked at him with such resentment it was near to hatred. She did not trust him. He and his entourage had been arrogant, careless of the safety of poor old Davy. She was uneasy at the thought of being escorted by such a trio, not least because undoubtedly they were all in the pay of the uncle who had used her mother so cruelly.

'When am I to go?' she asked bleakly.

'We set out in two days' time,' Sir Richard answered.

'We shall rest the horses tomorrow, and leave at dawn the day after.' His manner was coolly practical. He was simply undertaking a mission for his master.

Meg nodded. They would be up at dawn. Everyone in the nunnery was up early for prayers. She was pleased that she would also be able to make one last visit to old Betsy, as she had promised.

'May I take Sarah with me, if she is willing?' she asked.

'Sarah? Oh, your maid? Certainly,' the Prioress agreed easily. Sarah meant nothing to her.

'I would like to assure you, my lady, that you will be perfectly safe,' said Sir Richard.

Meg looked at him keenly but made no reply. She had nothing to say to him. She was deeply troubled about the whole arrangement. Why should her uncle have sent for her? She had nothing. He had robbed her mother of everything that should have been hers. He had forged papers purporting to show that not only was the title to pass to him, but that he should own all the worldly goods that had rightly been her mother's.

Her uncle was a villain—and therefore it followed that this man, Sir Richard, his henchman, who had been sent to fetch her, was not to be trusted either. She would go with him—she had no choice. But she would be on her guard—and she would have as little to do with him as possible.

Chapter Two

Meg was surprised and puzzled by the helpfulness of the Prioress over preparations for her departure. It might have been no more than relief that she would have no further responsibility, even though in past years the lady had shown only a minimum of interest in Meg's well-being. The Prioress had done her duty and no more—and now it became evident that she wished to impress Earl Thurton. She even provided a neat little bay mare for Meg to ride.

Did she know more about the marriage plans than she wished to divulge? Why was it all so sudden and so secretive? She fussed over Meg's apparel, all of which had been handed down from her mother, or had been woven, cut out and stitched by Sarah and the nuns. She seemed to be quite distressed that there was no time for new garments to be made, and presented Meg with an elaborate brooch with which to fasten her cape. She also hired a packhorse to transport Meg's few personal possessions, and a bundle belonging to Sarah.

Sarah had at first refused to undertake the journey. She had been indignant when it was suggested that she should ride pillion behind Alan Crompton, the third member of the party from Bixholm.

'Hosses!' she protested. 'Great big hairy things. I ain't used to 'em, and I don't like 'em. I'd probably fall off!' she had said vehemently.

Meg laughed, then was immediately contrite as she saw real fear on her friend's plumply pretty face. 'You won't fall off, Sarah! Honestly, you'll be perfectly safe. I promise we won't ride too fast.'

'It's all very well for you, my lady. You allus did like ridin'. I ain't never been on the back of a hoss, and I never want to!' Sarah clamped her mouth shut disapprovingly.

Meg was almost in despair. The prospect of going away quite alone was unbearable. 'Please, Sarah, do come with me. I have to go, and I can't manage without you.'

'Yes, you can, my lady. You're no fool.' Sarah could be really stubborn at times.

Meg gave a wry smile, remembering past altercations between them. This time she was determined to win the other girl over. 'I'll be so lonely without you, and anyway, what will you do when they close the priory?'

'Find work somewhere, I suppose.' Sarah's lips trembled slightly. 'Not that I want to work for anyone else. Couldn't I walk beside you, my lady?'

'Sarah, that's impossible—it's much too far. I really do need you. I can't possibly leave you here. We've always been such good friends. Please don't desert me—for I have to go.'

'We-ell.' The word was long drawn-out, showing her reluctance. 'All right. I suppose what is to be will be. I'll come with you—even if it kills me—for I've no wish to be parted from you, my lady.'

'Nor I from you, Sarah.' Meg threw her arms around the other girl and hugged her tightly. 'I'll look after you—always.'

Her feelings were mixed as they rode away from the priory. She realised that the natural course of life for a woman was to be married, and that it was normal for a husband to be chosen by her guardian. She had assumed that some day such an event would happen to her, but had expected that her wedding would be to a gentleman of her mother's choice and in the distant future.

Most particularly it alarmed her that from now on she would be entirely beholden to this uncle of whom she had never heard one single word that was good. Did he already have some marriage of convenience in mind for her? Whoever the gentleman was, he had to be a stranger to her—and she to him—for she knew no men who could be remotely considered as eligible. If he was abhorrent to her, would she be able to refuse? A priest would not perform a marriage ceremony without the bride's consent, but she had heard tales of some who were not as honourable as they should be.

The town was left behind. The horses trotted gently along stony tracks, through the fields and meadows of the open countryside. Villagers were working in their own strips of land, digging, raking, sowing seeds. Spring was a busy time, and they were making the most of the fine weather.

Sir Richard brought his big black charger up to ride alongside her. She was aware that he was there, but she did not turn her head; his nearness fired a tension that alerted previously unknown sensations which were disturbing—though not entirely unpleasant. For some inexplicable reason she had no wish to enter into conver-

sation with him. Her mind raced with questions, but she
was reluctant to reveal her anxiety.

'You ride very well, my lady,' he remarked.

'Thank you, sir,' she responded, coolly polite.

'Did you learn whilst you were at the priory?'

'Of course. I was only three years old when my
mother took me there. She saw to it that I acquired those
skills that would be necessary for life outside its walls.'

'I imagine it must have been restrictive at times. Will
you be glad to be free from that life?'

'Neither glad nor sorry, sir,' she replied truthfully. 'I
have known no other way.'

'You will find things very different at Bixholm.'

'I do not doubt it.'

'Every night there is feasting and dancing. There are
resident musicians and jesters, and sometimes they are
joined by travelling players,' he said.

'I am sure it is very entertaining,' she said. 'But that
will all be new to me.'

They rode side by side for some minutes. She glanced
at him, studied his well-chiselled profile and decided
that he looked much more friendly than when she had
first encountered him. Then he turned towards her and
his face was quite transformed by a smile—he seemed
contented, as if well pleased to be riding with her. How
ever was it that she had decided he was not handsome?

Suddenly it seemed easy and right to ask the question
that had been continually in her mind since that interview with the Prioress. 'My lord, can you tell me—
because I would very much like to know—does my uncle have a gentleman in mind to whom he wishes me
to become betrothed?'

The smile faded from Sir Richard's face. There was
a pause before he replied, and then his words were

vague. 'That is something that he will tell you in due course.'

'I suppose he must already have given some thought to the matter,' she persisted. 'Otherwise he would not have sent for me.'

'Perhaps. I am not privy to the Earl's plans.'

Despite his answer she was sure that he knew more than he was telling. 'Then I shall have to ask him when we arrive at Bixholm,' she said.

'In my opinion, Lady Margaret, it would be wise to leave the matter until the Earl raises it with you.'

His tone sounded ominous. The smile had been replaced by a closed and distant expression. Her fears were reawakened. Of course, he was no friend to her. Why should she expect it? He was in the pay of her uncle. She had allowed herself to be deceived because his face and bearing were attractive to her. She had been a fool to think he might be friendly. She wished he would go away, leave her to travel alone with her thoughts.

He was silent for a time, but continued to ride at her side. Uneasily she turned her head towards him, and was disconcerted to find his eyes looking directly into hers—brown eyes flecked with gold. They seemed gentle, caring, almost as if he was sorry for her—but why should that be? A flush spread up her cheeks and over her face; it made her feel vulnerable and foolish. She looked down at the nodding head of her mare, a pretty animal, and then straight ahead.

'What were you doing when I encountered you in the street?' he asked. His voice was low, pleasantly warm, but she would not allow herself to be cajoled by it.

'Visiting the sick and the poor.'

'Do you enjoy doing that?'

She turned her head sharply, her eyebrows raised. It struck her as a strange question. 'It is necessary,' she said, in a matter-of-fact tone. Did he not know the plight of the poor?

The look she cast upon him disturbed Sir Richard more than he cared to admit. He had felt little enthusiasm for this task when it had been imposed upon him by Earl Thurton, but for reasons of his own he had not cared to question the command. He had no love for the master of Bixholm, whom he knew, to his cost, to be a callous brute. He had simply been given the order to fetch a young woman from a nunnery in Norwich.

'She's just seventeen,' the Earl had said. 'A virgin, ripe for a man. Bring her back here, Richard, and who knows what may happen?'

'Don't tell me you've a mind to wed, after all these years,' Richard said.

'Not I! Nancy would have something to say if I did! Anyway this chit is my niece. There is someone more powerful than I am who is seeking a new wife. Someone who will bestow untold wealth and honours upon a relative who delivers the right goods into his hands—or perhaps, I should say, into his bed.' The Earl chuckled, well pleased with himself.

Richard repressed a shudder. 'The King?' he asked.

Edmund's cunning expression told all. He nodded. 'Exactly. And, as a good and loyal subject, do I not have a duty to bring pleasure and happiness to his majesty? He has suffered sadly since the death of his puny little wife in childbirth.'

It was two years since Queen Jane had died giving birth to the long-awaited heir, Prince Edward. Richard felt a knot tighten in the pit of his stomach as he remembered the fate of the King's previous wife, Lady

Anne Boleyn. The King had tired of her, mainly because, after three years of marriage, she had produced only one living child, and that a daughter, Princess Elizabeth.

The King had then declared that Queen Anne had committed treason, betrayed him by taking a lover. It was well-known that he had already transferred his affections to Jane Seymour, and had had no qualms about signing the death warrant for Anne to be executed on Tower Green. His first wife, Queen Catherine, had also given birth to only a daughter, Princess Mary. Her fate had been a little kinder, for she had been divorced and exiled to the country. It was sons the King wanted, as much to bolster his pride in his masculinity as for the sake of the country.

Richard's voice held a grim note as he answered the Earl. 'I have heard the King is seeking to remarry.'

'Exactly! And I'm told this niece of mine is a beauty! I'd go myself to fetch her, but this accursed gout is playing me up. Bring her back here, Richard, and mind you take good care of her. No nonsense, mind! You so much as touch her and I'll run you through with my own sword.'

'No fear of that, sir.' Richard understood the threat. In fair combat he would have taken the Earl on with the certainty of winning—but that was never Sir Edmund's way of disposing of enemies. A stab in the back by a henchman was more likely. 'I shall guard her honour with my life,' he said.

He had expected no difficulty in keeping that promise when he'd set out on the journey. Secretly he thought the Earl must be mad to believe the lusty King Henry would be tempted by a holy woman, however young and virginal. He had also doubted the Earl's assertion that the woman would be a beauty, especially when he'd heard she had lived all her life in a nunnery. He had expected her to be pale, an insipid creature, not the sort of woman to appeal to him. It had amused him to imagine a relative of the coarse, ugly Earl being in any way attractive to the King.

With regard to the lady's feelings, or to her fate, he had given them no more thought than if he had been sent to fetch a horse or a dog for his master. In any event he had assumed that the woman was amenable— possibly even eager to relinquish life in a nunnery to become Queen of England.

The clash of wills he had witnessed between Meg and the Prioress had changed his mind on that score! She had pleaded strongly not to be sent away—and not because she wished to take the veil! She had evidently rejected that idea some time previously. He commended her for that; it would have been a most regrettable loss to mankind for such a delectable young woman to become a nun. There was nothing insipid about Lady Margaret Thurton! She was of a fiery temperament, though at the moment she appeared to be hiding it. She was also the most fascinating woman he had ever met.

He had noticed her face when he had first seen her, that morning in the crowded street. The brave way she had stood up to him during that encounter had puzzled and interested him. Her habit had been of coarse material, splattered with mud—and worse! There had been a streak of dirt on her cheek. But still something about her had caught and held his attention. His presence had not cowed her in the least; that had been one indication of her breeding. And when he heard her voice, clear and melodious, it had confirmed his impression that she was no ordinary peasant girl.

He would never have harmed the blind man. It had annoyed him that Gervase Gisbon had flicked his whip at the old fellow. There had been no need, but it was typical of the man, who had no time for those less well placed than himself. Richard had been about to order Gervase to draw back when Meg had rushed forward. She had taken him completely by surprise, flung a challenge at him, and he had enjoyed pitting his wits against hers and watching her reaction. He had been disappointed when she'd made off so quickly. He had tried to follow her but had lost sight of her when she'd darted down that alleyway, where it had been impossible for horses to follow.

He had scarcely been able to believe it when she'd walked into the solar where he and the Prioress had been waiting. He had recognised her immediately, despite the change of clothing. Dressed in a gown that was twenty years out of fashion, she was still beautiful, and had a commanding presence. Suddenly he had feared for her—so vulnerable, so young and tender—not at all how he had envisaged the niece of Earl Thurton!

His first feeling at that second meeting had been of delight at seeing her again. Now, with every mile they covered, wending their way towards Bixholm Castle, he became less and less enthusiastic about the fate her uncle was planning for her. Indeed he began to feel quite ridiculously protective towards her. It was probably something to do with the size of her wondrous blue eyes, or perhaps it was the curvaceousness of her lissom figure, her liveliness, for that was evident even when she was silent—and her gentle voice. He was quite disturbed at the thought of any man touching her—other than himself. And he was banned from doing so on pain of death.

That was a sobering thought. No woman would be worth such a sacrifice, he told himself. He must have as little to do with Lady Margaret as he possibly could. His task was to deliver her to her uncle. He must put any other ideas out of his mind. He reminded himself that the Prioress had been more than willing to place her under the guardianship of her uncle. She knew the husband Earl Thurton hoped to bind her to, and he'd had the impression she was delighted at the prospect of the match. It was not for him to interfere. He had his own problems, and any entanglement would only add to those difficulties. He allowed his horse to slow its pace, to leave Meg's side.

Bringing up the rear of the little group was Gervase Gisbon, Earl Thurton's man. Gervase, who had no wish to ride with a serving wench behind him, was leading the packhorse. He regarded Richard with a supercilious smile on his face. There was no love lost between the two.

'Your blandishments aren't cutting much ice with the young lady, Richard?'

Richard bit back the angry answer that was almost on his tongue. Gervase was one of Thurton's most trusted men. He could make trouble if he chose, and he had evidently been keeping a close watch upon Richard as he had ridden alongside Lady Margaret.

'Just making sure the lady is all right,' Richard said.

'She's riding better than I expected,' Gervase admitted. 'Surprising, after being in a nunnery all her life.'

'She is indeed an accomplished horsewoman.' Richard was glad it was a point on which they could agree, but he took it as a warning that he was under surveillance on this journey.

Aware that he had dropped behind, Meg set her mount moving a little faster, until she came up alongside Sarah, who was riding pillion behind Alan. The pair did not immediately notice she was there, so she watched for a few moments and was delighted to see them both looking relaxed and happy. They were chatting and chaffing with each other, even chuckling in a friendly manner. Evidently Sarah had conquered her fear, although she was clinging very tightly to the young man—which he did not seem to mind in the least.

Although of noble birth, Alan had fallen on hard times. As a third son, there had been no inheritance for him. He and Richard had fought together in defence of England and he had suffered that terrible wound. He would have died had Richard not taken care of him. They had been friends ever since.

'Are you all right, Sarah?' Meg enquired.

'Oh, yes, thank you, my lady. I never thought it would be so comfortable, riding like this. An' the countryside's all so b'utiful, ain't it?'

'You've no need to worry about Sarah, my lady,' said Alan. 'I'll see she comes to no harm.'

Meg smiled wryly to herself. She was glad that they, at least, were happy as they continued along the road. She was in no hurry to reach Bixholm, especially when she thought about this plan of her uncle's to provide her with a husband. She hoped it would be a kindly and considerate young gentleman—perhaps even someone who looked a little like Sir Richard. Not that she would easily come to like, let alone love him! His remote manner towards her made her dismiss such a thought—it made her angry that it had even entered her head.

Deliberately she thrust aside those useless worries about what lay ahead. The weather was fine and, as Sarah had said, the countryside was beautiful. Sometimes the tracks took them through woodland, coppiced hazel and huge ancient oaks, the fresh growth of young leaves a delicate perfection of green. Sunlight dappled on primroses and dainty anemones, bejewelling the grass beneath. Deer and rabbits started away at their approach, and birds flew up into the canopy, anxious for the safety of their nests. At other times they rode over heathland, thickly covered with heather, brown now, with fresh fronds of bracken unfolding at the wood's edges.

Even though she had never before spent so many hours in the saddle, and had never been so far from Norwich, Meg found herself enjoying the ride—and there was not one word of complaint from Sarah.

The journey south, towards Essex, took three days. At night they stayed in the guest accommodation of great monasteries that would soon be dissolved on the orders of the King. Introductory letters from the Prioress assured that they were well catered for in every respect. The pace at which they travelled was unhurried, but every evening when they stopped Meg was tired, stiff and sore. In the women's quarters, she slept soundly.

'That's Bixholm,' Richard said.

She had grown accustomed to the sound of his voice. There was something in the timbre of it that caused a fluttering in her heart. It wasn't exactly fear. On the journey he had done nothing that could arouse the slightest suspicion of such an emotion. Yet she was always on edge when he was near, would feel an awareness, a tension heightened by the vibrancy with which he spoke.

It was late afternoon on the third day and he rode up alongside Meg as the castle came into view—the house which had belonged to her father and which, by right, should now be hers. Her first sight of it was of two tall towers. They formed part of the gatehouse. The spread of red tiled roofs denoted a place of considerable size, and many tall twisted chimneys suggested opulence, lots of fires to warm the rooms in winter.

Meg caught her breath. 'I was born there,' she said. Emotion flooded over her.

'At Bixholm?' Richard raised his expressive dark eyebrows.

'It belonged to my father. He was killed in the fighting in France.'

'So you know the castle?'

'I don't remember anything, really. My uncle forced my mother to leave. He insisted it all belonged to him, declared that he had papers to prove it.'

'You sound doubtful.'

'I cannot believe my father would have done such a thing. My mother tried to protest, but she did not have the strength to fight him—in addition to which she was afraid for my safety. We never came back.'

'Your mother was a wise lady.' He lowered his voice. Gervase Gisbon was not far behind. 'I advise you to say nothing to anyone about your doubts, Lady Margaret. Most especially do not challenge your uncle on the matter.'

'I am not a fool,' she said. 'I know there is nothing I can do about it.'

Richard's mouth was held in a tight line. He knew little about her story, yet what she said did not surprise him. More than ever he feared for her, and cursed that he was powerless to do anything other than deliver her to that monster who waited within.

Meg gazed at the impressive structure in silence. Her thoughts were running riot. This should have been her home. Here she should have grown up, in security and some affluence, but for the untimely death of her father and her uncle's subsequent treatment of her mother.

Only the clip-clop of the horses' hooves and the jangle of harness disturbed the silence as they rode toward the great house, for it was more a fortified manor house than a castle.

A square moat surrounded the buildings, and they crossed by the drawbridge, which was seldom lifted in these relatively peaceful days. The horses' hooves echoed as they passed through the guardhouse into a courtyard. Stablehands ran out to hold the horses, and, as he had done at the end of each day's riding, Sir Richard was there, his strong arms ready to assist her to dismount. Even in her tense state she found comfort in the way he held her, although she tried to suppress such thoughts. When he released her, very quickly, as always, loneliness swept over her.

'Tell the Earl that his niece, Lady Margaret Thurton, has arrived,' Richard instructed the porter who had stepped forward to greet them.

'The Earl is at dinner,' the porter replied. 'My instructions are to show you into the Great Hall, as soon as you are ready.'

Meg was nervous. With Sarah's assistance she had quickly washed and changed her clothes, which were still creased from being transported in the pannier on the packhorse. Sir Richard had also washed and changed from his outdoor riding gear. He waited outside the chamber that had been alloted to Meg, ready to escort her to the Great Hall.

Again she wore her best gown of blue-green velvet, as she had when she had been called into the solar at the nunnery. Sir Richard now presented an elegant figure in a doublet of damask, his silk shirt gathered into a high band which emphasised the strength and shapeliness of his neck. His hat was of matching crimson velvet and ornamented with a magnificent ostrich feather. Paler coloured hose encased his athletically muscular legs and he wore shoes with the highly fashionable square toes. Although he had remained aloof for most of the journey, he was no longer a complete stranger, and he had always attended to her needs with gallant courtesy.

'If you are ready, my lady, I will escort you to the Great Hall.'

'I am ready, Sir Richard. And Sarah has also washed and changed. She is as hungry and tired as I am; may she come with us to the Hall?'

Before Richard could answer Alan stepped out of the shadows. 'I am waiting to take Sarah to join the servants in the Hall,' he said.

'Oh, Alan—how smart you look!' beamed Sarah. Then anxiously, 'You won't leave me there on my own, will you?'

'Certainly not!' Alan said emphatically.

Satisfied that Sarah would be well looked after, Meg turned to Richard. She was grateful to place her hand upon his steadying arm as she walked from her chamber to the Great Hall. Alan and Sarah followed several yards behind and took their places at a table lower down the room. The aroma of roasted meats tickled Meg's tastebuds as they entered, reminding her that she was hungry.

About forty people must have been gathered there, but Meg's gaze went immediately to the high table at the end of the room, beneath banners and armorial artefacts. In the central position, with a carved wooden screen behind him and page boys waiting on either side, sat a large man. He was red-faced, wore a soft flat hat of brown taffeta, and was clad in a padded velvet jerkin with slashed sleeves over a silk shirt. Though his clothes were of rich fabrics he wore them untidily, and wine from his pewter goblet had been slopped down the front.

At his side was a woman, about thirty years of age, blowsy-looking, whose plump bosom seemed likely to spill over the top of her low-cut gown. She stared at Meg, looking her over, nodding her head, not really welcoming but with an expression of intense interest—even, perhaps, with her eyes half-closed, of speculation.

Lord Edmund speared a large slice of beef on his knife. He lifted it to his mouth and chewed on it as Richard led Meg forward to the high table.

'About time you got here!' he said loudly. 'I was beginning to think you'd got lost on the way.'

Richard ignored the jibe. He executed a polite bow. 'My lord, I assumed that you would not wish me to tire the lady with too much hard riding.'

'No, indeed. We can leave that for another time and another gentleman, can we not! Ho, ho!'

The company around him all laughed at his lewd joke. Meg did not understand the play on words, but sensed that it was in some way derogatory to herself.

Sir Richard spoke again, quickly, to cover the un-couth comment. 'Sir, allow me to introduce your niece, Lady Margaret Thurton.' He turned to Meg. 'My lady— this is your uncle, Edmund, Earl Thurton.'

Chapter Three

Meg found it difficult to repress a shudder at the impressions that whirled through her mind as she curtsied low. Everything was worse than she had anticipated. It was a ribald company that sat either alongside the Earl and his lady at the high table, or at long trestles down the Great Hall. There were men and women, one with a baby at her bare breast, older children too, and dogs quarrelling over morsels dropped or thrown to them.

'Bring her round here, Richard. Let me get a better look at her.'

The tone of the Earl's voice and his appearance and manners confirmed her worst suspicions. With her hand still lightly placed on Richard's arm, she allowed him to guide her round the end of the table. The Earl turned towards them as they approached his chair. She was acutely conscious that the eyes of everyone in the Hall were fixed upon her, and there were few signs of friendliness—except from one or two of the men, and there was undisguised lasciviousness in their expressions. She was trembling, but determined to hide her fear. Almost unconsciously her fingers gripped Richard's arm tighter.

Earl Thurton washed down the slice of beef with a

draught of red wine from his goblet. He wiped his mouth with the back of his hand, staring at her all the while.

'Stop,' he shouted suddenly.

They were close to where a circle of candles was suspended from a beam in the ceiling, casting more than the usual flickering light. They both stood still.

'Step back, Richard,' he commanded.

Gently Richard removed her hand from his arm. His fingers lingered, as if he was reluctant, but he obeyed his lord's order. She missed the reassurance that had emanated from him when at her side. How comforting his close presence had been! She clasped her hands together in front of her, held her head high and returned stare for stare, not liking what she saw.

'Turn around,' the Earl growled.

She did so woodenly, suppressing her anger and humiliation.

'Not bad, as far as looks go,' he commented. 'Not bad at all. Though she'd look better with a smile on her face. She'd be too thin for me, but could be right for—' He broke off, leaving Meg to wonder what he had been about to say.

'But those clothes! Aren't they awful?' commented the woman beside him. 'That style went out of fashion twenty years ago—they look as if they've come out of the ark!'

He grinned at the stupid joke. 'Wherever did you get that gown?' he asked.

'It was my mother's. I am proud to wear it.' Meg spoke defiantly.

He turned to the woman at his side. 'You'll have to take her in hand, eh, Nancy?'

'She certainly needs bringing up to date—lower

necklines, softer, more feminine fabrics. Give me the money, Edmund, and I'll get new gowns made for her.'

The Earl patted the woman's knee. 'Good. You see to it, Nan, and I'll make it worth your while. A woman's touch, that's what she needs.'

'A woman's touch to make her ready for a man's.' Nancy chuckled, digging Edmund in the ribs as she said it.

He guffawed loudly, and the laughter was echoed all down the Great Hall. Meg glowered at them, prepared to fight if anyone dared to touch her. 'She looks as if she doesn't belong in this world,' he said. 'I reckon you can change that, Nan. No expense spared at this stage, eh?'

'The nunnery has left its mark on her,' the woman agreed, running her eyes over Meg. 'But there's a good basis to work on. Leave it to me. You won't think it's the same girl when I've finished with her.'

Meg fumed at the manner in which they were talking about her, summing her up, as if she had no feelings, no mind of her own. She clenched her hands together till her nails bit into her palms, forcing herself to stand still, trying to ignore their comments. She would have liked to lift the skirts they so despised and run out of the Great Hall—but she had nowhere to go.

Suddenly she realised the Earl was actually addressing her. 'How about that, Meg? Lots of nice new clothes—I'll wager you'll like that, eh?' His thick-lipped face, flushed with over-indulgence, wore a semblance of a smile. 'You don't need to worry about a thing. We'll look after you now—get you fitted out in something more elegant. You'll look irresistible when Nan's finished with you.'

Meg stared at him coldly. Her scowl deepened. Did

he really expect her to be pleased? The Earl banged his fist down so hard on the table that the trenchers and pots jumped noisily.

'Don't look at me like that, girl. Give us a smile. This will cost me a deal of money and it's all for your own good. Smile, I tell you—smile!'

What had she to smile about? She felt more like weeping. But she controlled herself. She managed to lift the corners of her mouth, though there was no amusement in her heart.

'My lord.' Richard's voice rang out. 'The lady is tired and hungry—will you not invite her to sit down?'

'Huh! Is she another one of these mawkish wenches they breed nowadays?'

'I can assure you that Lady Margaret is nothing of the sort.' Richard spoke slowly and clearly. 'I am merely reminding you that she has ridden further in the past three days than ever before in her life, and she has stood the trial with great strength.'

He was challenging the Earl and speaking on her behalf. Meg could scarcely believe it! His words rang out clearly and immediately lifted her spirits.

'I am glad to hear it,' said Earl Thurton. 'For it doesn't show in her behaviour.'

'I should also remind you that Lady Margaret is still in mourning for her mother,' Richard added.

Meg listened to him gratefully. In this alien and hostile world, could she really hope that he might be her friend and champion?

It seemed that the Earl took note of his words, for he nodded in grudging acceptance. 'All right. Well, there's plenty of time to train her. Come, Meg. Sit here beside me. The page shall bring viands for you.'

She hoped his use of the diminutive of her name

meant that he was softening his attitude towards her, but it was with dragging steps that she moved to take the seat the Earl indicated. On the table before her a trencher bread was already in place, together with a knife, spoon, bread rolls, and a goblet. The company in the Hall had already started eating and were well into the first course.

A page approached Meg, bowed low and asked, 'Does my lady wish for a slice of the boar's head? There is also beef and roast swan—or may I bring slices of each?'

She was hungry, and the roasts were succulent, well flavoured with mixed herbs. She elected to have the swan, a delicacy which had not often been served in the refectory at the priory. It was accompanied by rich gravy and a good selection of vegetables: chopped turnips, parsnips and fresh spring cabbage. Her goblet was filled with wine.

Even before she had been served, the Earl and the lady he had addressed as Nancy resumed eating and drinking, as did all the others in the Great Hall. Sir Richard had taken his place at the High Table, a slight distance away on her left. She glanced in his direction. She had expected him to be engrossed in the repast, for the food was undoubtedly excellent, well cooked and accompanied by rich sauces and gravy. He caught her eye, smiled and nodded in her direction, as if he knew that meeting his eye gave her courage. Instinctively she smiled back—it was as if an invisible bond magically linked them, and in that moment it tightened.

Where previously she had doubted his friendship, after his intervention on her behalf her attitude towards him had softened—just a little. It strengthened her to know he was there, even though her head told her that was ridiculous. He, like all the other men and women gathered in the Great Hall, were under the patronage of the Earl. No one would dare to cross him. Her own dear mother had tried to assert her rights, but had been driven out in fear for her own life and that of her baby daughter.

Meg still seethed with anger at the rude manner of her reception, but common sense warned her, just as Richard had, that it would be unwise to defy the Earl openly.

She had been hungry when she had first been assailed by the delicious smell of roasted meats; now each mouthful seemed tasteless. She ate because she wished to keep up her strength, and took a draught of the full-bodied red wine because she was thirsty. It was never wise to drink water. She kept her eyes downcast, concentrating on her trencher, though with an occasional surreptitious glance around. The Earl was so absorbed in his food and wine that he ignored her. He and Nancy talked together and the rest of the household did the same, the chatter of voices swirling up in increasing volume.

Meg could see Sarah, well down the room, but not so far below as the roughly clad outdoor workers and their wives. She willed her to look up, but the message was slow to reach her. Sarah had eyes only for her trencher of meat or to engage those of Alan Crompton, who was close by her side. Then, suddenly, she looked up, a questioning expression on her honest, open face. To reassure her Meg winked, and with a cheeky grin Sarah winked back. That had been their way of communicating when they had been children in the nunnery and dragooned into long dull lectures.

There was nothing dull about that evening at the cas-

tle. The musicians in the gallery behind them played
and sang and the sound of the lutes and virginals was
pleasant, soothing to her ears. Meg almost began to enjoy herself. It was all so different from the nunnery—
the food, the wonderfully bright hues and variety of the
clothes, with the men being especially flamboyant. The
wine had gone to her head a little. Perhaps she should
be grateful for the money and the time and trouble her
uncle was prepared to spend on her. It would be nice
to have new gowns, pretty things to wear, soft silks and
beautiful damasks.

A group of strolling players came into the Hall, clad
in colourful costumes with bells jingling, and the atmosphere was changed again. They gestured, strutted
around and shouted obscenities which produced loud
roars of laughter from everybody—except for Meg. She
had never heard or seen such vulgarity and was
shocked. She could see nothing funny in the lewd jokes,
and revealed this by staring poker-faced at the players.
Her uncle and Nancy were wiping the tears from their
eyes at the antics. When the Earl noticed that Meg was
showing no sign of amusement, he turned towards her.

'What's the matter with you, wench? Let yourself
go—have a good laugh.'

'I beg your pardon, Uncle, but I do not find them
funny.'

'My God! You're hard to please. One of the best-
known troupes in the land, I pay them an exorbitant
amount of money—and you say they're not funny!' he
exploded.

'Not to me,' she said. 'But perhaps it is because I do
not understand what they are saying.'

'Then we'll have to see to it that you get some lessons in humour,' he snarled. 'You'll never catch the eye of H—' He broke off as Nancy jogged his arm.

'Whose attention?' asked Meg.

'Nobody's if you don't buck up a bit,' he snapped. Then he raised his voice and shouted, 'Richard!'

'Sir?'

Richard was laughing as he turned towards them, though not so uproariously as the Earl and Nancy. He was evidently amused by the performance, and that reminded Meg that he really was one of them. How foolish she had been to think that he might become a friend.

'Richard.' The Earl was not laughing now. 'Your duties with Lady Margaret are not yet finished. You will take her in hand and teach her how to enjoy herself. Wake her up to some of the fun in life.'

Richard drew in a deep breath. He could think of nothing he would like better. In the days he had been in her company he had learned a good deal about the delightful Lady Margaret Thurton. The cloistered life she had led until he had taken her from the priory was strongly imprinted upon her. He knew that she had much to learn of the ways of the world. But in his assessment—and he was not unversed in such matters— she was indeed ripe for a man. What a pleasure it would be to have the privilege of teaching her all those adult and worldly pleasures and pastimes that were so much a part of courtly life and from which she had been sheltered.

Then he remembered. She was destined to become the wife—or more likely the mistress—of the cruel and lecherous King Henry. It was a sobering thought.

'Tell me, Meg,' requested the Earl, 'do you know the galliard or lavolta?'

'I believe they are dances,' Meg replied.

'Of course they are dances! Everyone knows that—but can you dance them?'

'I have never learned,' she confessed.

'What about archery? Have you ever drawn a bow?' She shook her head.

'Do you sing?'

At last, an attribute she could claim with honesty. 'Oh, yes, my lord. I can sing. I have been praised for the quality of my voice, and I know most of the psalms in Latin.'

To her surprise and embarrassment the Earl burst out laughing. He turned to Nancy. 'Want to hear one of the psalms?' he chuckled.

'I think not, Edmund. Not here and now.'

'Exactly. We'll hand her over to you, Richard. See that my niece becomes well versed in all those necessary pleasantries to take her place properly in high society.'

'I shall deem it an honour, sir,' said Richard. Then he turned to Meg and smiled. 'We will start tomorrow, in the morning, if it pleases you, Lady Margaret.'

'You will start tomorrow whether it pleases the lady or not,' shouted the Earl. 'We have no time to waste. She has only a few weeks in which to acquire those graces necessary to take her place in society.'

Meg sat bolt upright, her face flushed with discomfort and anger. Again they were talking about her as if she was a performing animal that they owned. They offered her no voice in plans that seemed to be already made. A short training in pleasantries—and then what? Who was this mysterious suitor whose identity was never actually spoken? If it was a good match, to a pleasant and honourable gentleman, why was it all so secretive?

The future loomed menacingly before her, but she

was determined to face whatever it held bravely. She was alive and strong. She was here at Bixholm, back in the castle of which she had no real recollection. She had often dreamed of returning to the place where she had been born. She had never imagined it being like this, but she told herself she must be prepared to face life here in the real world. Even though there was much that disturbed her she was willing to learn these additional graces—though it might be difficult to concentrate since her teacher was to be Sir Richard.

'I shall be ready to start tomorrow,' Meg said firmly.

'You may find it quite strenuous as you are unaccustomed to the dance or to outdoor pursuits,' Richard suggested. His voice was polite and gentle. 'I would therefore suggest that you retire when you have finished your repast.'

'I am indeed very tired,' she murmured.

It would be a relief to exchange this rumbustious company for the privacy of her own bed-chamber. She flashed a grateful smile at Richard.

Earl Thurton noticed. His eyes narrowed suspiciously. 'Hah! You have a smile for Sir Richard. Let me make it absolutely clear to you, Meg, he is not the one for you. You will regard him only as your mentor in matters of social etiquette, and especially he is to teach you to take that prim look off your face. I am proposing to take you to Court. You will be mixing with the liveliest and most fashionable people in England. I want you to shine among them.'

How would she ever manage to do that? The very thought of meeting and conversing with such people made her nervous. 'I understand what you require and I shall do my best—' She choked on the words and stood up. 'Pray excuse me—'

Richard was at her side immediately, offering his arm.

'Allow me to escort you to your chamber, my lady.'

'Thank you, Sir Richard.' She had control of her voice again.

The Earl waved her away, with a dismissive gesture, then picked up a bone and began to gnaw at it. With unhurried steps Richard led her away from the top table and down the length of the Great Hall. The entertainers were still at their nonsense, and the Lord of Misrule, playing his part, bowed mockingly in front of them. He capered and tried to persuade Meg to dance with him. Shyly she shook her head, and he pretended to look crestfallen—but she was aware that when his head was turned from her, he made another ribald comment. It sparked a great burst of laughter from the top table and made Meg feel foolish.

Richard tightened his arm against his side, a gesture of support that trapped her hand protectively close. There was something possessive in his touch, as if he wanted her to belong to him. If only it were so! She was sure he would never have made these unreasonable demands of her. She would have gone with him gladly, but the Earl's warning rang in her ears—*'He is not the one for you.'*

'Do not trouble yourself over their antics, my lady,' Richard said. 'It is not really personal. They only act thus because it is what they are paid to do.'

Would she ever understand this extraordinary world she had been precipitated into? Who could it be who would make such demands upon a wife?

Sarah and Alan stood up and followed, several steps behind, side by side. It seemed to take for ever to reach the door that led them into a stone passageway. Meg glanced at her companion and said, 'I fear I am a great disappointment.'

'Far from it, my lady. They find you too good to be true.'

'Now you are laughing at me, too.'

'Not at all. I assure you they are delighted with you. I know them. I can read the signs. They have never met anyone quite like you before and they do not know how to behave.'

'On that point I agree with you.'

He smiled. 'You even charmed Nancy.'

'How can you say that? She did nothing but criticise me.'

'Your clothing, not you. She was eager to undertake the task of introducing you to her dressmaker and ordering garments that will enhance your beauty.'

Meg blushed when he said that. She did not believe he could possibly mean it. She knew perfectly well that she was not beautiful. People had said that about her mother, never about her. It was a fact that she had inherited some of her mother's features, but she was only too aware that her mouth was rather too wide, her nose not aristocratically aquiline and her hair of a pale colour. Clothes, of course, would make a difference. She knew enough of the world to see that she had to look as if she belonged to a wealthy family, as if she had a good dowry. Men of the aristocracy did not marry for looks alone, and almost never for love. If that came later it was a bonus—as it had been for her mother.

She ignored Richard's statement, dismissed it as meaningless pleasantry, the language of the courtier. She asked, 'Is Nancy the wife of the Earl?'

'In all respects other than having a ceremony to bless their union. She holds considerable power over him, even though her youthful beauty has left her. They suit each other well. Two of a kind. Be advised by me, my lady, take care not to upset Nancy.'

'I suppose I should be grateful that I am to have new gowns,' she said.

'Most young ladies would be,' he agreed easily.

'I will admit to being a little excited at the prospect,'

'Good.' His eyes twinkled—she could not help liking him. If only she could trust him!

'Are you really quite willing to teach me how to behave properly?' she asked.

'I think you know more about proper behaviour than the Earl and Nancy will ever do,' he said.

'My uncle wishes me to be different from the way I am, Sir Richard. I have to learn to dance, and to sing songs other than the psalms, and to shoot with a bow and arrow—and a whole plethora of things besides.'

He nodded. 'I am convinced you will make a very apt pupil, Lady Margaret.'

'I'm willing to try,' she sighed. 'But I am not at all sure I shall be able to change enough to please my uncle. It's all to do with finding me a husband, is it not, sir?'

She noticed the tightening of his mouth.

'Yes.' His response was brief.

'Truly I am not ill educated,' she said, suddenly feeling a need to defend herself. 'There are many things I can do, and do well—I can read and write, and indeed I am better educated than most women. I could easily undertake to run a household, oversee the servants, and I have a considerable knowledge of the merits of various herbs and lotions. I nursed my mother until her death. What more should a husband need?' She paused, and then asked, 'Who is this gentleman I am to marry?'

'That I cannot say.'

'You mean you will not,' she said scornfully.

'I mean exactly what I say.'

The comradeship she thought had been spun between them was snapped in an instant. She wished she had not persisted—but it was too late. At least it told her exactly where she stood with him. He was no friend to her. He would obey the Earl to the letter. His next words confirmed that.

'Your uncle will reveal his plans when he is ready.'

She snatched her hand away from his arm. They had reached her chambers. Sarah hurried up to open the door ahead of her mistress.

He bowed. 'At what hour shall I come for you in the morning, Lady Margaret?'

'As early as you wish.' She tossed her head. 'I am not accustomed to sleeping late.'

'There is no need to start too early. At half past nine, then?'

'Certainly,' she agreed.

Half past nine! He had no eagerness to commence the task which the Earl had assigned him. Tears pricked behind her eyes. He had been quick to offer to escort her to her chamber. No doubt he would now hurry back to the Great Hall and would stay up, drinking and dancing and having fun into the small hours of the morning.

There was nothing more to say other than to bid each other goodnight. She did so with a heavy heart.

Sarah shut the door firmly behind her.

'Cor, my lady—what a carry on! I ain't never seen nor heard anything like it in all my born days!'

'I know, Sarah. Those players were quite disgraceful.' Meg heaved a sigh.

'So rude, wasn't they?' said Sarah.

She was smiling—though she held her hand over her face to hide it, moved behind her mistress and began to unlace her gown.

Suddenly, unbelievably, Meg heard a sound that sounded like a chuckle. She listened. It came again, louder, exploding from Sarah's mouth.

'Sarah?' she questioned.

'Sorry, my lady. I just couldn't help a-thinkin' when we was there in the Great Hall—' She broke off as her laughter pealed out.

'What were you thinking?' Meg asked. She was finding it difficult to keep a straight face herself, as Sarah's laughter was beginning to be infectious, just as it always had been ever since they were little girls together.

'Oh, my lady! I just couldn't help a-wonderin'—what would the Prioress have thought if she'd been here? Couldn't you just imagine her face?'

Meg could. All too easily! The stern face of the Prioress flashed into her mind and it was so ridiculous that she, too, burst out laughing!'

'She'd have had a fit!' chortled Sarah. 'An' it'd have done her a power of good!'

'Oh, Sarah, you must not talk so.'

Meg felt she should speak firmly, and she tried to do so, but it was useless. The disapproving figure of the Prioress, with narrow pursed lips and spiteful tongue, came into her mind so vividly that she doubled up with laughter.

'Thank goodness—you came—here with me,' she spluttered, almost too convulsed to speak.

But later, mirth having subsided, curled up in bed, Meg thought again of her extraordinary situation, and felt afraid.

Chapter Four

Meg had not expected to be able to sleep at all, but she had been so tired that she had dropped off quite quickly. She awoke to a day that was fine and sunny. It lifted her spirits so greatly that she leapt out of bed and rushed to the window to look out. The little she could see made her eager to explore the castle and its surroundings.

Sarah must have woken up even earlier, for she was not in the room. Her truckle bed, still at the foot of Meg's was empty. Later it would be pushed beneath the large bed in which Meg had slept so comfortably. Without waiting for her maid, Meg attended to her toilette and dressed herself. A few minutes later Sarah appeared, bearing a tray with ale and hot buttered oatcakes.

'It's a fine morning, my lady,' she said cheerfully. 'I've been down to the kitchens an' got summat for your breakfast.'

'Thank you, Sarah.'

'The Hall's in a right ole mess, an' some of 'em are still asleep there.'

Was Richard among them? Meg wondered, and

wished that the thought was not so distressing. She was not hungry, but she ate and drank a little. It would be more than an hour before Richard would call for her. She was too restless to remain in her chamber.

'It's such a beautiful morning, Sarah. I shall go outside for a walk.'

'Just hold you hard a moment, my lady, whilst I dress your hair.'

'I've already run a comb through it, and it will be covered with my hood,' Meg protested.

'It's not good enough,' Sarah insisted. 'It'd be more than my job's worth if I let you go outside without having it done right. They reckon that Mistress Nancy is a right sharp one. If I don't look after you properly, she'll bring in some other woman, an' send me packing.'

'I'd never let her do that,' said Meg.

'You might not be able to stop her,' Sarah countered. 'An' then you'd be spied upon every moment of the day.'

Meg sat down meekly. Sarah might well be right, and certainly her maid was the only friend she had in Bixholm. There was no one else she could trust—though she thought the girl was being somewhat fussy. It couldn't really matter what she looked like at this hour of the morning.

Sarah dressed her hair carefully, then placed her cap and gable hood on her head. She stood back and cast a critical eye over her mistress. 'There. That's better.' She nodded with satisfaction.

'May I go now?' Meg asked, with a smile.

'You may laugh at me, my lady. But there's truth in what I say.'

'I know, Sarah dear. But I can't bear to stay indoors a moment longer.'

She avoided the Great Hall and moved through a series of passages until she came out into the courtyard through which they had entered. Guards were lounging about, presumably on duty, but standing at ease, chatting together. They glanced at Meg, but made no move to challenge her as she walked out into the sunshine and over the drawbridge.

She looked back and saw the castle was an impressive building, well constructed of brick and flint, rising from the top of a slight hill and surrounded by a moat. A river flowed gently on one side, and beyond that were wide acres of water meadows, where cattle grazed. Woods darkened the background. Undoubtedly it was a site of consequence. How different her life would have been if she had grown up here! But it was useless to harbour such thoughts, and she pushed them to the back of her mind.

She walked on and found the herb garden. She noted with approval that it was well stocked with a variety of pot-herbs: thyme, rosemary, celery and lovage among others. She ran her fingers over fragrant leaves, delighting in their scents. Automatically she pulled a few weeds from a bed of parsley. The gardeners arrived, and, not wanting to intrude, she spoke to them briefly, wishing them a good day and moved on.

It was impossible not to enjoy such a beautiful morning. She lingered for a little while by the stew ponds, watching the fish darting through the translucent water. As was customary for a gentleman's residence, Bixholm Castle had a bowling alley and butts for archery practice. Soon she discovered it also had a tiltyard.

The pounding of horses' hooves, shouts of command,

the thump of wood and rattle of harness told her that other people were already up and about. She walked towards the sounds which came from behind a barn. Four young men were practising for the joust, Sir Richard and Alan Crompton among them.

Fear leapt into her heart as she watched Richard galloping his steed towards the quintain, a crossbar on a pivot. On one end of the bar was a flat piece of wood, which the rider had to strike with his lance. At the other hung a bag filled with sand; when struck, the crossbar swivelled. She saw it swing and closed her eyes, convinced that the heavy sandbag would strike the back of his head, that he would be unseated.

When she looked again he was well past, and riding with his lance triumphantly high in the air. She chided herself for being so stupid. Why should she have experienced even the slightest concern for his safety? He was one of the Earl's men, no friend to her. He turned his horse and, seeing her, slowed it to a trot and rode to where she stood.

'I bid you good morning, my lady,' he exclaimed, doffing the flat hat of green velvet that topped his handsome head. 'I trust you slept well?'

'Very well, thank you, sir. Pray do not interrupt your sport on my account.'

'I've almost finished my exercise for today. We are practising for a great tournament that is to be held at Hampton Court when we are in London. If you'll excuse me, I shall ride at the quintain a couple of times more, then I will join you.'

He turned his horse and was off again, riding full tilt. He struck the wooden bar dead centre and spurred his horse forward, well ahead of the swinging sandbag. This time Meg was able to watch with only a tiny contraction of her nerves. He was capable. He knew what he was doing. It was the same with Alan Crompton when he took his turn. One of the other men, less able, was struck, and only just managed to hold his horse and keep his seat. The expertise of Richard and Alan had made it look easy.

Richard turned his snorting charger, galloped to where Meg stood, and drew the huge animal to a halt immediately in front of her. Leaping down, he handed the reins to a groom, who had run up ready to lead the horse away.

'I'm a bit out of practice,' Richard said. 'This is my first morning at the tilt for almost two weeks.'

'I thought you did very well,' Meg felt obliged to say.

'Thank you, my lady. But real jousting is another matter. The opposition will be very strong when we go to Hampton Court.'

Despite his doubts she could see he was in high spirits after the energetic session. Meg made to move away. She would have been quite happy to continue her walk alone.

'Don't go,' he said.

'I've been exploring the grounds,' she told him.

'And do you approve of what you've seen?'

'It is impressive.'

'It is, and it is well run. You haven't forgotten that I am to give you tuition in various sports and pastimes?'

She felt shy in his presence and shrugged her shoulders to indicate her indifference.

'Then, my lady, I think we should start with archery.'

He took her arm and guided her to the butts a short distance away. Men, boys and a few women were already at practice, loosing volleys of arrows towards targets set on top of tall mounds at the end of the field. The young gentlemen were of the nobility or gentry, fledgeling officials, destined to join the governing classes. They and their ladies lowered their bows and gathered around Richard and Meg. Most had witnessed her arrival, but she had not yet been properly introduced to them.

'May I present Lady Margaret Thurton, niece of the Earl, who is now his lordship's ward?' Richard said.

He named all those in the group, and they exchanged greetings with the utmost civility, but Meg was overwhelmed by meeting so many all at once, and afterwards could not remember the names of any of them.

She was grateful that they soon strolled away to resume their practice. Skill with longbows was essential, not only as a military art, but also for hunting. The pursuit of game was one of the most popular sports, and women hunted with bows as well as men. Meg had never done so, and it was not an activity she looked forward to.

Hunting was only for the privileged few, and severe laws and harsh punishments prohibited commoners from taking game from the royal forests. In Meg's eyes that was quite wrong. It was the poor who really needed the food. But she knew it would be useless to make such a suggestion. She felt lost and helpless. Everything and everyone was strange to her. She almost wished she was back in the nunnery. Then she looked at Richard and knew that being with him was more exciting than any experience in the whole of her past life.

'I'll show you what to do,' he said. 'You'll soon learn.'

Meg doubted that, but it delighted her to watch. Richard stood tall, his velvet cap set on his head at a jaunty angle, decorated with gold and blue feathers. He lifted the bow, and his muscles flexed beneath his sleeveless jerkin as he drew back the string and took aim. He loosed arrow after arrow. They shuddered with the force of their impetus and ended their flight clustered in a tight circle around the bull's-eye. He made it look easy.

Meg would have been content to watch him all morning, but as one servant retrieved the arrows, another handed him a smaller bow.

Richard passed it to her. 'Right, Meg. Now it's your turn.'

Although the bow was lighter than the one Richard had used she had difficulty in pulling the string. Every arrow fell short of the target and dropped limply, sticking into the ground in a zigzag line.

'It's useless,' she moaned. 'I'll never manage it.'

'Of course you will. Practice, that's all it takes.' Richard said encouragingly. 'I'll help you.'

He moved behind her, so close his body was touching hers. His arms reached around her, his hands, warm and strong, covered hers. She was unnervingly conscious of his nearness, and the warm, musky masculinity of him caused her to tremble.

'Stand steady,' he whispered in her ear. 'You can do it. Just concentrate. Place your legs firmly, a little apart.'

She obeyed, and could not avoid knowledge of his hard, strong thighs pressing against her skirts. She hoped he did not know why it was that she was shaking! She blushed with shame, especially as it seemed that, for him, being so close had no such effect.

She wished she could shrug his hands off, but that would have been foolish, for there was no doubt she needed assistance, especially as she was aware that some of the other archers were watching them. Pride made her determined to succeed. She gritted her teeth, forced herself to clear her mind of his presence and concentrate only on the target.

'Lift the bow a little higher. Hold it out at arm's length. Now gently pull the string back—further—further—till it touches your nose. Aim a little above the bull's-eye.'

His hands guided hers as he gave each instruction, and when she released the arrow it flew towards the butt. It did not quite hit its mark, but to her joy it stuck firmly in the target.

She turned her head triumphantly, so excited she forgot how close Richard was. He had not released his hold on her and seemed to be in no hurry to do so. She felt his breath warm on her cheek, saw his eyes smiling down at her, and felt hot colour leap into her cheeks.

'You see,' he said softly. 'You'll soon learn.'

From the corner of her eye Meg noticed a gentleman among the archers who was watching them keenly. She recognised him as Gervase Gisbon. She had disliked him at that initial meeting, when he had flicked the whip at old blind Davy. Since then he had shown her nothing but courtesy, yet she could not bring herself to like him and felt uneasy in his company. Richard stepped back, as if he too was unnerved by those staring eyes. He took the bow from her and notched another arrow, ready for her to try again.

'You must shoot this one without my assistance. Remember what I told you. Stand firm and keep your eye on the target. I know you can do it.'

She wished she had that same faith in herself. She knew she would never find archery easy, and would never become as adept as some of the other women.

But she persevered, and as the morning progressed there was no doubt her aim was beginning to improve.

'That's better,' Richard told her. 'Practice, that's all you need. But you've had enough for your first morning.' He took the bow from her, adding, 'I believe Mistress Nancy is seeking you.'

Meg turned and watched Nancy walking towards them with a determined air. She had lifted her skirts off the ground, revealing sturdy shoes and knitted stockings. Irreverently Meg thought she looked more like a milkmaid than the Earl's lady.

Richard greeted Nancy in his customary friendly manner. 'You see Lady Margaret is already starting to acquire social skills, as his lordship wishes,' he said.

'And pleased I am to see it, Richard.' Nancy smiled, but there was an edge to her voice as she added, 'Just be sure you confine your instruction only to those achievements and nothing else!'

'I assure you, mistress, no other thought has ever entered my mind,' Richard answered easily. He deliberately changed the tone of the conversation by turning to Meg. 'Nancy is one of the most accomplished women with the bow,' he said. 'She is also more skilled in the hunt than many a man.'

Meg bobbed a curtsey. 'I fear I have much to learn, Mistress Nancy,' she said. 'For I have never taken part in either sport.'

'It's not necessary for you to become expert; for that you have to be born to it, and even then it takes years of practice,' Nancy said. 'Anyway 'tis not of the greatest importance. Come with me now, Meg. My dressmaker and her sewing maids are awaiting you in my chamber.'

'I was about to take Lady Margaret riding in the woods. It's such a fine morning,' said Richard.

'Indeed it is, and I'm sure you'd enjoy that whole-heartedly, Richard,' Nancy said. 'However, I fear you'll have to take the exercise alone. There is a great deal of work to be done, and only a short time in which to have a whole new wardrobe cut and stitched and ready to wear.'

'A formidable task,' Richard agreed. 'For how long will you require Lady Margaret?'

'A couple of hours, perhaps.'

'And after that she will be free to join me again?'

'Certainly.'

'I've arranged for the musicians to play for us,' he told Meg. 'Then it will be my pleasure to instruct you in the dance. I am sure Mistress Nancy will agree that to dance well and gracefully is one of the most important accomplishments for a young lady of quality?'

'I cannot argue with that,' Nancy agreed. 'She shall be returned to you when the dressmakers have finished.'

'Then for the moment, adieu.' Richard bowed.

Allowing Meg time for only a brief word of thanks to Richard for his tuition, Nancy hurried her into the castle.

'I've arranged for your maid to attend,' she said, hustling Meg up the winding stone stairs and into her private chamber.

The dressmaker, a middle-aged woman, was introduced as Mrs Goodley. She and her two assistants curtsied as Nancy and Meg entered.

The large room was sumptuous, dominated by a huge four-poster bed, made up with down-filled pillows and a damask quilt. The sides were hung with tapestries, now looped back, worked in shades of brown, gold and green threads. Similar rich tapestries decorated the high walls of the chamber. Sweet-smelling herbs and rushes were strewn on the floor. There were chests, chairs and a court-cupboard. The whole effect was of wealth and comfort. Bolts of taffeta, velvet, silk, satin and damask were lying on the bed.

Sarah assisted Meg to strip down to her kirtle while Nancy poured out a list of instructions regarding the garments that would be required. The women looked her over. They turned her this way and that, and discussed how she should be clothed as if she was deaf, blind and entirely without feeling.

'Good complexion,' said one.

'Neat figure,' commented another.

'Pale colours will complement that innocent look she has.'

'Good teeth—she should smile more.'

'Just what his lordship said last night!' commented Nancy.

They unrolled a purple silk and held it against her.

'Too harsh,' said Nancy.

Meg glanced at Sarah and raised her eyebrows. Sarah smiled and nodded. She seemed to understand exactly how her mistress was feeling, and indeed Meg was fuming. But, since there was nothing she could do or say to improve her position, she accepted their pushing and prodding in silence. They measured, and spoke of darts and pleats, trimming, frilling and cut-work, slashing and embroidery till Meg's head was spinning. Their expertise was impressive, and she could not help but admire their skill, for they worked with the deftness of experts.

'It's a beautiful shade of purple, my lady,' said Mistress Goodley.

'Not for Lady Margaret,' said Nancy. 'It takes away some of her youth and innocence. Try the apple-green.'

'You were right! That is quite delightful!' Mistress Goodley clapped her hands together approvingly. 'It's not everyone who can wear green, but that colour is perfect for the young lady. It should be cut with a close-fitted bodice, worn over tight stays to lift the bosom. And a wide, square neckline—quite low.'

'A narrow frilling, decorated with tiny pearls,' suggested one of the sewing maids timidly.

'The skirt full, open at the front, revealing a decorative petticoat and a glimpse of ankle,' insisted Nancy.

'Certainly, mistress. Perhaps it should be gored from the waist, fitting neatly over the young lady's hips rather than gathered. It's the newest look—more alluring, I think.'

Meg was delighted with the beautiful materials that were held up to her. There were to be other garments too, and silken underwear such as she had never imagined even in her wildest dreams.

'Surely that is wasteful, for nobody will see it,' she said.

Her protest was greeted with a scream of delighted laughter from the dressmakers.

'You never know what may happen when we go to Court,' said Nancy, a statement that provoked more chuckles and brought hot colour to Meg's face.

'To court?' Meg questioned. She was becoming more and more uneasy as the session continued. 'Is it at Court that I shall meet the gentleman I am to marry?'

'Indeed that is so.'

'But will he want me, when I have no dowry?'

'It will be your duty to charm him. That is why you

are being robed so elegantly and Sir Richard is teaching you so many accomplishments.'

'Mistress Nancy, I cannot understand why I am not to be told the name, or indeed anything of this gentleman,'

'You'll find that out soon enough. Just do as you are told and don't make a fuss.'

'But it would be so much easier for me if I knew—'

'Easier? What could be easier than having beautiful garments made for you? You should be grateful that his lordship is willing to spend so much money to make you look presentable.'

'But why is he doing all this for me? He has never done anything for me before, and he drove my poor mama—'

'I don't know anything about that, nor do I wish to hear,' snapped Nancy. 'Not another word.'

Meg sighed. She was becoming more and more alarmed at this secrecy. Despite Nancy's assertion that she did not know about the terrible way Lord Thurton had treated her mama, Meg didn't believe her. She could read in the other woman's face that she knew, but was not prepared to admit it. Nancy was too young to have played any part in the cruel and evil event when the Earl drove Lady Elizabeth from Bixholm. She knew about it, but made it clear that she had closed her mind to it.

Nancy clapped her hands commandingly. 'Come on, Mistress Goodley. Don't stand there gawping. Get back to work on these gowns. And I don't want any more interruptions from you, Meg.'

Again Meg was turned this way and that. The dressmakers took measurements. They discussed other garments that would be necessary. Riding clothes, capes with and without collars, stockings with garters tied just above the knee, and shoes of velvet, silk and leather.

Meg was dazzled by the speed at which the dressmakers made decisions, and amazed at the points of fashion which were discussed at length. She could scarcely believe the ease with which Nancy ordered gowns, even in the very expensive cloth of gold. What a different world this was from the nunnery, with its emphasis on poverty and chastity, and from the streets of Norwich, thronging with the poor and disadvantaged. The women talked of hooks and pins and cut-work, of girdles and sashes, ribbons for her hair, purses and pomanders which would be ordered from the goldsmith. Despite her reservations she could not help a mounting excitement at the prospect of so many beautiful clothes being made just for her.

She began to wonder how she would look when all was finished. The image of Richard leapt into her mind. What would he think? Would he find her attractive in all this expensive finery?

It was a far cry from the way she had looked when he had first encountered her in the street. In that bespattered state, dressed in old rough clothes, she had seen a spark of interest in his dark, unfathomable eyes. She recalled that she had, quite shamefully, found the way he had looked at her then both exciting and threatening. However, his attitude since their formal introduction in the parlour of the Prioress had been different, distant. At times he seemed to be almost aloof, and yet surely he had not needed to touch her quite so intimately as he had that morning, when he'd guided her at archery! Always at the back of her mind were her uncle's words, *'He is not the one for you,'* and loneliness squeezed her heart.

'Enough for today.' Nancy brought the session to an abrupt end. 'Get on with making up as quickly as you can,' she instructed the dressmaker. 'Take on as many sewing maidens as you require. We must have a really good wardrobe ready to wear within three weeks.' With that she swept out of the room.

Sarah assisted Meg to dress again, in the plain garments that were such a contrast to the magnificent materials that had been draped over and around her.

'Bossy woman, that!' commented Sarah when Nancy and the dressmakers had left. 'Wouldn't do to get on the wrong side of her. You'd best be careful, my lady.'

'I know, Sarah. I just wish I knew why they're doing it.'

'I reckon they're hopin' you'll marry some bigwig who's got even more money than they have, an' no doubt they expect to get their hands on some of it.'

'I expect you're right,' Meg said, with a sigh. 'And all I can do is wait and hope that my intended husband will be honourable and kindly.' Even as she said it the thought jumped into her mind that, whoever it was, it was unlikely she'd find him as attractive as Sir Richard.

'Whoever he is, he won't be good enough for you,' Sarah said.

Meg gave her a hug. 'Thank goodness I've got you!'

'I'm rather glad of that myself,' Sarah said. To Meg's astonishment she blushed and hung her head. 'Now turn around, do, and let me finish fastening this gown.'

'My next lesson is to be dancing,' Meg said.

'You'll enjoy that, my lady,' said Sarah.

Meg was not so sure. Impulsively she said, 'You must come with me, Sarah.'

She felt a need for the familiar loyalty of her maid. With so much happening, and for reasons she could not fully understand, she felt a desperate sense of unease.

Chapter Five

The musicians had assembled in a room of moderate size, situated close to the Great Hall. The sweet sounds of their lutes, virginals, flutes and tabors met Meg's ears as she and Sarah approached.

A broad smile lit Sarah's face. 'Remember that tune?' she said. 'The travelling musicians used to play it in the streets of Norwich at fair time.'

Meg smiled. 'What fun we had!'

'Didn't we just! Remember when we managed to escape from the nunnery?'

Dear Sarah, who so loved life and fun, yet had such a practical streak to her nature.

There was no time for further comment for they had reached the Music Room. Richard had been lolling on a settle, but leapt to his feet immediately they entered. He greeted Meg with a smile, warm and welcoming. If he was surprised to see her maid accompanying her, he gave no sign of it. Again she felt a sensation of pleasure which lifted her spirits. Even though their behaviour towards each other was strictly formal, just to be in his company brought happiness—although she assured herself it was simply relief at seeing a friendly face.

Sarah slipped away, quiet and self-effacing, to sit on a bench by the wall. Richard bowed and took Meg's hand as the musicians continued to play. He led her towards them, his steps keeping time with the music. Side by side they moved forward, at a walking pace. Instinctively she fell into step with him and picked up the rhythm of the movement. With her hand cupped lightly in his, she followed his lead, forward and back. He turned her to face him, then released her hand.

'Set and turn single,' he said.

She watched him and mirrored the movement.

'Again,' he commanded. Then, 'Up a double, and back.'

Next it was 'siding'.

Even though she had not heard the call before, as he walked towards her she knew what to do, and passed by him, turned and swept back again. His head was held proudly high, his eyes fixed on hers, half shielded, and with that same expression that she had found so disturbing when she had first encountered him in the street. His body, too, had been part of the sensuality of the movement, almost touching hers before turning away.

'Arming.'

That too was simple to understand, for he swaggered towards her with his right elbow crooked and she slipped her arm into it. They turned, then repeated the movement with the left arm. Stepping back from her, he swept an elegant bow, then looked up, smiling, obviously delighted.

'After that you can't pretend you haven't danced before.'

'Only as a child, out in the street,' she told him shyly. 'Just simple country dancing.'

That admission did not disturb him in the least. 'You can dance, Meg!' His voice was enthusiastic.

'I've always enjoyed it,' she said. 'The lovely melodies and crowds dancing in the streets and open places. Sarah couldn't bear to stay within the walls of the priory when the fair was on.' She glanced over to where her maid was sitting, in the shadows at the back of the room. Their eyes met and Meg smiled.

'And you went out with her?' Richard prompted.

'I shouldn't have done so, but it was such fun,' Meg admitted merrily. 'Sarah knew most of the dances, and she taught me. We joined in, dancing up and down the street.'

'I wish I could have seen you.'

'I'm sure you'd have been horrified! We just galloped around together. We didn't even try to be graceful, but we were so happy in those days! Sometimes we danced together in the garden, while the nuns were at prayer.'

'What about music?'

'Sarah knew the tunes, so we sang and hummed them together.'

'And the Prioress permitted this?'

Meg chuckled at the idea. 'She didn't know. She would have been shocked! But the younger nuns saw us and they just smiled; I believe they wished they could join in.'

'I'm sure they did. Correctly performed, the dance is both a pleasure and an art. You will see what I mean when I show you the steps of the galliard and, better still, the lavolta. It's fast and energetic; I believe you'll enjoy it.'

He led her towards the musicians and introduced her to their leader. As they talked he kept hold of her hand and gently stroked the back of it with his thumb. It was done without looking at her, in an absent-minded manner. The touch meant nothing, but it was pleasant and friendly. He consulted with the musicians and together they decided on the next tune.

'Listen to the music, Meg.' His enthusiasm was infectious. 'The galliard is a running dance in triple time; it has phrases of five steps—like this.'

She watched as he demonstrated, leaping high, capering, deliberately showing off his agility and strength. She began to dance opposite him.

'You're a natural dancer, Meg,' he encouraged her. 'You've picked up the steps and movements, but there are one or two points that can be improved.'

The musicians launched into another melody. He took her hand, led her to the middle of the empty floor and they danced again.

'Don't look down at your feet. Keep your eyes on me.'

Obediently she looked up, and found herself spellbound by the nimbleness with which he was performing, leaping so high and kicking with great vigour. She was caught also by the sensuality that emanated from him, the same tension as had taken her unaware at their first meeting. She faltered and looked down. Instantly he admonished her.

'Look up, Meg. Head and body erect. Step it boldly. You must always appear self-possessed. Leave the complicated steps for your partner. The man's part is to flaunt his agility. He will be inspired to even greater feats on the dance floor if his partner shows approval.'

Was he really serious? she wondered. He was teaching her the dance steps but he was flirting with her quite outrageously.

'Sir Richard,' she said, 'I do not think you should be looking at me in that manner.'

'Ah, my lady, you must understand that flirting is all part of the dance. Look into my eyes. Relax, Meg, and smile. It is but part of the game of courtly love.'

'What do you mean by that? Surely love is not a game.'

'At Windsor it is, sweet lady. All the gentlemen play it. One does not need to mean anything by it, but it will be expected of you. Be warned, for the gentlemen will take dalliance as far as you are willing to allow them to go.'

He was a master at the game, using tender touches, kissing her fingers, and the palm of her hand. She remembered that her uncle had particularly instructed him to teach such things to her. It seemed strange that such behaviour was only a pastime, but, if that was so, perhaps there was no harm in it.

She stifled her doubts. It wasn't that she found it difficult to smile, for she had a naturally happy disposition, and as she mastered one new step after another, gaining Richard's approval, smiles came as naturally to her as breathing. She was surprised at how easily she talked with him, and he encouraged her, as if they were friends.

'The dance that is sweeping the Court at the moment is the lavolta. If you are not weary, would you like to learn that also?'

'I'm not the least bit tired.' She was enjoying herself too much for that.

'This dance originated in Provence,' he explained. 'It's in triple time, with turning movements.'

Those 'turning movements' brought her shoulder to shoulder with Richard, and another flirtatious meeting of the eyes, but this time she was on her guard. Coolly she wondered how many dancing partners he had seduced with those movements.

'Regard me as the centre of a circle around which we are dancing,' Richard instructed.

Amused, she obeyed with genuine pleasure.

'Now we come to the movement that makes this dance different from all the others. You must place your right hand on my shoulder, and hold on to your petticoats with your left—'

She did as he asked, though she was amazed at such an instruction. She was even more amazed when suddenly he grasped her around the waist, his hand holding her firmly just above her hip. He followed this by placing his right hand just below her bosom. She was about to protest, but in that instant he impelled her up off her feet, by applying strong pressure with his thigh.

She was shocked to find she was virtually sitting on his lap! She screamed. Ignoring that, he swung her up into the air and spun around and around. She hung on with both hands, helpless as her skirts and petticoats swirled up, revealing a disgraceful length of bare leg. Her brain was reeling. She felt quite dizzy when he set her down on her feet again.

'Bravo! Bravo!' the Earl's loud voice rang out. He had come into the room whilst she had been swung around like a doll.

'Sir Richard!' she exclaimed breathlessly. 'Are you sure that is how it is danced at Court?'

'Exactly,' he said. 'You did very well.'

'It was a question of survival,' she snapped.

The musicians finished the melody and clapped their hands in approval. Everyone had found their dance highly entertaining, except Meg, who was convinced she had been made a fool of.

'Magnificent,' Richard exclaimed. 'But you should keep your hand on your skirts to keep them from flying around you.'

'Don't tell her that,' cried the Earl. 'That was the part I enjoyed most of all. A mightily pleasing spectacle.'

'I do not wish to be made a spectacle of!' exclaimed Meg. She glared at the Earl, but he was no longer looking at her. Nancy and Gervase had sauntered into the room.

'You missed a treat!' he told them. 'Richard and Meg have just danced the lavolta—the most revealing I've ever seen. Let's have an encore, Richard.'

Meg stepped back. 'I'm sure Mistress Nancy would like to dance with Richard now,' she said. 'I do not wish to do more today.'

Richard cast a sharp look at her. For a moment she thought he was about to insist, but evidently he took note of her furious expression, for he bowed and said, 'We will practise again tomorrow, my lady.' Then he advanced to Nancy, holding out his hand in invitation. 'May I have the pleasure?'

Perversely Meg now wished she had agreed to dance again. It gave her no pleasure to watch them circling around each other, eyes locked, playing the game of love. She turned away. That proved she meant nothing to him. Dancing alone with Richard was dangerous.

For comfort she looked to where Sarah was sitting, and noticed with surprise that Alan Crompton had joined her. They were chatting together just as they had done on the journey, absorbed in each other. Meg was pleased for them, of course, but their togetherness made her feel terribly alone.

She turned again to watch Richard and Nancy, saw Nancy smile at her partner, place her hand on his shoulder. He grasped her, swung her up and around. Her weight prevented him turning as fast as when she'd been in his arms, and he seemed relieved to set Nancy back on her feet, which gave Meg some satisfaction.

Gervase stepped forward to dance with Nancy, and Meg walked over to Sarah and Alan. She had never before thought of Sarah as beautiful, but the light shining in her eyes transformed her. She must warn her not to show her feelings so transparently.

But was her maid the only one in need of such a warning? Wasn't she in danger of doing just the same?

The following days passed in a flurry of activity such as Meg had never known before. Life in the nunnery had not prepared her for any of the things she was supposed to take part in at Bixholm.

Richard insisted that she should try everything—all the activities that to him were a normal part of life but which were so strange to her. In vain did she plead that she needed more time to master each new sport or dance, but he would not allow it.

'We have so little time,' he said. 'It's better for you to know something of everything rather than perfect your skill at only one or two.'

'Why is there such a hurry?' That question was always on Meg's mind. 'I have not yet been introduced to any particular gentleman. So how does anyone know that he will wish to marry me?'

'Oh, he will. I am sure of that, and they are sure of it too. You must not question me on the matter, my lady, for truly I am able to tell you nothing.'

Richard gave a wry smile. Something in his expression, as well as his words, made her heart sink. She felt that he was sorry for her, but, under orders from the Earl, was determined to maintain silence on the matter. Since she did not wish to incur his displeasure she could only bow to his wish. Yet that did not still the rebelliousness that was building up within her.

She knew that Richard held high office in Lord Thurton's household, yet he was not a free man. She sensed that the Earl had some hold over him, but could not imagine what it could be. His instructions were to educate her in a variety of social accomplishments and it was clear that he would carry out that task and nothing more. Yet were the times when he showed warmth towards her only figments of her imagination? Was it always a pretence? An affectation? Part of the duplicity that surrounded her now?

She toyed with the idea of acting stupidly, pretending she was unable to learn anything. But when Richard demonstrated something new, her natural eagerness and desire to please made her do her best. She loved dancing, and would practise for hours on end without tiring. And she enjoyed archery—more so as every day her skill with the bow improved. She became accustomed to watching the tilt. She still feared that Richard might be hurt, whilst at the same time she could now appreciate his skill and enthusiasm.

It was a pleasure to watch the falconers out in the field as they exercised and trained the birds. She was fascinated by their beauty: the peregrines, dark-eyed, long-tailed, graceful in flight with tapered wings, and the goshawks and sparrowhawks, too. Though she drew back when Richard suggested she should take part. It was her first act of rebellion.

'Please do not ask me.'

'It's a merlin,' Richard explained. 'A lady's hawk. Is she not a lovely creature?' He held the bird towards her.

'The bird is indeed beautiful,' Meg agreed, running a tentative finger over its slate-blue back. 'But I confess I am a little frightened by it.'

'I promise it will not hurt you.'

'No, sir. I cannot hold it. It has such a sharp hooked beak, and those talons!' She shuddered.

'I would give you covering for your wrist and hand.'

'I know it is natural for hawks to hunt and kill, but I do not wish to take part in such a sport.'

'Will you not even try?'

'I cannot. I will not.' Nothing he said would persuade her to change her mind. Her attitude hardened. In a small way she felt she was making a point. She would enter into those activities which pleased her, but refuse to take part in any that did not. She scanned his face with some anxiety, waiting for his reaction. She was prepared for a clash of wills and determined to stand her ground.

'Very well.' He shrugged and smiled disarmingly. 'It's of no consequence. I realise hawking is not to everybody's taste. Shall we return to the castle?'

He offered his arm and chatted pleasantly as they strolled over the field. His relaxed attitude showed that he bore no resentment at her rebellion. Perversely she was not sure if she should be pleased or resentful that her act of defiance had made so little impact.

As they entered the castle her spirits were uplifted by the sound of the musicians at practice.

'Shall we join them?' Richard said. 'You have not yet had the opportunity of learning the latest songs. Would you like to do that?'

She wondered if there was a tinge of sarcasm in his

voice, for he was asking her most politely. However, he was smiling, and his suggestion was one that pleased her.

'I should find that enjoyable,' she agreed. Then, after a pause, added, 'I recall that I was ridiculed because I thought only of the singing of psalms, as we did in the choir at the nunnery, but I shall be happy to learn other songs.'

'They should not have behaved towards you as they did on your arrival,' Richard said. His voice was no more than a whisper in her ear. 'I thought you bore their churlish remarks with great dignity on that occasion.'

'Thank you.' The compliment pleased her.

The musicians were rehearsing the tune that was one of the most popular at Court, not least because it was said to have been composed by the King himself. One of the musicians began to sing.

> *Greensleeves was all my joy,*
> *Greensleeves was my delight,*
> *Greensleeves was my heart of gold,*
> *And who but my lady Greensleeves?*

Meg found it pleasant and easy to join in. Her voice had been trained for singing in the choir, and that made it easy for her to pick up the rhythm.

From that they moved on to some of John Tavener's songs: 'My Harte, my Mynde?' and 'Love will I Never Love thee More'.

They were accompanied by expert lute players, one of whom taught her the words. 'You have a lovely voice, my lady,' he said. 'It has obviously been trained.'

'I've always enjoyed singing,' Meg told him. He was a charming young man, to whom music was more than just a job. He was immersed in its intricacies and always sought perfection.

'Where did you learn?' he asked.

'In the nunnery.' She smiled at his expression of surprise. 'My mother sought sanctuary there when I was but a baby.'

'They taught you well.'

'The nuns had an excellent choir and I was encouraged to join. It was all church music.'

'Religious music is some of the most wonderful ever written. But it is not to the taste of everyone.' He paused, his face expressive. She knew he was thinking of the Earl and Nancy. 'Fortunately I also enjoy the popular songs for entertainment.'

Time slipped away quickly and pleasantly that afternoon. She was surprised when Richard said they should change in readiness for the evening meal.

'Tomorrow there is to be a great gathering for a hunt,' Richard told her.

'So I have heard,' Meg said.

For several days the castle had been a-buzz with talk of the hunt to come. All the young men and women had been looking forward to it with great excitement, and others had come to join in—noblemen and their ladies from neighbouring estates.

Meg did not say so, but she had no intention of joining them.

That evening, when all had eaten and drunk their fill—and more besides—the Earl turned towards her. 'I hear you've learned some songs, Meg, is that so?'

'Yes, Uncle.'

He leaned back in his huge chair, replete and well-pleased. 'Just what we need. You can sing for us now.'

'Now?' She hesitated. She had not thought to perform so publicly or so soon.

'Now!' thundered the Earl. 'Let's hear what you can do.'

Richard offered her his arm. 'Allow me to escort you to the musicians.'

'I—I can't. I've forgotten all the words.'

'If you la-la-la, most of them won't know the difference.'

She chuckled. She did not believe him, but it helped her to relax.

The musicians stood up as she approached; they bowed. They had been kind to her that afternoon. She must not let them down. For if she failed the Earl's wrath might spill over to them also.

They began to play 'Greensleeves'. On the first note the words came back to her. The melody lifted her. She had never sung before with such a gifted accompaniment, and all the chattering voices in the Great Hall fell silent.

They applauded loudly. The Earl was among those expressing delight. 'More!' he shouted. 'More!'

She sang one more song, then begged to be excused. 'I have not yet learned any other songs,' she said.

'Very well,' Thurton said. He looked delighted as he turned to Nancy. Sarah just made out his words as she was being escorted by Richard back to her seat. 'She'll be a sensation at Court,' he said. 'The King's own song. I've never heard it sung so well. He'll love it!'

Meg was horrified at the thought—did they really expect her to sing before the King? She hoped she had not heard correctly. Then peals of laughter reeled around the Great Hall. The usual entertainers were already at their antics. The Earl was soon convulsed with laughter. The more vulgar the jokes, the louder he and Nancy laughed.

Now that she knew what to expect Meg had prepared herself. She conjured up the thought that Sarah had put into her mind. She ignored the words and antics and imagined the face of the Prioress, had she been there. That invariably brought a smile to her lips, and the Earl was deceived into believing she was changing her ideas. He nodded towards her with approval and leaned over to pat her hand. With considerable self-control she managed not to cringe.

The party broke up sooner than usual that evening.

'Up and about early tomorrow, ready for the hunt,' the Earl announced.

Meg intended to indulge in a pleasantly long lie in bed.

Sarah brought the breakfast tray very early. Then, surprisingly, dashed back to the kitchen, as if she hadn't a moment to lose. Meg began her breakfast in a leisurely manner. Long before she had finished Sarah bustled back into the chamber, bringing a ewer of hot water.

'You better hurry, my lady,' she said. 'They'll soon be a-mustering, ready for the hunt.'

'I know. I've heard the commotion outside.' Meg yawned and stretched. 'But, since I'm not taking part in it, I've no need to hurry.'

'Oh, but you must, my lady!' Sarah was aghast. 'Sir Richard particularly made me promise to have you ready in good time.'

Meg sat up, buttered an oatcake and nibbled the edge of it delicately. Sarah watched her with an expression of horrified disbelief.

'Sir Richard said if you wasn't up and out in good time, he'd come in and fetch you himself.' Sarah paused, then added, 'Probably dress you himself, too, the way he was carrying on.'

Meg almost choked on the oatcake! Would he dare to do that? Would he come into her chamber and forcibly make her get ready for the hunt? She decided he probably would.

'Well, if I must!'

'I should think so, my lady,' Sarah said cheekily, as she poured water into a basin. Her mistress would not be late if she could help it. She hustled Meg through the routine of dressing and hairbrushing and braiding without relaxing one iota her normal standard. Meg felt less urgency than usual.

Determined to take no part in the hunt, she sauntered out into the courtyard and stood lazily surveying the busy, colourful scene around her. Horses and riders, men, women and children were milling about. The verderers were on foot, keeping control of the greyhounds and mastiffs.

Richard came up to her, leading his own mount and also her mare, saddled and ready.

'Good morning, Meg. Excellent weather for the chase,' he observed.

'It is, indeed, a delightful morning.'

She seemed to have no option but to allow him to help her up into the saddle. Especially as at that moment Nancy rode up alongside. She was accompanied by another younger companion, who was, Meg decided, one of the most beautiful ladies she had ever seen. Her costume was magnificent and she handled a large, very restive grey horse with consummate ease.

'Isabelle, may I introduce Thurton's niece, Lady Margaret? Meg, this charming lady is the Marchioness of Belaugh.'

They bowed their heads to each other with cool civility.

'Ah! The young lady on whom Edmund's hopes are riding,' commented the Marchioness. 'Very pretty. Very pretty, indeed.'

Nancy smiled, as if the compliment was directed at her. 'We are in the process of creating a magnificent new wardrobe for her,' she said.

Talking about her again as if she was not there! Evidently the Marchioness had heard about her in advance. Their attitude caused Meg's anger to flare, but she held her tongue. She was about to wheel Molly and move away when Sarah appeared. She carried a silver tray with beakers of wine and held it up to Nancy and the Marchioness, then to Meg.

'Sarah, you shouldn't have been asked to perform that task,' Meg objected.

'Nobody asked me, my lady. I volunteered,' Sarah said merrily. 'Didn't see why I should be left out.'

'But you're afraid of horses!'

'I know better now. Mr Crompton's been taking me out riding every day. Not just pillion to him, either, but on a horse of my own!'

'Goodness!' exclaimed Meg.

'He says I got a good seat—an' he tells me that's a compliment!'

With a merry laugh, Sarah curtsied and moved on to offer her tray to other riders.

Nancy finished her wine and turned back to Meg. 'The Marchioness is a great friend of mine,' she remarked. 'And also of Richard's.'

Richard doffed his cap and bowed low. 'Now that

you are here, dear lady, the gathering is complete,' he said.

The Marchioness chuckled. 'Such words fall easily off your tongue,' she said. 'But they are not borne out by facts. You have not ridden over to visit me these past two months.'

'Alas, no. But I have heard that you have not been short of visitors, dear lady.'

'It is true. I have not. But you know you have always—'

The sounding of the hunting-horn drowned out her words. The meet was preparing to move off. The Earl shouted to Richard to ride up at the front, for he was to lead the great gathering. The Marchioness moved forward and cantered alongside him. She obviously assumed it was her right to share the leadership of the hunt. She was sure also of Richard's welcome, Meg thought, noticing how he turned his head, smiled at the lady and made some seemingly intimate comment.

She watched until they passed out of sight, hidden by the concourse of riders. She wished she had not observed the looks that had passed between them, for undoubtedly the arrival of the beautiful Marchioness had driven all thought of her from Richard's mind. Then she frowned at her own stupidity, reminding herself to be glad he had gone. She would never have been able to carry out her plan if he had remained close to her, but she could not entirely suppress a twinge of jealousy.

When all was ready the horn sounded again and the whole company moved forward at a gentle walking pace. As soon as they were beyond the confines of the castle and had reached the open countryside the horses were spurred on to a canter and then a gallop. Meg held

Molly back and watched them go. She had no wish to keep up.

She allowed Molly to carry her at a gentle trot towards the forest, following the well-worn track. Before long the Earl and Nancy, and all the great company of huntsmen and women, their servants, the verderers and the dogs were so far ahead that she could not even hear them crashing through the undergrowth. She had no idea what they were chasing, and she most certainly had no wish to know. She allowed her mare to amble along at her own pace, walking now. Her quiet rebellion was progressing.

It was peaceful in the forest. Meg decided to keep to the edge of the woodland, ambling along a narrow path that seemed to be very little used. In a small clearing Molly stopped, lowered her head and began to graze on a patch of grass. Meg dismounted, keeping a loose hold on the reins. She sat down on the dry, leaf-strewn ground and leaned back against a tree.

The peace of the woodland calmed her. In its immense depth she was but a minute part of the world, her life a brief span compared to the majesty of the ancient trees. She'd had little chance to think her own thoughts, or be her own person since she had arrived at Bixholm. All day long she'd had to struggle to master some new skill, and the evenings had been endured at the high table beside the Earl, constantly watched by Nancy and dominated by the rough, boisterous company.

It was a pleasure to be on her own, half dozing, absorbing the earth scents, enjoying the dappled sunlight on her face. Time passed without her being aware of it.

Then the jingle of a horse's harness came to her ears. Someone was riding nearby. She stayed still and silent, hoping whoever it was would pass without seeing her. She experienced a frisson of fear.

Molly neighed.

The rider halted. She held her breath.

Chapter Six

Richard crashed into the clearing.

The wild, angry expression on his face was frightening. He leapt from his horse and dashed towards her.

'Meg!' he cried. 'What are you doing here?'

Her mind reacted furiously. Why had he returned? Could she not be away from him for a few hours, or not so much away from him as his efforts to 'improve' her? She wished he had not disturbed her solitude—and yet the sight of him set her heart racing.

'Meg?' His voice was more gentle, questioning. He strode towards her, reaching out his arms. 'Are you hurt?'

'No.'

He halted. He dropped his arms just as she was about to lift hers towards him. She froze when he suddenly stood still. He was regarding her with a puzzled expression. 'Are you sure all is well with you?'

'Most certainly, thank you, Sir Richard.'

He turned his gaze upon the little mare, who continued to pull at the short grass with strong teeth.

'I am perfectly sound in mind and limb,' she assured him. 'And so is Molly.'

He looked relieved, though still puzzled. 'So? What are you doing here?'

'That is what I wonder every day,' she answered. 'Why am I here, Richard? Why are you trying so hard to change me? What was wrong with me before you brought me to this place?'

'Nothing, Meg.'

A grin spread over his face. He threw himself down on the ground beside her. The sudden movement startled her. She looked down, for he was below her now, lying on his side. Only a few blades of grass separated them. She met the challenge of his gaze and felt mesmerised and strangely happy. Every nerve in her body was on edge, alive, throbbing.

'I have no wish to change you,' he said. A husky note deepened his voice. The tone in which he spoke, caressingly soft, affected her. It weakened her, as if she had been struck by a blow in the ribs, but there was no pain, only an overwhelming joy.

It disconcerted her. They were quite alone in the beauty of the woodland glade. The air was sweet and still. Neither of them moved, yet emotion, intangible, but as real as life itself, was drawing them closer.

In desperation she tried to keep the conversation light, wanting to deny there was any deeper sensibility between them.

'No wish to change me?' she mocked. 'Even though I refuse to go hunting?'

'Not even that.' He did not laugh. He replied seriously, picked up one of her hands, turned it over and fondled it.

She withdrew it hastily. 'Have they finished?' she asked, determinedly prosaic.

'No. They'll go on for hours yet.'

Then she had to ask. 'Why did you come back?'

'To look for you, my lady.'

That was pleasing, but she was not quite ready to accept it. 'Did the Earl send you?'

'No.'

Then, with a hint of mischief, and because she needed to hear his reaction, 'The Marchioness will miss you.'

'I doubt it. She's in her element in the chase, especially of males, wild or human.'

He recaptured her hand and kissed it. The tingling sensation that had unnerved her when he settled on the ground at her side intensified. He raised his head, sat up and leaned towards her. Slowly, gently, he brought his face closer to hers. She shut her eyes, and he kissed her.

His soft, sweet lips touched hers lightly, experimentally. She had never before been kissed by a man, not even within the family—no father, uncle or brother—and not on any part of her face. Yet instinctively she responded, allowing her lips to brush his with only the briefest of butterfly touches. She drew away, savouring the delight of that kiss, running her tongue over her lips. After a few moments she opened her eyes and regarded him wonderingly.

Richard guessed it was a new experience for her and he was anxious not to awaken fear in her. His blood pounded hotly through his veins. He longed to clasp her tightly, to plunder her mouth with his, to stroke and caress every inch of her beautiful body. But he checked himself; he had to be careful. He must not lose the trust she had in him. He smiled at her and simply ran his forefinger over her cheek.

'Richard,' she breathed. 'Kiss me again.'

He could not resist—it was a deeper kiss this time.

He had wanted this from the very first time he saw her, dressed in that awful soiled gown, bravely protecting old blind Davy. She lifted her arms and wound them around his neck. He drew her close against him. At that moment he seemed unable to save himself from drowning in the rich sensuality of arousal.

Yet he remained alert. His eyes were wide open, his ears tuned to the sounds of the wind in the trees, the birds, the woodland creatures. He could not, would not allow desire to lower his defences. There was always danger in the forest, and more for him than for most men. He reminded himself how much was at stake. He could so easily have allowed passion to overwhelm him, but fought against it. To be caught off guard could bring death. He must take no risks. Meg had no protector other than he. It was a bitter irony that she could never be his. His lips parted from hers reluctantly.

'We shouldn't be doing this,' he said.

She tried to draw him back into her embrace, but he sprang to his feet.

'You must forget this ever happened,' he said.

'Why? We have done no wrong, have we?'

'In the eyes of the world we have.'

'You told me it was essential to flirt,' she objected.

'At Court—yes,' he agreed. 'Not here. And not when we both know there can never be anything between us.'

To emphasise the point he stepped away from her. He listened intently, put a finger to his lips.

'Someone is approaching,'

She held her breath. She heard a jingling harness, a horse's hooves, moving at a slow walking pace. Richard's hand was on his sword. Meg crouched back. His stance suggested danger. The sounds came nearer. There was no doubt they would be discovered.

A moment later Gervase Gisbon rode into the clearing. His eyes darted from her to Richard. Meg felt sure he guessed that Richard had kissed her. His sly expression deepened the dislike and distrust she felt for him. Undeniably he was handsome, his skin cleanshaven and smooth, his manners polished—why was it the very sight of him made her flesh creep?

'What a delightful bower you have found,' he said. There was a sneer in his voice.

'It is charming,' Richard agreed easily, but Meg detected the tension in his voice.

'The Earl has been asking for you, Richard,' Gervase announced. 'And more particularly for Lady Margaret.'

'How very considerate of him,' said Richard.

'In fact,' Gervase continued, 'he is so disturbed by your absence—or more especially that of your fair companion—that he has turned the entire company back to search for you.'

'There was no need for alarm,' Richard assured him. 'Lady Margaret's pony was unable to keep up with the hunt, that is all.'

'Strange. I do not recollect that Lady Margaret's mount had any difficulty in carrying her from Norwich to Bixholm.'

'That was on well-worn tracks. The mare is unused to the woodland paths.'

That was not the full truth, and Meg's conscience made her feel obliged to explain properly. 'That is true,' she said, for she did not wish to suggest that what Richard had said was wrong. 'But I did not try to keep up, for I did not wish to take part in the hunt.'

Gervase raised his eyebrows. 'How extraordinary!'

'It may seem so to you, but it is the truth,' she assured him.

Gervase looked from Meg to Richard with a disbelieving grin. Then he shrugged his broad shoulders. 'You'll have difficulty explaining that to his lordship. He'll be here shortly, and I warn you, he is not in the best of tempers.'

'I'm sorry if I have spoiled the day. But I have no wish to hunt.'

Gervase shrugged. 'I believe you—the question is, will the Earl?' He backed his horse out of the clearing. 'He will, I think be particularly interested to know that Richard is here with you.'

'Richard turned back only because he realised I was missing and he was afraid some ill chance might have befallen me. Just as you did, did you not, Master Gisbon?'

Gervase did not answer.

Richard was becoming impatient. 'I suggest we ride back to the castle,' he said. 'There is no point in wasting time here.'

'Do you think he'll send me back to the nunnery?' Meg asked apprehensively. Insecure though she was at Bixholm, she had no wish to return and face the disapproval of the Prioress.

'Not unless his plans come to naught,' said Richard.

Meg shivered. A few minutes previously, lying in his arms, life had seemed vibrant and joyous. Now all was changed. Richard had changed, too. There was no loving tolerance about him now.

'Back on to your mare,' he ordered.

He tossed her up into the saddle as if she was no more than a bundle of straw. She felt humiliated and angry. She did not wait for him. She set Molly moving forward immediately. She feared that Gervase Gisbon would try to prevent her from leaving, but he moved aside to allow her to pass.

Out of the clearing, she was about to turn into the path along which she had ambled contentedly such a short time before. Loud shouts, crashing sounds, the tooting of the hunting-horn, baying dogs, told her the hunting party was close. A moment later they burst out of the woods and surrounded her.

'Ah-ha, Meg. There you are! What's afoot?' demanded the Earl. 'Why are you back here?'

'My lord, I meant no harm, but I know nothing of hunting. I was just enjoying the ride in my own way—'

He wheeled his mighty horse, which seemed double the height of Molly. He scowled. His face was a livid colour. 'Ha! In your own way? What the devil does that mean?'

'I did not wish to join the hunt, my lord.'

'Didn't want to hunt! Never heard of such a thing! Was that your only reason?' He stared at her in disbelief. 'You're sure you were not up to some mischief?'

She regarded him unflinchingly. She did not believe that allowing Richard to kiss her could be categorised as mischief. 'Certainly not, sir!'

'Richard!' the Earl yelled.

'Yes, sir.'

'What is your part in this nonsense?'

'When I realised that Lady Margaret had not managed to keep up with the hunt I turned back. I thought her mare might have found the going difficult. I arrived here only a short time before you, sir. As did Master Gisbon.'

'Hmmph! Well, I suppose there's been no harm done. See that Lady Margaret is better mounted before we commence the ride to London.'

'I will, sir.'

The Earl turned back to Meg. 'Next time we hunt, you shall ride alongside me.'

Meg sighed. As usual he had not listened to a word she had said. She did not argue, but she had no intention of hunting with him, or with anyone else! If this prospective husband expected it of her, he would have to be dissuaded.

'You don't know what you've missed, Meg.' The Earl beamed. 'We've killed a magnificent boar. Biggest beast I've seen for many a month. I intend to make a present of it to the King. We'll move on to London at the end of this week.'

Despite the hunt having been turned back early, all the members were in high spirits. The Earl's excitement and pleasure in such a successful day was reflected in the general boisterous behaviour. Meg turned Molly and rode towards the castle. Richard was nearby, but there was no opportunity for private conversation as the whole concourse was moving together.

She did not encourage Molly to hurry; she moved aside and allowed other riders to canter past. Although she no longer had the pleasure of being alone in the peace of the forest, she still enjoyed its beauty. It was some time before she emerged from the shadows of the huge old trees into the bright sunshine. From the greensward that then stretched before her the castle rose, majestic and strong. It was impressive, of gleaming cream stone, with towers and turrets and mullioned windows that caught the sun's rays. She had developed a great liking for the place, and daydreamed as she trotted towards it, imagining improvements she would make if it only belonged to her, as in law it should.

Two riders came into view—not members of the

hunting party. They were some distance away, yet she thought she recognised the young woman. It was a moment before she could be sure—then she gazed in amazement, for it was Sarah! Her maid, who had always expressed such an overwhelming fear of horses, was out riding with a gentleman! And not on pillion either, but in the saddle, and cantering! They passed over the brow of a small hill and were soon out of sight. Meg decided to make no mention of it, but to leave it to Sarah to tell her, if she wished. She held the view that what her maid did in her free time was entirely her affair.

That evening Sarah was in an effervescent mood as she helped Meg to prepare for the feast that was to finish the day's hunt.

'I bin out riding today too, miss,' she said.

'I know, Sarah. I saw you.'

'Never thought as I'd do that, did yer?'

'I must admit, I was surprised.'

Sarah was thoughtful for a moment. Then she spoke again, hesitantly, 'My lady, may I ask you a question?'

'Of course, Sarah. When have you ever felt that you needed to ask my permission to speak to me of anything?'

'Never.' Sarah grinned. 'But it's so different here, with you being with Sir Richard almost all the time, and sitting at the top table with the Earl at meals. Nothing's like it used to be, is it?'

'That's true. But I haven't changed, Sarah. You mustn't think I don't wish to speak with you, or spend more time with you. It is simply because his lordship and Nancy and Richard all demand so much of my time. You must never—ever—think that I don't care for you.' She threw her arms around the girl and hugged her tightly.

Sarah hugged her back and kissed Meg's cheek. 'I know you do, my lady. It's hard for you here, more so than for me, not knowing what's to happen an' all. Truly sometimes I fear for the future.'

'I do, too, Sarah,' Meg said seriously. 'They say I am to be married to someone, but they won't tell me who, no matter how often I ask.'

'It's not fair that they should treat you like that!'

'But there's nothing I can do about it,' Meg replied. 'Now, tell me, what is it you wish to speak to me about?'

'Well, my lady.' Sarah blushed and hung her head, and seemed unusually tongue-tied for one who was normally so loquacious. 'It—it's just that—well, I was wondering—do you like Alan Crompton?'

'Why, yes, Sarah. I do. And I have the impression that you also like him.'

Sarah looked up with bright eyes, wide open. 'He says he likes me too, my lady. But I'm afeared that it's wrong, because he's of noble birth and my father was nothing but a labourer in the fields. He didn't even have his own land, or at least only a little bit.'

'But you have been educated, Sarah. You learned your lessons alongside me. I think that must make a difference. You could hold up your head in any society. Has Alan spoken to you about this?'

'I spoke to him, my lady. I didn't want him thinking me better than I am.'

'What did he say to that?'

'He said as I didn't seem like a peasant girl and he'd never met anyone like me before and it's what I am now that matters.'

'Quite right.' Meg nodded emphatically.

'Then he said that although he was of noble birth, he

was really quite poor. His older brother inherited everything and he's had to live on his wits and get by as best he can, and that's why he's here in the service of the Earl. Then he looked at me, silly idiot that he is, and he asked if I found him very ugly, an' of course I said, "No, not at all." I told him it was how he behaved to me that mattered, not what he looked like. An' anyway, he couldn't help it if he had a scar on his face, an' it didn't make no difference to me. In fact I don't see it no more, now.'

'I know, Sarah,' Meg said. 'When you get to know people well you don't think so much about appearance. It's other things that count then.'

Sarah was silent for a moment. Her eyes were shining. Her cheeks were shining too. Meg knew her well enough to realise she was about to say something that she thought was unbelievable! Like the time when she'd taken Meg into the stable at the nunnery to watch a litter of kittens being born.

'What is it?' she asked gently.

Sarah took a deep breath. 'Alan Crompton—' she rolled the name round on her tongue '—said as how he'd ask me to marry him, only he'd nothing to give me. 'Course I said as how that didn't matter to me. I ain't got nothing either.'

'Oh, Sarah. I'm so happy for you.'

'Thank you, my lady. I was quite overcome. An' I told him how proud I was to be asked. An' I would have liked to say yes, but I had to say no, because I couldn't leave you, my lady.'

'Dear Sarah.' Meg had tears in her eyes. 'I won't stop you. If you wish to go away with Alan—'

'No, my lady. That I'll never do. At least not until I know as you're properly settled an' safe.'

'I don't want to stand in the way of your happiness,' Meg insisted, though her heart was heavy. She knew how greatly she would miss Sarah, her constant friendship, her sensibility, humour and high spirits.

'I mean it, my lady. Alan Crompton'll have to wait. It won't do him no harm. If he won't do that for me, then he's not worth having. That's what I say.'

'But, Sarah, it's your happiness—'

'There'd be no happiness for me unless you were happy as well!' Sarah was adamant.

Every day Meg had to spend several hours with Nancy and the dressmakers. They discussed the latest fashions, held up beautiful material to see its effect. Sometimes they asked if she liked this or that, then completely ignored her response. So mostly she took the easiest course and simply left it to them.

She always took Sarah with her to these fittings, not only to assist with the interminable dressing and undressing, but because she needed her maid's companionship, even though she had to remain quietly in the background. If she uttered a word she was threatened with being summarily expelled from the chamber.

Once Meg had remonstrated when she'd considered a gown to be too revealing. Her objections had been brushed aside.

'Nonsense,' Nancy had said. 'You must leave those convent pruderies behind you now.'

'It's the fashion, my dear,' Mrs Goodley had cooed.

'The Court would be more surprised if you hid the upper part of your bosom,' Nancy had said. 'They would be sure you had some hideous blemish that you wished to cover, and such a rumour would totally ruin your chances.'

'You have such a lovely complexion!' one of the sewing maids had said. 'Not a mark from the small-pox. You don't know how lucky you are.'

Meg was disturbed when one afternoon Earl Thurton joined them in Nancy's chamber. Mrs Goodley and her assistants immediately drew back and curtsied.

'Carry on, ladies.' He waved his hand magnanimously and seated himself upon the bed. 'I've come to see how the robing is progressing.'

'You are most welcome, my lord.' Nancy was all smiles. 'I am sure you will find we are assembling a very becoming wardrobe for your niece—'

'Excuse me,' interrupted Meg. 'Surely it is not seemly for a gentleman to see me in my underwear?'

'Don't be so prissy,' Nancy snapped. 'The Earl is paying the bills; he has a right to see what he'll get for his money. Besides, he's well used to seeing ladies in their underwear.'

'Quite right,' the Earl chuckled. 'You've no need to be bothered by my presence. As I've said before, you're too skinny for my taste.'

Nancy laughed loudly, taking the comment as a compliment to her own buxom form. Meg hung her head. Perhaps she was being foolish. The Earl was old enough to be her father.

'Very well,' she said. That was foolish too, for she'd been told, not asked.

A moment later she heard the ring of quick footsteps on the stone-flagged passage. The door was flung open and Richard stood on the threshold.

Meg gasped. She was about to protest, until she saw the welcoming smile Nancy was bestowing on him.

'I invited Richard to give us his opinion. Please enter.'

He bowed to them all, then strolled forward, relaxed and at ease, pleasantly smiling. Meg froze. Was he also accustomed to seeing ladies in a state of semi-undress?

Cold fury seized her. Like a statue she stood as they continued with the fitting. Tight-lipped, showing her disapproval with silent rebellion. Mrs Goodley and her sewing maidens busied themselves around her, tacking and tucking. They lifted her arms and put them down again, turned her this way and that.

'What's the matter with the girl?' exploded the Earl. 'Does nothing make her happy? That's a magnificent gown, enough to turn any man's head. What do you say, Richard?'

'Lady Margaret does indeed look very beautiful in it.' Richard spoke softly, sincerely.

'There, Meg,' said Nancy. 'What more can you wish for? Aren't you one of the most fortunate girls in the land?'

Meg made no answer. She stared straight ahead, looking at no one. She felt humiliated, a spectacle. When Mrs Goodley began to remove the gown, which in any event only partly covered her, Meg instinctively stepped back.

'We are merely educating you into the ways of the Court, of the very highest people in the land. Who are you to object? You are infuriating!' Nancy moved to slap her face.

'No.' The one word from Richard stopped her with her hand raised. 'You told me Lady Margaret wished for my opinion,' he said quietly. 'I see now that was not the truth.'

'I was sure Meg would wish to be guided by what you think, Richard.' There was malice in Nancy's face.

'What nonsense!' he snapped. 'I shall leave.'

Meg did not move an inch. She held her head high, dissociating herself entirely from the conversation. She felt angry and humiliated. In the silence, she heard his footsteps crossing the floor as he left the room. Part of her wanted to turn and look at him, but she could not—would not—do so. She maintained her silence for the rest of the session.

It put Nancy into an ill-temper. She ranted at the dressmakers, insisted that the bodice of a gown be lowered yet further, although she knew well that Meg had previously objected to its cut. The dressmakers complied with Nancy's wishes, then stood back, looking at the new line critically.

'Do you not think it was more fetching as it was, Mistress Nancy?' said one of the dressmakers. She regarded Meg with a look of sympathy. 'A little modesty can have great appeal, especially in one so young—'

'Modesty be damned!' Nancy turned to the Earl. 'What is your opinion, my dear one? Am I not right? A man wants to see what he is being offered.' Nancy gave a harsh laugh.

'You have a point there,' agreed Thurton. 'I would say it reveals just enough, not too much. Quite luscious. You've made a good choice, Nan.'

Nancy smiled broadly, pleased to have her opinion vindicated.

'There is just one point, your ladyship,' said Mrs Goodley. 'If it is lowered, as you suggest, there is a possibility that the gown will fall off the shoulder.'

'Let it,' snapped Nancy.

'That's my girl!' The Earl chuckled.

Meg thought there was a distinct possibility that her bosom would spill out over the top, even if the gown did not fall off altogether, but she said nothing. She would refuse to wear that gown, even though it was intended to be the most beautiful, and was the most expensive in the whole magnificent collection.

Nancy's lip curled as she spoke to the woman. 'If you cannot make the alteration, I shall take it to a better dressmaker when we get to London.'

The sewing maids exchanged anxious glances.

'I'm not saying we can't do it, my lady. Indeed it's quite a simple job. I was merely making a suggestion.' She could not afford to lose the custom of her wealthiest client.

Nancy would have none of it. 'I've made up my mind. I shall have this gown finished in London, and we'll have more made when we get there. There will be a better choice of materials than you can provide. If we had more time I'd suggest to his lordship that I should take her to Paris—there they really understand how to make clothes!' She turned from the mortified women and spoke directly to Meg. 'You can go and join Richard, who will no doubt be expecting you for further instruction on behaviour.'

Nancy held out her hand to the Earl and together, looking well pleased with themselves, they sauntered from the chamber.

Chapter Seven

Richard paced up and down in the passageway that led to the Music Room. It had been almost unbearable to walk away from Nancy's chamber, to leave Meg's delightful form partially exposed, then covered in alluringly rich garments. He had seen the expression in the Earl's eyes as he had watched, and no matter what he said, Richard could not believe that any man could look at Meg without lusting for her.

His pulse-rate had quickened when Nancy had said, 'Meg would like you to attend her next fitting, and I should value your opinion of the styles I have chosen for her.' He had been unbelievably excited, as feverish as a schoolboy rushing to his first assignation with a woman.

It had taken all his will-power to wrench himself away from the delectable sight of her in the shimmering silken underwear which had clung so revealingly to the curves of her lovely body. He'd yearned then to cover her, to comfort her and carry her off to his own private chamber. He broke off the thoughts. How could they treat her like that? It had been evident the moment he saw her frozen face that all had not been well with her.

He had seen Meg in many different moods during their daily contact, and he could readily recall her anger at their first encounter in the crowded street in Norwich. But that had been different from this. Then she had been proud and unafraid. He knew her face when she was concentrating, so willingly trying her best at archery. He had seen fear in her eyes at the tilt, and delight when under his patient tuition she had mastered a new step in the dance. He was entranced by the sound of her laugh, which would ring out with uninhibited gaiety when she was amused.

Hers was the most expressive face he had ever seen, and never had she looked so thunderous as in the dress-makers' hands. Rage was tight-bottled within her, fanned by her helplessness. Like a prisoner in chains she had stood stock-still, but her eyes had darted about, seeking escape and seeing no way out. He sensed that they were trying to break her spirit, forcing her to bend to their will.

He felt anger for her, and fury that his helplessness was as great as her own. He longed to gather her into his arms and carry her away—but he had no place to take her. No home, no fortune, no means to support her as a lady of her rank had a right to expect.

Nancy's invitation had suggested that she suspected there was an attachment between them. Had it been a trap, set up to test him? The Earl's expression had been watchful and mistrustful.

He was no fool. He was ambitious and he was play-ing for high stakes in this enterprise of arranging a mar-riage between Meg and the King.

Richard feared that his outburst might have fanned suspicions already harboured by the Earl and Nancy, but he'd been unable to prevent himself. Had he witnessed any further indignities inflicted upon Meg his anger would have exploded even more forcefully. She did not deserve such treatment. She was beautiful, intelligent, a truly delightful character. Of course he liked her, but he had taken care that it should be no more than that. He ought not to have kissed her as he had done that day in the woods, but what did a few delicious kisses mean? He'd kissed many women, and lain in the arms of several, but this was different—because Meg was different.

It had been a pleasure to spend so much time with her, but that was all. Most definitely there was not the least suspicion that he had fallen in love. He assured himself that he would have felt the same concern for any woman who was destined to be married to Henry VIII. It was his pride in chivalry, his training in knight-errantry that demanded he should make the tuition he was giving to Meg as pleasant as possible.

He had last seen the King during the Christmas festivities, and had been horrified to see how gross His Majesty had grown, especially for a man who was only in his mid-forties. Some said Henry had never fully recovered from that fall he'd had when jousting, when he'd lain unconscious for two hours or more. Could that have had an effect upon the regal brain? Heaven forbid—and heaven forbid also that anyone could read such thoughts, for surely they were treasonable.

Henry had been handsome, vigorous and popular in his youth. Then he might have made a fair match with Meg. Now it sickened Richard to think of it. If only he could devise some means to protect her! He must redouble his guard. If any mischance befell him there would be no one to watch over her, and she was so vulnerable. There was little he could do except remain vigilant for her welfare, and that meant taking care of himself also. A knife in the back was not a fate to which he intended to expose himself.

His unease increased as he entered the Music Room and saw Gervase Gisbon sprawled on a bench. They exchanged perfunctory greetings as Richard walked over to the musicians. One of them handed him a lute. He settled himself in their midst and began to play. The music was soothing, but could not entirely dowse the anxiety he felt as he waited.

Would Meg come to him for tuition as trustingly as before? She had made her feelings abundantly clear when he'd seen her with the dressmakers. Had he lost her good opinion for ever? He was surprised at how deeply that thought distressed him. His fingers slipped on the strings of the lute, making such an ugly twang that he laid the instrument aside. He was too disturbed to make music. The other musicians continued to play. Richard sat with his head bowed.

Perhaps it was time for him to step aside from Meg? Time for someone else to take on the task of preparing for her launch into high society? It would be sensible to say he had done all he could, but even the thought of that was unbearable.

'Richard.'

The Earl's voice boomed into the room, thunderous above the gentle music of the lutes.

He looked up uneasily. It was the last sound he wished to hear. Nancy was with the Earl, the two of them standing in the open doorway. Thurton with thick legs placed sturdily apart, his heavy frame accentuated by his fashionable padded doublet, slashed sleeves puffed to the elbow. Nancy plumply filling her gown, expensive necklaces decorating the bare flesh above the fitted bodice. Her sleeves had exaggerated cuffs hanging loose, revealing elaborate undersleeves of richly patterned silk. Despite the richness of their clothing, their appearance was coarse.

'Yes, my lord?'

They watched as Richard walked towards them. He bowed.

'We expected to see Lady Margaret here with you,' said Nancy.

'She has not yet arrived,' Richard replied stiffly. 'Perhaps she is changing her gown. She has several now from which to choose.'

'And the minx is hard to please,' growled the Earl. Then sharply he asked, 'What was that scene about?'

'In Mistress Nancy's chamber?' Richard enquired.

'You know perfectly well what I am talking about. No prevarication. I want the truth.'

'There was no more to it than you saw for yourself,' Richard said. 'You must remember that Lady Margaret was brought up in a nunnery. She is not accustomed to the ways of the world.'

'I'm not blind, Richard. She would have dismissed me if she had been able, but it was when you came into the room that she became really upset. Why should that be, I wonder? Is there something between you? Some— attachment, perhaps?'

'No, sir. I think her shyness springs entirely from her convent upbringing. She thinks of me as a friend.'

'Only that? A friend?'

'Just that. I am no relation to her, and in truth I had no right to be there.'

The Earl brushed that aside. 'You were there at the invitation of Mistress Nancy. Perhaps it was a mistake. It is the extent of this "friendship" that I am querying.'

'It was but part of the task you entrusted me with, sir. It was necessary to gain the young lady's confidence as I educated her in those sports and pastimes necessary for her to enter the sophisticated circle at Court.'

The Earl's small eyes narrowed till they were but slits in his big florid face.

'I also gave instructions that you were not to ingratiate yourself into her affections.'

'I assure you I have done only that which was necessary to fulfil the task you entrusted to me.' Richard stood straight and returned the Earl's searching gaze unwaveringly.

'I have to believe you,' he said grudgingly. 'I admit you have greatly improved the wench. She begins to act almost as if she belongs in the real world. If we play our cards right she should catch the amorous eye of our lusty King.'

'I have no doubt about that,' Richard agreed. He believed it, but had difficulty in saying it without a note of despondency in his voice. It pained him to think of the future mapped out for Meg, who was still so lovely, fresh and innocent.

'It is crucial that nothing should go amiss at this stage.'

Richard nodded acceptance. He could not trust himself to speak.

'Mistress Nancy and I have talked it over,' the Earl continued. 'It is clear that my niece has blossomed from the shy child that she was into ripe womanhood.'

Richard's feelings were of deepening gloom, but he spoke coolly. 'She is now an enchanting young woman.'

'Exactly!' said the Earl. 'An enchanting young woman! Tempting to any man, eh?' Richard did not answer. He was wondering what was the purpose of this interview. 'Tempting, eh?' pressed Thurton. 'And you spend all day, every day, often alone with her.'

It seemed to Richard that he had seldom been alone with Meg—except for that delightful, all too brief occasion in the woods, which had no doubt been reported to Thurton by Gervase.

'You wish to appoint someone else?' he asked cautiously.

'No. You are to keep on with the good work—'

'We think it essential for you to continue schooling Meg,' Nancy interrupted the Earl. 'For despite your efforts, Richard, she is as yet by no means perfect.' There was a carping note in her voice.

'Quite,' agreed the Earl. 'Now we wish you to accompany us to the chapel.'

'Certainly.' Richard shrugged.

Gallantly he offered his arm to Nancy, but all his senses were alerted, his eyes darting left and right. Was it a trap? Had Gervase Gisbon poured poison into the Earl's ears? Was a hired assassin poised ready to strike?

The castle chapel was large and cold, the lime-washed walls extensively decorated with paintings of saints and sinners in ochres, vermilions, and copper-salt green. The Earl strode down the centre of the nave towards the colourful stained glass window above the altar. He stopped beside the lectern, on which a Bible was chained.

The Earl turned sharply and faced Richard. Nancy stepped aside. 'A safeguard, Richard,' he said. 'This enterprise is too important for it to be ruined by some unexpected slip. We fear that being in close company with my niece, whom you yourself describe as enchanting, may present too great a temptation—'

'My lord, I gave you my word.' Richard interrupted sharply. 'My honour—'

'Honour has been forgotten before this, when passion has taken over,' the Earl said. 'I know men—and their weaknesses. I know how a woman's beauty can make stronger men than you are forget their duty. If you wish to remain as mentor to Lady Margaret, you must take an oath on the Bible.'

'I assure you it is unnecessary,' Richard insisted.

'Then it can do you no harm to take it. Come here. Swear before almighty God that Lady Margaret is still a maid.'

'To the best of my knowledge and belief that is so,' said Richard.

'Secondly you must swear that she will remain inviolate.'

'I cannot take responsibility for the lady for ever,' Richard demurred. 'But I will willingly swear that I shall protect Lady Margaret's chastity, with my life, if need be, until she shall marry.'

'Then put your hand on the book and repeat those words.'

Solemnly Richard obeyed.

'Good.'

The Earl and Nancy walked away. Just before they left, Thurton turned. 'Have you seen to providing Lady Margaret with a faster mount?'

'I will do so immediately, sir.'

'We shall depart for Westminster any day now and I intend to make our arrival as notable as possible.'

'I will see to it, my lord.'

Richard stayed in the quiet of the church for a few minutes more. He had no regret over the solemn oath he had taken. He had worded it with care. In that moment he had been forced to face the reality of his feelings. When he had said 'until she shall marry' his mind had suddenly focused. He had almost added the word 'me'. What a foolish thought that was! Meg was far beyond him. He shook his head, then walked briskly to the stables.

Meg knew Richard would be expecting her to join him for another dancing session but her mood remained rebellious. Let him wait! Smouldering with rage, she picked up the skirts of the newly finished gown she was wearing and walked quickly along the castle corridors. Sarah hurried behind her, keeping silent. She knew the time was not right even to try and talk her mistress out of this mood. In her own chamber, Meg began to tug at the fastenings of the elegant gown.

'Sarah—help me out of this—this thing!' she commanded.

'Yes, my lady,' Sarah murmured. 'But truly this gown is very becoming to you, and it is by no means immodest—'

'It's one *they've* had made for me. I want to be my own self again. Bring out the clothes I wore at the nunnery.'

Sarah was shocked. 'You cannot wish to wear those things again!'

'I do. And I will. I take it they are clean?'

'Of course! I washed them myself.'

'Thank you, Sarah. Now please fetch them.'

It took very little time to put them on. 'Ah! How comfortable they feel!'

'Ugly, though,' said Sarah.

'I don't care. You and the nuns made them for me,

and they were stitched with care and love, not for showing me off to potential suitors.'

With a feeling of freedom such as she had not experienced since her arrival at Bixholm Meg walked out of the castle. She wandered around, just as she had done on her first morning. The gardeners were busy tending the herb garden and the vegetable plot. She leaned on a wall and watched them. The soft cooing of doves was in the air, the dainty birds fluttering in and out of the dovehouse. The scene was peaceful but it did not calm her.

She had felt humiliated by Richard's intrusion into the fitting session. How dared he assume that she would accept his presence? She chewed over the hurt, telling herself he was no different from the Earl or Nancy. It was yet another instance of treating her as a nonentity. He had never done that before. His actions had always been courteous, kind, considerate. It seemed quite out of character. The only thing in his favour was that when he had realised his presence was unwelcome he had departed.

They had spent so much time together that it was strange not to be with him. She had enjoyed most of the activities to which he had introduced her. Best of all had been dancing, for she had a natural sense of rhythm. She could not help wishing she could be with him now, stepping out a gay galliard, a stately pavane or even the risqué lavolta.

'Look at me. Smile. Make eyes at me—just pretend,' he had instructed. Then added with a light laugh, 'You don't know how to flirt, do you?'

'Why should I? It is insincere.'

'Not at Court, because everyone knows it is meaningless pleasantry.'

She had been shocked. Then, as time went by, she had begun to find it rather pleasant to return those flirtatious gestures. Was that all it had been when he had kissed her so sweetly in the woods? She was too honest not to know that her response had been meaningful. His kisses had effectively lifted her away from all that was mundane. She had felt she could renounce everything else in the world, as if she had been born just for that day. She had wanted no other heaven than to lie there with him, had yearned for him to continue loving her for ever. It had been like an eclipse of the sun when they had been disturbed.

They had so seldom been on their own together. When he tutored her in various pastimes and recreations, almost always there were other people around, watching, laughing, shouting encouragement or the reverse. Her days had been so full. He had led her from one activity to the next. She had danced late into the night, until she was so tired that she had almost fallen asleep on her feet. But she had been learning fast, and mostly she enjoyed what she was doing.

She had scarcely realised it, but those long hours with Richard had awakened in her a yearning for something more. She had felt the quickening of her blood, the racing of her heart. When she had lived in the nunnery love had been only a concept, something that might happen in the distant future. Now, as she wandered moodily over the turf that surrounded the castle, the truth came to her. She had fallen in love with Richard.

It was shameful, because Richard had never spoken of love; he was only interested in playing the game of courtly love. Moreover, the Earl had made it abundantly clear—*he is not the one for you*. And he had full control over her future.

The sound of cantering hooves interrupted her reverie. She turned and saw Richard approaching, riding one horse and leading another. He reined in beside her. She expected to be reprimanded for not attending the dance session. He even smiled and, noticing her simple clothes, raised his eyebrows. She tossed her head with a haughty gesture, expecting him to make some disparaging remark. She would make no apology. Her mood was still defiant.

To her amazement, he chuckled. Although it seemed to be a friendly sort of chuckle it made her angry. Did she look so funny? If he had not been so high up on that great horse she would probably have slapped his face.

'My lady.' He spoke with deference, and as ever his voice sent a shiver of delight coursing through her. 'The Earl was disturbed that you were unable to keep up with the hunt and has ordered me to provide a more powerful mount for you.'

'That was not the reason I lagged behind.'

'Nevertheless he is right. We ride to London in a few days' time.' He swung himself out of the saddle. 'I've chosen this mare. What do you think of her?'

Meg stroked the hard forehead, patted the strong neck. Brown and white. She and Meg took to each other immediately.

'She is beautiful. What is her name?'

'Bella,' he answered. 'I rode her yesterday and found her lively but with a commendably good temperament.'

Meg looked Bella over and loved her almost as much as she did Molly.

'Will you ride with me, to see how you get on with her?'

He made no mention of the previous incident. She

wished he would apologise, but, being realistic, knew he would not do so. Whatever her feelings, she decided that a good hard ride was just what she needed.

'If indeed I am to ride her to London in the near future, it would seem sensible for me to try her out.'

He helped her up into the saddle and, without even waiting for him to remount, she wheeled the mare and set off at full speed. In her mind she was trying to get away from him—even though her heart told her that was impossible.

The mare was fast and strong, eager to gallop. The fresh air blew into Meg's face and through her hair. The power of the animal excited her as they raced away over the pastureland that surrounded the castle. She glanced over her shoulder. Richard was chasing after her. She urged Bella to go faster, wanting to get away, to leave him behind. She hoped it would humiliate him, as he had done her. Easily and rapidly he closed the gap between them.

'Slow down, Meg,' he shouted above the pounding of the horses' hooves.

She would have ignored his call, still rebellious, but they were approaching the forest. To have continued at such a pace beneath the overhanging trees would have been madness. Reluctantly she reined in, but did not stop. She wondered, with ridiculous inconsistency, if he would suggest they might meander through the trees. Part of her yearned to find again that secluded spot where she had discovered such happiness. Would it—could it—be repeated if she was again alone with Richard? The mare moved on at a walking pace towards the opening in the trees, where a track invited them into its depths.

Richard called again, more sharply. 'Stop, my lady.'

So it was my lady again now! It had been Meg when he had kissed her. The defiance dropped away. She waited for him.

'We have to return. The farrier is waiting to look over the horses' shoes.'

She turned Bella and gently, side by side, they trotted back.

'You ride very well,' he said.

'Thank you.' She was studiously polite.

'I thought you might have difficulty in managing such a spirited animal.'

'The Prioress at the nunnery kept a fine stable.'

'And she permitted you to ride?'

Meg gave a wry smile. 'My mama persuaded her to allow me to have riding lessons on a very gentle old horse.'

'Bella does not fit that description,' he remarked dryly.

'No, well, I've always enjoyed riding. I love horses too. I spent hours and hours at the stables, and I persuaded the grooms to take me with them when they went out exercising the horses. Some of them were really fast.'

'That explains it. What do you think of Bella?'

'She's wonderful.' She leaned over and patted the mare's neck. As they talked the atmosphere between them became normal again. 'When do we go to London?' she asked.

'In a day or two, I believe.'

'It's strange, but I have no wish to leave here.'

'It has not been too unpleasant, then?'

'You know it has not. But I confess I am more than a little afraid of going to Court.'

He wanted to reassure her, but found himself tongue-tied. It would be a lie to say she had nothing to fear.

'Do you think I shall find a husband there?' she asked.

'I have no doubt of it.'

That deepened her anguish.

Chapter Eight

The journey to London was uneventful, but to Meg no less interesting and enjoyable for that. Every village they passed through was new to her, and the countryfolk bowed or curtsied and ragged children capered merrily alongside the horses. She wished she had money to throw for them, but when she suggested this, Nancy told her not to be so silly.

The riding party consisted of Meg, Nancy, the Earl, Richard and Gervase, together with their servants. As before, Sarah was riding pillion behind Alan. There were also outriders, for defence should they be attacked by highwaymen. Grooms and stablehands led pack-horses with personal possessions, including the elabo-rate clothing which had caused Meg so much anguish. Carts had been sent on in advance, packed with addi-tional items.

Fortunately the weather was warm and dry, so that the state of the roads was less treacherous than might have been. Even so there were deep holes and ruts, which could have caused a rider to be thrown or a horse lamed if care was not taken. Bella was sweetly behaved, strong and willing, and Meg began to think of the mare as a friend.

Quite often, and for long periods, Richard rode at her side. They talked companionably, but always there were other members of the party within earshot.

Sometimes Nancy joined them. 'Everyone that's anyone is in London.' She exuded an air of excitement. 'There'll be so much to do—balls and pageants, and a Great Tournament is planned! How I wish we were there already! This journey is so tedious!'

Meg did not agree, but she did not wish to enter into an argument and remained silent. It was easier just to nod amiably.

Sometimes the Earl brought his great horse up alongside her. He had a look of delighted anticipation which had the effect of making Meg nervous. Those things that were enjoyed by Thurton and Nancy were usually very different from her own inclinations.

'How do you like the new mare?' he asked. 'You handle her well.'

'Thank you, Uncle Edmund. She's a lovely creature.' Meg smiled at him, because that was something upon which she was fully in agreement with him.

'Ha! You've learned to smile! You've blossomed since you've been with us. No longer the frightened waif from the nunnery, eh? Richard has worked wonders with you.'

That was an unpleasant reminder that those days and evenings she had spent so happily with Richard had been at his lordship's bidding. She had no comment, but Thurton was so pleased with himself, and with her, that he did not notice.

'It's all for your advancement. I have great plans for you. You know that, don't you?'

Meg's belief was that it had been more for her uncle's advancement than hers. 'All I know is that your intention is to find a husband for me,' she said.

'Exactly! The best match in the land, no less.' The Earl was beaming; she had never seen him in a better mood. 'Oh, Meg! My own dear little niece! What a sensation you'll make when I take you to Court. Bless my soul if you won't!'

He was in an exceptionally genial mood. She had never seen him so mellow, and was emboldened to ask, 'Is it at Court that I shall be introduced to the gentleman you hope will offer for my hand?'

'You will. You will, my dear.'

'Then should I not know the gentleman's name and something about him? I would then take special care to be on my best behaviour when we meet?'

'Anxious to meet with the gentleman, are you?' He chuckled happily. 'Patience, wench. Just do as you are told. Keep that smile on your pretty face and the whole world will be at your feet. I promise you will meet him very soon.'

The world at her feet! What nonsense was that? Had he perhaps been imbibing too freely at the alehouse where they had rested? She was about to question him further, but he spurred his great charger forward.

'Soon,' he called back to her. 'Very soon. Be patient, my beauty.'

Be patient, indeed! Did he really think she was so anxious to be wed? If it had been to Richard she would have welcomed the announcement, but how could she feel anything for a stranger? She uttered a silent prayer that this fine gentleman whom she was expected to marry would not be like the Earl in any respect. Sometimes she wondered if he was ill in the head. Why should anyone wish to marry her? She had not even the smallest of dowries. If Bixholm had belonged to her, as in truth it should, then her prospects would have been quite different. That would have been an estate to bargain with—but her uncle had forcibly possessed it all those years ago, and most definitely he did not intend to part with it now.

She was of good blood. Her mother had been proud to tell her that she was descended from one of the earlier kings of England. But who would care a jot about that? Meg certainly didn't.

They passed through the hamlet of Islington, and rode into the inner city through the great gate at Bishopsgate. The wall on one side was crumbling, and on the other it had recently been patched up, probably paid for by a rich merchant who lived nearby. The streets were narrow and unpaved, and her nose was unpleasantly assailed by the smell of rotting refuse at which ravens and kites scavenged. Patches of green, trees and gardens, showed between some of the fine houses of the rich merchants. Lesser dwellings crowded shoulder to shoulder.

The Earl's town house was on the south side of the Strand, one of the most sought-after areas in London. It was three storeys high, built of stone, with mullioned windows and the Thurton arms carved above the heavy doorway. An oriel window in the parlour overlooked the street. Meg was pleased to be allocated a small chamber on the first floor, but dismayed to discover it was next door to that occupied by the Earl and Nancy.

'Reckon they intend to keep a close eye on you whilst you're here in the big city,' said Sarah.

Meg had thought exactly the same.

'Nice, though, ain't it?' Sarah said approvingly.

The chamber was well furnished. The estate at Bix-holm must be rich to be able to support such an affluent town house. A stab of anger shot through Meg as she remembered how simply and frugally her mother had been forced to live in the nunnery.

Thurton had been callous and ruthless in his treatment of his gentle sister-in-law, widowed, alone with a small child. Meg shuddered as she wondered why he was now bringing her to London. Of one thing she was certain: whatever plan he had it was for his benefit rather than hers. His secrecy added to her fears.

The gardens sloped to the river, and the palaces occupied by the King were close by. For health reasons the royal household moved along the banks of the Thames, from Richmond to Windsor, Greenwich, Eltham and Westminster. As one site became polluted everyone moved to the next. The huge Palace of Whitehall, an intricate mass of apartments and galleries, also had gardens, covered tennis courts, a tiltyard and bowling green.

Within days of their arrival in London the Earl had arranged a banquet, to which he invited all the most powerful men and women he knew, or could get introductions to. Invitations to pageants, balls and banquets flowed back. He and Nancy were smugly delighted, but Meg became increasingly puzzled and despondent. She was decked out in the elegant gowns newly made for her. Jewels which, she suspected, should have belonged to her mother were hung around her neck, decorated her hair, or were pinned to her garments. Meg squired to think that more recently they had been worn by Nancy.

The Court lay at the centre of everything. The palaces and great houses were thronging with ambitious men and women, all vying with each other for the King's favour. Those who were not high-born enough to be within his orbit bowed and scraped to those who were now, or might one day be there. She began to understand that those courtesies Richard had been teaching her were, as he said, 'the only way of getting promotion or of gaining wealth'.

He might have added that the rich and aristocratic never expected to have to earn a living. Wealth was available more abundantly than ever before. With the dissolution of the monasteries the King had acquired land, fine buildings, gold, silver and jewels. They were his to sell, or bestow upon those he favoured.

Meg was uncomfortable at being thrust into the company of so many strangers. Everyone was lavishly attired, the men just as flamboyant as the women. You would think it was a sin not to spend freely and dress brilliantly, she thought. Meg had never felt so alone as she did in that throng, and more so because Nancy was never far away. Meg curtsied and smiled. She answered politely when she was spoken to and regarded the glittering scene with such open amazement that it brought smiles to those who watched her. She had never known that such wealth and splendour existed, and she could not help being excited by it.

In every gathering she looked around, seeking Richard, but he was seldom present, and when he was there it was impossible to speak with him privately. She had become accustomed to his attentiveness and realised how much she had relied upon his companionship. She missed him terribly. At banquets she was always seated with the Earl on one side of her and a stranger on the other. That should have been pleasant, for normally she enjoyed talking to people, but the main topic was always concerned with events at Court, of which she knew little.

There was endless speculation as to who was in favour with the King. Even greater relish was shown when the talk concentrated upon those who were said to have fallen foul of His Majesty and had been dismissed. More than anything there were always a multitude of suggestions as to whom the King might choose as his new wife. The Court chuckled at the joke that one foreign princess had refused, saying she would not marry him even if she had two necks!

One wife divorced, another beheaded, and it had been said that when Queen Jane had had such a terrible time in childbirth Henry had been more concerned with saving the child than with care for his wife! After her death he had shown great remorse, but he was still sending envoys to all the European countries, seeking princesses whose fathers or brothers were seeking an alliance with England. Two of his previous wives had been chosen from among the ladies-in-waiting at Court, and there was always the possibility that might happen again. Various names were mentioned and their family connections discussed in minute detail. Meg understood only half of all that was said, for she had little knowledge of modern politics.

Nancy glowed, gossiped and giggled at scandals regarding people of whom Meg knew nothing. She preened and was complimented by other ladies and gentlemen with words that Meg was sure were falsely uttered. She was surprised to observe that the Earl was treated as a high-ranking gentleman of considerable consequence. Even more amazingly, she noticed that those to whom she was introduced were fawningly flattering.

'It is as if they think I am a person of importance,' she whispered one day to Richard.

It was late in the afternoon and they were attending a pageant which had been performed in the streets by one of the guilds. She had managed to draw him a little aside from the throng, so as not to be overheard by Gervase, though they remained within sight of his ever-watchful eyes.

'You will become accustomed to that, if the Earl has his way.' Richard's voice had a grim undertone which was reflected in the set of his face.

'What do you mean, Richard? Why should it be? I don't understand.'

'No, of course you don't, my sweet innocent. But soon you will be introduced to the King—'

'That's arranged for tomorrow,' she told him, with a light little laugh. 'I'm so nervous! Just imagine it! I had never met any aristocratic people at all until I encountered you, Richard. To tell the truth I find the prospect rather alarming. I've been practising my curtsey, and I've been told to smile at him and to listen to him and agree with everything he says to me.'

'Good advice,' Richard said curtly.

'Naturally I shall be civil. I hope that I always am to strangers. Anyway, I don't suppose I shall be in the company of the King for more than a few minutes.'

'Meg—take care—'

'Ah, Richard—and Lady Margaret.' The unwelcome voice of Gervase Gisbon came insidiously between them. 'My apologies to be the cause of breaking up this delightful tête-à-tête.' The sneer was unmistakable. 'His lordship sends compliments and requests that you join him and Mistress Nancy. They are about to move on to another gathering.'

Meg tried to read from Richard's face what he had been about to say. *Take care.* Why now especially? A sense of insecurity had been with her ever since she had left the nunnery.

'Will you accompany us, Richard?' she asked.

'Alas, I cannot,' he said. 'I have to practise for the Great Tournament in a few days' time. But I shall be with you tomorrow when you are formally introduced to the King. You know that you have already been noticed by His Majesty?'

Meg gasped. 'No! I had no idea! I have been at events where the King has been present—but you are teasing me, are you not, Richard?'

'It is true, my lady.'

She shook her head, genuinely puzzled. 'But why should His Majesty have noticed me?'

Gervase gave Richard no chance to answer. He stepped between them, lifted Meg's hand and tucked it within his arm, drawing her away from Richard.

'I understand we are all to accompany you tomorrow,' he said. 'The occasion may include some dancing, and it is proposed that Sir Richard shall partner you.'

'We are to dance before His Majesty?' Meg gasped. She turned to Richard accusingly. 'You did not tell me.'

'I didn't know, until this moment,' said Richard. 'But of course I shall be happy to do so.' Despite his words, he looked far from happy. His expression puzzled her. He'd always appeared to enjoy the dance almost as much as he enjoyed jousting. She thought he would have been pleased and proud to perform before the royal party.

'The Earl had intended to partner you personally, my lady,' Gervase said. 'But Nancy convinced him that your sweetness would be shown to better advantage with a younger man. Your lively stepping will also bring you to his notice.'

Meg stared at Gervase. 'Why would the King care how well I dance?' she asked. 'Surely he has professional entertainers?'

'He does, naturally. The best in the land. But he particularly enjoys watching delicate young maidens disporting themselves.'

Meg was relieved to hear that, taking it to mean that there would be several couples dancing for the King's pleasure.

'You will find it a truly memorable occasion,' Gervase said. He bowed. 'Now, my lady, we must move on. The Earl and Mistress Nancy are waiting for us.'

The following day, when the Earl escorted Meg into the Great Hall, he strutted like a peacock and was as brightly gowned as the bird itself. Nancy, Richard and Gervase followed a short distance behind. Meg's nervousness increased with every step. The grandeur of the huge room far outshone all the other wondrous palaces she had seen since her arrival in London. She gazed up at the elaborate ceiling, at the magnificent tapestries on the walls and the rich carpets on the floor. Brilliant colours and intricate designs clamoured to be noticed, but gold and scarlet predominated.

Her wonder and amazement grew as her attention turned to the people gathered there. Magnificence and artistic splendour were on blatant display. All were hoping for an audience with the King. A hundred or more ladies and gentlemen lined the sides of the great reception hall. The soft chatter suggested an underlying but unmistakable excitement, yet was kept within bounds. The men's caps, of the richest materials, made a sea of colour, were decorated with flashing jewels and nodding plumes. The ladies' hoods framed fashionably pale faces.

Meg understood then why so much trouble had been taken over her appearance that day. She was clad in one of the most elegant of her new gowns, though not the one which had offended her. Never—never—would she be seen in public wearing that! The gown Nancy had chosen on this occasion was of a rich russet colour. It had a tight-fitting bodice, heavily embroidered in gold around the delicately curved neckline, and elaborately slashed sleeves. The full skirt trailed on the ground and was open in front to reveal a jewel-encrusted petticoat.

Sarah had, of course, accompanied Meg to her robing, but Nancy's maid had been called to dress Meg's hair. Meg would have protested, but Sarah had whispered to her that she did not mind in the least. This was to be a great occasion, and it was possible that the other girl knew more about current trends than she did.

The maid had worked on Meg's hair for almost an hour. She'd smoothed it till every hair was lying straight from the central parting, in exactly the right shape. Her long tresses had been combed to ripple thickly down her back—a style that denoted her maidenhood—and the undercap set slightly back on her head. Lastly the gable hood had been placed in position, framing Meg's youthful face in the most becoming way. A rope of pearls finished the picture, opulent, fresh and charming.

Meg had been shown a portrait of the King, and it seemed to her that several of the gentlemen present looked much like him. Perhaps they all believed that imitation was the sincerest form of flattery, for each one of them looked big, in broad-shouldered doublets, flat hats, and shoes with square toes. Many adopted a pose with their legs slightly apart too.

She was led forward, with her hand lightly resting on the Earl's arm. 'Which is the King?' she asked.

'His Majesty has not yet arrived,' Thurton said. 'We will move close to that dais on which he will be seated, for he knows of our coming.'

'My lord, is it to one of the gentlemen here that I am to be wedded?'

The Earl did not answer immediately. He negotiated a place near the front, to the obvious annoyance of some who had been standing there for a considerable time. Thurton brushed them aside, aided by a few sharp comments from Nancy and a shoulder applied by Gervase.

'He is not yet here,' the Earl said.

Meg was not sure if he was referring to her question or to the King. She did not bother to pursue the matter; she had just noticed that Richard was standing almost beside her. As always his presence was reassuring, giving her a feeling of warmth and well-being. She wished she dared reach out and take hold of his hand. His eyes met hers, and she thought she read a longing in them that matched her own feelings. Why—oh, why could he not be the one for her? She smiled, but the expression on Richard's face was solemn.

The air of expectation among those in the Great Hall intensified as time passed and the hour at which it was thought King Henry might arrive drew nearer. When at last that moment came, the musicians trumpeted loud and clear. The King entered, and with one accord those multi-coloured caps were swept from the men's heads as they bowed low. The women lowered themselves in deep curtsies. The Earl and Meg paid homage in the same manner, but she could not resist lifting her head slightly to get a glimpse of the King.

Her disappointment was intense. He was a large man, tall, but also overweight, even allowing for the widening effect of his clothing. As he processed close to her she noticed that if he had taken off his cap, which he wore dashingly aslant, he would have shown himself quite bald. He walked with a slow, waddling movement, and she recalled that Sarah had told her that His Majesty suffered from ulcers. His legs were painful.

'Just like that old priest who took confessions,' Sarah had said.

'That's just gossip,' Meg had reprimanded her, and had refused to listen when Sarah had protested. 'You shouldn't repeat such things.'

Meg pretended to look down humbly as he passed by in front of her, but her eyes were fixed on his legs. Beneath the silken stockings they were obviously wrapped around with thick bandages. She had never expected that the most important man in the whole land would suffer such a disability. She felt sorry for him, as she would have for any person with such an affliction. Then she looked around in dismay, fearing that someone might be able to read her thoughts—for surely that could be treason! No one would be permitted to think of the greatest man in the land as a 'poor gentleman'.

He passed by, and the company raised themselves to normal height again. The King was seated in a throne-like chair on a dais. It was beneath a huge canopy of cloth of gold. Servants offered refreshments but he waved them away. The musicians who had followed him, playing a march of triumph as he processed along the length of the Great Hall, now grouped themselves to one side. They began to play some of the popular tunes, including several which had been composed by the King himself. The conversation, which had been flowing freely before the entry of His Majesty, started again, in whispers and hushed tones.

Nancy began to fiddle with the skirts of Meg's gown, as if she thought it had been ruffled. Of course it had not! She had taken the greatest possible care to ensure that it had not been crushed or creased.

For the first time an anxious expression came over the Earl's face. 'We shall soon be in the royal presence, Meg,' he said. 'Don't forget what I've told you.'

'Smile and wait for His Majesty to speak to you before you make any comments,' said Nancy.

The King was graciously offering audience to courtiers and their wives and daughters, who moved gradually towards him. A queue had formed and the Earl, with Meg on his arm, slowly led her towards the presence.

Most people were with His Majesty for only a short time, then, with a leisurely gesture of his fat beringed hand, the King would wave them aside. Meg watched with a sense of relief. At this rate her ordeal would soon be over. She might as well enjoy the occasion; it would be something to tell her grandchildren about when she was an old lady. He said so little to any of them that she was confident she would remember every word. Thurton removed his cap. There were only a few people before them now.

The King lifted his head, which had slumped slightly. In that moment he looked directly at her, and to her amazement an eager twinkle sprang into his eyes. Abruptly he dismissed the family who were in front of her.

Bowing low, Thurton swept the floor with his elegant cap. Meg lowered herself into the graceful curtsey she had spent so long practising, and was pleased that she managed it without the slightest tremor. She stood up and smiled, warmly and honestly, for she did indeed feel she was greatly honoured to be in this position.

'Ah, Thurton,' said the King. 'And the pretty young lady I've been hearing so much about.'

'Your Majesty. I have the honour to introduce my very dear niece, Lady Margaret Thurton.'

The King's eyes roved over Meg, from her demurely hooded head down over the bare flesh above the tight bodice. They rested for a moment on her tiny waist, then flashed back up to her face, and he nodded as if in approval. Her cheeks flushed with pleasure and embarrassment.

'Charming,' he said. He smiled at her, then turned to the Earl. 'Just as well your niece does not take after you in looks, eh?'

The Earl turned a good deal redder than usual and forced out a loud laugh. He would not have accepted such a comment from any other man.

'I am told that I take after my mother, Your Majesty,' Meg interposed, quite forgetting that she should not speak until she was spoken to.

The King seemed not to mind at all. 'Your mother was Lady Elizabeth Thurton, was she not?'

'She was indeed, Your Majesty,' Meg said, warmly. 'A kind and gentle lady. I loved her dearly.'

'Lady Elizabeth was a great beauty,' said the Earl. 'Not surprising, sire, for she was descended from the same regal ancestors as yourself, but on the female side.'

'So you have royal blood, my lovely.' Henry seemed

pleased with the information. 'Then you should come and sit here alongside me, how would you like that?'

Meg felt some alarm, but overcame it and answered honestly, 'I should be most honoured, sire.'

'A chair. Bring a chair for Lady Margaret,' he ordered.

It was produced with remarkable speed. Thurton took hold of Meg's hand and assisted her to mount the shallow steps on to the dais. 'All is going well, Meg,' he whispered. 'The King likes you. Don't forget to smile, and agree with everything he says.' When Meg was seated he bowed to the King and backed away.

His face was so brightly red that Meg feared he might take a fit of apoplexy. She watched as he moved to the side of the great room, taking his place beside Nancy, Richard and Gervase. All except Richard were smiling broadly, as if her being seated beside the King was something they had planned.

The King reached over and took hold of her hand. 'Are you comfortable, my dear?' he asked.

'Perfectly, thank you, Your Majesty.' She smiled at him quite naturally as she answered. It was not in the least bit difficult, for there was something very pleasant in his face, despite it being heavy and with obvious signs of ageing. He did not seem at all like the terrible creature who had been so cruel to his wives. There was admiration in his eyes as he looked at her, and she would not have been feminine if she had not responded to it. To her he seemed like the father she would have dearly liked, or perhaps a kindly uncle. Not at all like her real one.

'So, you are Lady Margaret!' he said. 'What do they call you? Maggie, perhaps?'

'Usually Meg, sire.'

'I like that. You are more lovely than I was told, Meg. That makes a change. You wouldn't believe the portraits they have been trying to palm me off with. Foreign princesses with faces like horses.'

'I am sorry to hear that, Your Majesty,' Meg said. 'But do you not think that goodness can be more important than beauty?'

'Not in a bedmate,' the King said.

Meg was so shocked that the smile on her face became fixed there.

The King looked pleased. He smiled back at her and patted her hand again. 'I've been a lonely man since my dear Queen Jane died,' he said.

Suddenly the awful truth dawned on Meg. Had she been brought here as a possible wife? Or, worse, to become Henry's mistress! One glance at the expressions of joy on the faces of the Earl and Nancy made terror clutch at Meg's heart.

Chapter Nine

King Henry resumed receiving the courtiers with their wives and families. Meg sat beside him, struggling with the thoughts that raged through her head. Most of the people who came to him had some request; others merely wished to give their greetings. Obsequiously they told him of their undying loyalty, probably with an eye to some future need. She paid little attention to them for her mind was in turmoil.

Then reason began to exert itself. How could such a foolish thought have entered her head? Some of the young ladies who were introduced to the King were truly beautiful, much more lovely than she. They were also more experienced in the ways of Court. They talked with confidence and knowledge and they smiled with beguiling warmth. He could take his pick of any of them—it was unbelievable that he should choose her. How foolish she had been even to think it!

By nature Meg was a practical young woman. Her mind challenged her imagination and insisted there was nothing extraordinary in the King's behaviour. He was quite polite to almost everyone. She scoffed at herself. Of course it wasn't true. He had merely asked her to sit by him because she was of royal blood, distant though it was. He had said he was lonely, and no doubt that was true, but it was absurd to think that he might contemplate marriage with her! She was so relieved that she almost chuckled aloud at the thought. She was getting ideas beyond her station, she told herself. As for becoming his mistress, the Church did not allow that, did it? And the King was Head of the Church, so he couldn't possibly take a mistress—could he?

She relaxed. He was still holding her hand, and gave it a little squeeze. The queue had disappeared.

He turned to her. 'I'm told you sing, Meg, is that true?'

'I can sing a little, Your Majesty, but I am not sure my voice is good enough to perform in public.'

'I shall be the judge of that,' declared Henry. 'You shall sing for the company here and I shall accompany you on the harp. Let us see how we fit together in a musical way.'

He beckoned to the musicians and they gathered at the side of the dais. One of them handed a small harp to the King.

'Now, my dear, what song will you choose?'

'I do not know many songs, sire. I was brought up in a nunnery and in the choir we always sang psalms.'

He brushed that aside. 'This is not the time for psalms. I was told you had recently learned some songs of a lighter nature.'

'"Greensleeves"?' she suggested, since obviously his request could not be refused.

'Splendid. Did they tell you I composed that?'

'They did, and I find it quite delightful.'

Henry smiled, pleased by her remark. He ran his fingers over the strings of the harp, and large though they were his touch was light. Meg stood up and began to sing.

> *Greensleeves was all my joy*
> *Greensleeves was my delight—*

The King was an accomplished harpist and the other musicians joined in softly, adding depth. She sang, putting her whole heart into the words, controlling her voice as she had been taught. Unable to prevent herself, she looked over to where Richard was standing. He had taught her this song, she was singing it for him, and it pleased her to see that he was listening raptly.

Then her eyes slipped from Richard's face to those around him. Most of the assembled company listened with signs of pleasure, but Gervase stood with folded arms and a supercilious air, as if bored with everyone and everything. By contrast the Earl and Nancy were looking at each other, their faces glowing with delight. Did they think, as she had done momentarily, that the King's interest in her had some deeper meaning? She would have to disillusion them on that score as quickly as possible.

Doubts flowed back into her mind and she almost forgot the words of the final line. She faltered, but quickly pulled herself together and finished on a strong note. Great applause followed. She was well aware that it was mostly because the King himself had played the accompaniment. Meg curtsied to him and he reached out for her hand, took it and kissed it.

'That was delightful, sweet Meg,' he said. 'We shall make more music together in the future. I shall teach you more of my favourite airs.'

'That is most gracious of you.' She smiled to cover the apprehension that threatened to envelop her.

'It will be my pleasure. Something I shall look forward to. For truly I have been starved of congenial company of late. But now it is time for the dancing to begin.'

'Will you dance, sire?' she asked.

'I would be charmed to partner you, but my leg is troubling me. You shall perform and I shall watch. Name the partner of your choice.'

'Sir Richard de Heigham has been my dancing master,' she responded immediately.

The King beckoned him over. Richard's face was inscrutable as he led her on to the floor. The musicians took up their instruments and music flowed into the Great Hall.

With her lips close to Richard's ear, she whispered, 'I did not expect this. What shall I do?'

'There is no need to distress yourself,' he said. 'I shall lead you into the steps.'

He seemed to be thinking only of the dance. Her eyes pleaded with him, but with all those people watching it was impossible to say more. She was not even sure that he understood her concern. His demeanour showed he was as much at ease as if they had been at practice at Bixholm.

He swept her a bow. 'You sang delightfully, and now together we shall perform a spectacular gay galliard.'

They began to dance. Each in turn leaping high into the air. It was a dance in which the man in particular was showing off his spritely stepping, making much play of the shapeliness of his leg. The movement separated them. She waited until they were close again.

'I must speak with you, Richard,' she whispered urgently.

Again his elegant stepping opened a gap between them, then brought them together.

'Later,' he said. 'After the Tournament.'

'This evening,' she insisted. 'I will walk in the garden after dinner.'

He did not answer immediately. His brow was furrowed. Was he trying to find an excuse? Then it was too late. The dance ended. Richard took her hand.

'After dinner,' she repeated.

'It may not be possible,' he replied.

She did not look at him as he led her back to the King, who greeted them with warm applause. They had danced vigorously, and were breathing hard as they stood together before the dais. Richard was still holding her hand.

'Splendid! Splendid! What a wonderful dance the galliard is. I used to be an expert myself,' Henry boasted. 'I could do it yet, you know, but for these accursed legs.'

'I am sorry that you suffer so.' Meg spoke with honest sympathy.

'The physician has hopes that he can cure me. When I am recovered I shall lead you on to the floor myself, Meg. You will see. You will see.'

'That will be a great pleasure to me, Your Majesty.'

Gervase approached and bowed to the King.

'Ah, Gisbon. Was that not a fine performance?'

'Fine indeed, sire,' Gervase responded. 'As it was also when Lady Margaret and yourself entertained us royally with that delightful rendering of "Greensleeves".'

'Lady Margaret is a very talented young lady,' the

King agreed. To Meg he added, 'You are a credit to your royal blood.'

For once she was grateful that Gervase gave her no opportunity to respond. 'Your Majesty,' he said. 'May I ask for Sir Richard to be released? He is required to assist with preparations for the Tournament.'

'Ah, yes, the Tournament. I have great expectations of both you and Richard.' Henry waved them away.

Bowing and stepping backwards, they retreated, until protocol permitted them to turn. Their departure was too abrupt for further speech with Richard. She watched his back, disappointed that he had not been more forthcoming about her suggested assignation.

The King's voice interrupted her thoughts. 'Have you seen a Great Tournament?' he asked.

'Never, sire. Neither great nor small.'

'Then this will be a treat for you. A year or so ago I took great pleasure in jousting myself. Now I can only watch whilst other men ride. At the Tournament you shall sit with me in the royal stand. We'll cheer them on together, eh?'

Meg curtsied in acknowledgement of the honour that was being bestowed upon her. She lowered her head and hoped it veiled the dismay she was certain must show on her face.

'That is exceedingly kind, Your Majesty.'

'Until then, sweet Meg, it must be *adieu*. Unfortunately I have matters of state which require my attention, so I must take my leave of you.'

His attendants sprang forward. They assisted him to his feet, adjusted his robes, then stood to attention. The trumpeters sounded a fanfare and followed the King as he progressed down the Hall. Everyone made elaborate obeisance and remained with heads lowered until he had slowly and painfully walked the length of the room. He left as he had entered, through the golden double doors.

The silence that had persisted whilst the King was present was dissipated instantly. Voices were raised, as if all the assembled company were speaking at once. Several times Meg heard her own name as people questioned. Who was she? Where had she come from? What did the King mean about royal blood? The Earl was surrounded by a dozen or more fashionable gentlemen and Nancy rushed over, holding her arms open, and, giving Meg no chance to escape, caught her in a great hug.

'What a fortunate young lady you are, Meg! This morning's audience has been beyond my wildest dreams! The King is fascinated—and you conducted yourself well, my dear. Everything you did was just right! You have pleased your uncle enormously.'

Meg felt intense dislike at being pressed so tightly to that fleshy bosom, and struggled until she managed to detach herself from the cloying embrace.

Nancy was too excited to notice the rebuff. She drew back, but kept one possessive arm around Meg's waist. Other women crowded around, eager to know exactly what the King had said.

At first Meg was reluctant to say anything, except that His Majesty had been very kind. But they pestered to know more, and, as nothing of a private nature had passed between them, she recounted all that she could recall. Finally she said, quite simply, 'I am to sit beside the King at the Great Tournament.'

'Oh, Meg, my darling girl! That's wonderful!' exclaimed Nancy. 'We must tell Edmund. Come.'

With her arm still tightly around Meg's waist, as if she feared she might lose her in the crowd, Nancy propelled her in the direction of the Earl. The news had just as dramatic an effect upon Thurton as it had had on Nancy. He threw his arms around Meg and hugged her, and it was only by turning her head sharply that she evaded having a kiss smacked full on her mouth.

That movement attracted Nancy's attention, but far from chiding her, as she would certainly have done in the past, she showed sympathy. 'Edmund, I think it has all been rather too much for Meg. Let us go home so that we may discuss this in greater privacy and make preparations for the day of the Tournament.'

For once Meg was grateful for a suggestion from Nancy. Her uncle tucked her hand in the crook of his arm and positively strutted through the crowd. More than once he was stopped by courtiers and their wives. It seemed as if they already believed that through Meg he had been invested with special power. She was aware, too, of how closely she was scrutinised, and on many faces she read disturbing expressions of envy.

Nancy followed them, with an unmistakable swagger of pride, bestowing smiles on those who pleased her with flattering comments. Meg was uncomfortably aware that she had become an object of curiosity. It was a relief when they reached the privacy of the Earl's house.

'It's working out just as I hoped!' Thurton exclaimed as soon as they were inside. 'Like a dream come true. I had a presentiment the moment I heard about you, Meg. I knew it!' He flung himself down in his big chair and shouted for the servants to bring wine.

Meg remained standing. 'What did you know, Uncle?' she asked coldly.

'I knew you could charm the King! And you have. You have! He chose you to sit beside him, didn't he?

All others were waved aside. What a wonderful occasion! Today has made everything worthwhile, hasn't it?'

'Exactly what do you mean?' Meg asked. 'What has been worthwhile?'

'The money I've spent on clothes. And the training. The lessons in dancing and singing. Henry was enchanted. I know. I've seen it before, when he met young Anne Boleyn, and then again little Jane Seymour. He was ready to fall in love again, and you've woken him up. You are what he needs, Meg. Keep on exactly as you did today and you'll have him eating out of your hand—if he isn't there already!'

He quaffed a goblet of wine. Nancy drank too. It was offered to Meg, but she refused. She felt befuddled enough already, without risking the effects of alcohol.

'The King married Anne Boleyn and Jane Seymour,' Meg said. 'Now they are both dead.'

'Exactly! So the King is in need of another wife.'

'And you hope that will be me?' Meg whispered.

'The highest in the land! Didn't I tell you that, when you asked me?' He chuckled. Triumph was written all over his big florid face.

'Couldn't have been better,' Nancy agreed. 'Did you see the faces of some of those people when he showed his preference for our Meg! It was wonderful.' Nancy was slumped on a settle, and her buxom body began to shake with laughter at the recollection.

They had schemed and planned and their dreams now showed signs of reaching fruition. What a great achievement for them both!

At that moment Meg knew for certain it was for this, and this alone, that she had been brought to Bixholm. She was expected to become the wife—or perhaps the mistress—of the gross and ageing King. Fear and help-lessness ate into her soul.

Bleakly she said, 'He had Queen Anne beheaded.'

'No need for that to happen again,' Nancy said. 'Anne was no better than she should be. An unfaithful hussy. I'm sure that won't happen with you, Meg.'

'It was murder.'

'Hush! It would be treason if the King heard you.' The Earl glanced around as he spoke, as if he feared the walls had ears. 'Don't speak of that, ever.'

'Queen Jane died a natural death,' Nancy pointed out. 'It was in childbirth. She was never strong, nothing like as healthy as you, Meg. Anyway, that's a risk women have to take, isn't it?'

'I suppose so,' Meg murmured. 'But he divorced Queen Catherine and treated her ill, so 'tis said.'

'That was never a proper marriage,' the Earl snapped. 'She had been his brother's wife. All past and done with. Forget it. Think of the bright future that lies before you. The King is always generous. You'll have jewels and rich clothes and servants of your own. Everything and anything your heart could desire.'

'Those people were green with envy.' Nancy chuck-led again, immensely pleased. 'That'll teach them! I reckon they'll be looking up to me from now on.'

'They will indeed! It was written in their faces!' bel-lowed the Earl. 'If looks could have killed, you would have had a knife through your heart, Meg. You were the only one he had eyes for.'

They laughed and took more wine, and repeated things that had been said, the envy that had been evoked. Their imaginations raced ahead, over wonderful times to come. With every new idea their merriment increased. The Earl listed some of the gifts that had been showered on Jane Seymour's family. Great estates and riches would be theirs for the asking when their Meg became Queen Margaret.

For Meg such a terrible fate was a nightmare. She was far too upset to say anything more. Besides, what would be the use? Her feelings were of no consequence to them. She walked out of the room and the Earl and Nancy were so pleased with themselves they did not even notice.

She wandered around the house and out into the garden. Would Richard meet her there tonight? Would he help her? There was no one else to whom she could turn. If she showed any reluctance her uncle and Nancy would put pressure on her. Probably they would beat her and lock her in the cellar, try to starve her into submission. Their anger would know no bounds. She must be strong. She would not give in. Yet she feared that if the King knew she rejected his advances she would incur his wrath. He had a reputation for killing those that disagreed with him—she did not want to die, not yet. Nor would she willingly submit to this proposed marriage.

The only escape she could think of was to ask Richard to marry her. They could be wedded quickly, then when the King learned she was a married lady, he would lose all interest in her. She and Richard would both be banished from Court and turned out of Bixholm, but she could think of no other way out. Restlessly she walked to the river's edge. The great Thames, carrying trade in and out of London, its water relentlessly flowing under the bridge, reminded her how fragile was life. She thought of flinging herself in and allowing the water to carry her away, to end it all, to be free!

But when she peered down the sight of the filth swirling past her made her draw back. The sewer smell from the river reached her nose and she knew she could never fling herself into that. It was too disgusting! Anyway, suicide was not on her mind. Not yet. Not until she had spoken to Richard. He was her only hope—but would he be willing? She turned and made her way back to the house.

She decided to say nothing of the day's events to Sarah, and forced herself to chatter normally as she changed for dinner.

'What do you think of London?' she asked Sarah.

'Phew, big, isn't it? Smelly, too! Alan and me walked over London Bridge. I'd heard of it, of course—never thought I'd walk over it! All those houses! I was afraid it'd fall down, like in the song, but Alan held my hand all the way, so I was all right.'

Dear Sarah. She chatted on happily, not seeming to notice how quiet her mistress was. Meg smiled and listened and envied her maid. Her simple walk had been with a man who loved her. How much more pleasant than her own encounter with the King!

The meal seemed unending, and there was no sign of Richard. The Earl and Nancy were still in a celebratory mood. The entire company, knowing something of the day's events, ate and drank right merrily. Meg picked at her food, turned it over on her trencher and slipped several choice cuts to the dogs that wandered, ever hopeful, under the tables. Where was Richard? She wondered and worried, praying he had not been injured in practising at the tilt.

Gervase Gisbon was enjoying himself. He was flirting quite outrageously with one of the ladies, a woman several years older than himself, who seemed to find his advances pleasing. Alan and Sarah were together, further down the line of tables. An elderly nobleman, a guest of the Earl, was seated on Meg's left. She tried to make polite conversation with him, but as he was extremely deaf it was almost impossible. The entertainment was ribald, as always. She was not so shocked as she had been previously, and once or twice she laughed quite spontaneously. She was invited to dance, but declined, declaring that she was feeling a little unwell.

'It's the excitement, I expect,' said Nancy.

'Probably,' Meg agreed.

'Not surprising,' said the Earl. 'Been a momentous day for all of us.' He nodded benignly.

'If you'll excuse me, I shall retire.' As soon as she moved, Sarah leapt to her feet and followed her mistress out of the Hall.

'Is something the matter, my lady?' she asked anxiously.

'No, Sarah. I am a little overtired, that is all.'

'I thought you was a bit quiet earlier on,' persisted Sarah. 'Is it true, my lady? You know what I mean, don't you? They're a-sayin' you've met the King an' he's taken a fancy to you?'

Meg nodded. She couldn't bring herself to speak.

'But you don't fancy him? That's the trouble, isn't it?'

'Yes, Sarah. That's the trouble. But nobody cares what I feel.'

'I care. You know that,' Sarah said stoutly. 'Oh, I'd like to screw their necks, the lot of them! They've no business to treat you so! Is there anything I can do?'

'No, thank you, Sarah. It was rather warm in there— I shall take a turn in the garden before I go to bed.'

'I don't like—'

'Don't fuss, Sarah. I wish to be on my own. Go back to the Hall.'

'You're quite sure?' Sarah said doubtfully.

'Positive.' She spoke so sharply that Sarah obeyed, though it was with evident reluctance that she walked away.

Meg fetched a dark-coloured shawl from her chamber, then hurried out of the house. The garden covered about an acre of ground. Darkness was falling. She looked all around, wandered here and there, but there was no sign of Richard. She sat on a stone seat among a cluster of hazel trees, her mind filled with doubt. Had he understood? Had some injury befallen him? Was he deliberately avoiding this meeting? Did he know how repugnant this proposed union with the King was to her? She brooded over the awfulness of her predicament.

Half an hour later Richard came to her. She heard his footsteps before she saw him, and jumped to her feet. She stepped forward to meet him.

'My apologies, sweet lady, for being late. There was a problem with the construction of the stand for the royal party.'

She smiled forgiveness and held out her hands to him. He clasped them, raised them to his lips and kissed first one then the other.

'Richard,' she breathed. 'What can I do? I'm terrified.'

'Hush,' he said. 'Let us walk through the trees, to the wall. We can be more private there.' He slipped an arm around her waist.

She allowed him to guide her into the shadows of the trees. The garden was protected by a high brick wall, and beneath the trees it seemed as secluded as when they had lain together in the woods at Bixholm. He turned her to face him and gently kissed her.

Only a light touch, but passion stirred immediately. He kissed her again, long and lingering. The magic of his lips on hers added to her sense of security. She was so deeply in love with him that she believed he must be able to rescue her. He was strong, capable, resourceful; she trusted him totally. Care fell from her shoulders like the wrap she discarded as she lifted her arms and with loving hands took hold of his head to keep him there, kissing and kissing her. Surely for him, as well as for her, there must be a depth of meaning in this embrace? Her response was instinctively warm. She opened her mouth slightly as his lips, moist and soft, pressed against hers with an almost greedy movement.

It was a kiss that awakened desire in her, that reached some intrinsically primitive part of her being. She wanted it to go on for ever, feeling she belonged to him, that her life on this earth needed no other reason. She had been born solely so that she could be made love to by this man. By Richard. She wanted no one else. Riches were nothing to her compared to the sensations that coursed through her. Her body was awakened, tingling with desire, her flesh delighting in this wondrous contact with him.

He drew her closer into his embrace. His arms so tight around her that she seemed no longer to be a separate being, but part of him. When love was as powerful as this, surely nothing could separate them?

He lowered his head and nibbled with his lips along the line of her throat. She lifted her head to receive his kisses and arched her back as she did so. She felt his loins through her flimsy skirts, and, although she scarcely knew why it should be so, the hardness there pressing against her intensified the sensations that enveloped her. Her body melted and softened to the power of his.

Again his lips found hers. With one arm he clasped her pliant waist; the other moved lower, caressing her back. Her fingers played in the hair at the nape of his neck. That dark, springy hair she had thought so attractive when she'd first met him. The way he had looked at her then had presaged this embrace—but how little she had known then of the ways of men. How little did she know now, even! But she trusted him. She loved him. Her mind and body both told her so. She had no defence against him. She yearned to belong to him entirely.

Then a tiny flip of fear broke into her mind. Not about Richard—but the continual fear that perhaps they could be seen. They were in the gardens, close to her uncle's town house. Others might have wandered out. She tensed. She had to speak about her future—to seek his assistance.

She released her lips from Richard's. She recalled how he had spoken about the 'game of love'. But surely this was different? A suspicion of doubt crept in. She was in no position to play games. She had come to Richard with only one thought in mind, to make serious promises, each to the other, that they would join their lives in marriage. She had rehearsed the words and they had been at the forefront of her mind—until he had swept her into his arms and kissed her. She should never have allowed herself to succumb to the joy of the moment.

She pulled herself together. She must speak to him. But she had forgotten the words she'd intended to say. Distraught, she simply blurted out the question.

'Will you marry me?'
There was a moment's taut silence.
'Please, Richard?' she added.
'Marry you?' he questioned.
Obviously no such thought had been in his mind.

Chapter Ten

Meg shivered, suddenly cold. She tore her arms away from where they had been resting, lovingly and trustingly, on Richard's shoulders. She stepped back, stooped to snatch up her shawl from the dank, leaf-strewn ground.

'Dearest Meg—there is nothing I would like better than to marry you. I'd do it, here and now. But I cannot. It would be the height of folly—'

'How else can I save myself from being forced into this liaison with the King? Can you imagine what it is like? I have to pretend a liking I do not and cannot feel—'

'I know it is hard for you, Meg. But you must be patient—'

'Patient! For the rest of my life? Or until he tires of me and sends me to the block?'

'Hush! Do not speak so! For God's sake, guard your tongue.'

'If you will not marry me, how otherwise can I escape?' Her voice was dulled. She had been so full of hope, and he had failed her.

'It would do no good, Meg, and it would be most unwise just now. Just wait awhile—'

'Wait!' She interrupted. She was seething with anger, finding it difficult not to scream at him. How dared he continue to pretend? 'You always say you cannot when you mean that you will not! You pretended you could not tell me what fate was in store for me when you brought me away, when all along you knew. Had you given me warning then I could have sought sanctuary in one of the religious houses, or hired myself out as a servant—'

'Hush, my dearest.' His fingers covered her lips to quieten her. 'You must believe me. It will be all right. I have a plan—'

He would have taken her into his arms again, but she would not. She side-stepped.

'Tell me,' she whispered angrily.

'The time is not yet right. I promise—'

'Let me be the judge of that. Tell me.'

'Trust me—'

She did not waste her breath by answering. She rushed past him, hurrying through the trees. She was past caring how much noise she made, crashing into branches, scuffling leaves with her feet and skirts.

She stopped abruptly when she heard someone call out, 'Who's there?' It came from ahead, not far away. She halted, listening intently. Now all was silent, but she had recognised that voice. Gervase Gisbon. She had no wish to be discovered in such a compromising situation, especially by him.

A woman's voice spoke softly, dreamily, 'What is it, my sweetheart?'

'I thought I heard footsteps among the trees,' Gervase answered. 'I was afraid it might be your husband.'

'No need to worry about him, dear one. He's returned to the country. He has to quell a revolt and hang one or two of the peasants.'

'He is a good man. It has to be done for there is no other way to keep order. I am grateful that he takes his duties so seriously, and leaves you here…' Gervase's voice trailed away.

The woman chuckled. There was a brief silence. Then she spoke again. 'There's no one here.' Her voice was a seductive purr. 'And here is a soft bed of leaves—'

There were scuffling sounds, murmurs and giggles. Meg moved on carefully, slowly, silently, fearful of being seen. She wondered if Richard was aware that Gervase and his lady were there, but she felt no real concern for him. Richard could look after himself—he was good at doing that!

She'd been a fool to think that he cared for her. Fine words and kisses meant nothing! She had almost allowed herself to be duped by him. Thank goodness she had now recovered her senses. It was obvious his comfortable position in the Thurton household meant more to him than she did. He would not take the slightest risk for her sake.

She moved quietly towards the house, keeping in the shadow, and with each wary step her mind became more firmly made up. She would leave London and return to Norwich, throw herself on the mercy of the Prioress, ask for sanctuary within the nunnery. She would fall on her knees and plead if need be. She could not believe that the Prioress would wish her to marry that monster. Her talents had been useful in the past and could be again. She could sew, write, even produce artistically illuminated manuscripts if she tried hard enough.

Richard's rejection had destroyed her last hope. It seared her soul that he was unwilling to assist her. What a fool she had been to think that he loved her! He had been horrified at her suggestion that they should marry.

Trust him! That was all he'd been able to say. Why should she trust him? It was obvious that those kisses and caresses meant nothing to him. It was only the 'game of courtly love'. A meaningless flirtation. No more than the carry-on between Gervase and the married lady. She remembered how Richard had told her that all the gentlemen at Court played the game—it was a sport for them, and they would take it as far as the woman was willing.

What a terrible world she had come into! Her life was shattered. It came into her mind that she had nothing to live for. She did not wish to die, would not deliberately attempt to take her own life, but if death came it would be preferable to the fate being planned for her by her guardian. She knew there were dangers on the road for lone travellers. Robbers and murderers lay in wait for victims. But her fear of marriage to Henry was greater than that—and if she took care she ought to be able to make her way back to Norwich. She would seek shelter overnight at the monasteries where they had rested on the journey to London.

It was late when she entered the house. With confident, swinging strides she walked along the passageway and entered her chamber. Sarah was waiting for her. A smile of relief spread over her face. 'My lady! Thank goodness you're back. I've been so worried. I looked out into the garden, but I couldn't see you nowhere.'

'I stayed in the shadows,' Meg said briefly.

'Did you see that Gervase Gisbon?' Sarah asked. 'He was out there, gallivanting wi' some woman twice his age. Reckon she must be rich, or he wouldn't bother.'

'I didn't see them,' Meg said.

She felt no need to add that she had heard them. She was too engrossed in her own plans, for her mind was quite made up. She would run away from her uncle, from London, from Richard. She wanted nothing more to do with any of them. Not even Richard. She must put him right out of her mind, forget him, even though it tore her heart in two. There was no other way. She blessed the fact that Sarah was there, for she needed help.

'You remember what I told you earlier, Sarah?' she said.

'Coss I do, my lady. I bin thinkin' about it all evenin'. If I could get my hands on those scheming devils, I'd make them scream for mercy! That I would!' Her anger was all the greater because she was powerless.

'I'm going to run away.'

Sarah was aghast! 'You'll be caught,' was her immediate comment.

'I shall disguise myself. I know it's a risk, but I believe I can do it.'

'Where would you go?'

'To Norwich.'

'Not back to the nunnery?' Sarah asked, wrinkling her nose in distaste.

'I know nowhere else. I don't suppose the Prioress will welcome me, but I shall plead with her to take me in, for the sake of my dear mother.'

'I wouldn't be sure about that! She's a rum 'un! But you know that. I'm sore a-feared you'll get caught before you get that far.'

'I must try.'

''Tis right foolhardy, if you ask me, my lady. All you'll get for your pains is a beating. An' you could be sent to the Tower if the King got to hear of it.'

Meg shuddered. 'I might get sent to the Tower if I married him. He had Queen Anne beheaded when he grew tired of her.'

Sarah turned quite pale. 'It's terrible—terrible!' She was wringing her hands in agitation.

'I won't ask you to come with me, Sarah, but I do need your help.'

Sarah regarded her cautiously. 'You know I don't approve, my lady—but what is it you wish me to do?'

'Get me some men's clothing.'

'Men's clothing?'

'Anything will do—I don't want to be a grand gentleman—the sort of garments that servants wear. I'll pretend to be one of the stable lads, exercising his master's horses. Can you do that for me? Please, Sarah.'

'Well, that's possible, I suppose.'

Meg's heart lifted. 'Bless you, Sarah. Nothing special. I shan't be fussy.'

'I'd have a word with Alan, but then he'd ask why I wanted it,' Sarah said, thinking aloud.

'No one must know,' Meg said sharply. 'You mustn't mention this to anyone.'

'I won't. Don't you worry about that.'

'But can you—?'

'Yeh, I think so. I've got to know most of the lads in the stable. Trouble is, they won't have much in the way of clothing to spare. I'd have to pay for them.'

'That's another thing I need. Money. I've some pieces of my mother's jewellery. I hate to part with them, but needs must.'

'There's no end of dealers in gold and gems in the City,' Sarah said. 'Shall I look about for you, my lady?'

'I'd be grateful if you'd sell it for me, Sarah. I'll fetch it—'

'If you please, my lady, could you make it enough for two sets of clothing?' Meg shot a sharp glance at her maid's cheeky face and saw she was grinning. 'You don't think I'd let you go off on your own, do you?'

'Even though you know it could be dangerous? You realise I can't be sure of a welcome back at the nunnery—or even if the place still exists?'

'Aye. And even though I think you're stupid!' Sarah sighed with an air of resignation. 'I've taken many a risk with you in the past, so I may as well go along with you now.'

'But what about leaving Alan? And your wedding?'

'I'll be sorry about that—but if he really loves me, I reckon he'll wait.'

'No, Sarah. I'll go alone. I can't let you risk your happiness for me—'

'If he won't wait, then he won't be worth havin'. First things first, my lady. That's what I allus say. You've been good to me. I'll see you through this muddle, if it's the last thing I do. And in my opinion it may well be that!'

Meg flung her arms around Sarah and hugged her and kissed her cheeks that were wet with tears. 'Dear Sarah. What a blessing you are to me.'

'That's as may be,' grumbled Sarah. 'I reckon I must be as soft in the head as you are! When do you want to leave?'

'As soon as possible. But you'll need time to get the money and clothes.'

'I should think a couple of days will be enough. The

quicker the better, before that Nancy woman starts fer-
reting around an' gettin' suspicious.'

'I can't thank you enough—'

'Then don't bother to try.' Sarah grinned, softening
her words. 'I'll be right glad to be away from her and
the Earl.'

'We'll try and make it the day after the Tournament,'
Meg suggested. 'There's to be a great banquet that evening. With luck everyone will be barrel-fevered and
they'll all lie late. We'll slip away first thing next morning.'

Sarah nodded. 'I'll start makin' enquiries tomorrow.'

By chance, on that same day Richard was also in the
City. Since coming to London he had made several visits to his lawyer, an elderly gentleman whose name was
Browhouses. Today's had not been a satisfactory interview and he was deeply disturbed that no progress
seemed to have been made.

When Meg had told him how her mother had been
forced out of Bixholm Manor by Thurton, he had easily
understood. He knew of many other misdeeds perpe-
trated by the Earl, not least how the cunning old devil
had swindled him of his own birthright.

It had happened when he'd been too young to understand. Not until he'd reached the age of twenty-one
had he discovered that he should have been heir to a
small estate east of London. Thurton had taken it over,
claiming authority to manage it on Richard's behalf.
Not surprisingly, though very suspiciously, in the inter-
vening years the deeds had disappeared! It had been in
an attempt to discover some proof of his claim that
Richard had attached himself to Thurton's household.
Surreptitiously and methodically, whenever possible, he

had searched among the manorial documents for evidence that might substantiate his claim—so far with little success.

In the course of this he had recently discovered charters and deeds regarding Bixholm, and he had no doubt that all Meg had told him was true. He had passed this information to Mr Browhouses, who had suggested it might be possible to bring a case against Thurton on both counts. Richard hesitated to tell Meg, however, feeling it would be cruel to raise her hopes if nothing came of it. He also had a deep-seated fear of Thurton's reaction, should his plan to marry her to the King be unsuccessful.

He knew from bitter experience how vicious the Earl could be. He'd had men, and women too, put to death for defying him, using trumped-up charges against them. Thurton was banking everything on this marriage of his niece. He would have no use for her otherwise. Marriage to any other nobleman would require a dowry, and, as Meg herself knew, his lordship wouldn't part with a penny to provide that. Richard felt angry and frustrated as he strolled back through the City.

He had delivered letters which in his opinion established his rights beyond doubt. Mr Browhouses had agreed that it might be so—but then again, he'd added, humming and hawing, it might not. It all depended on the interpretation of one word, or maybe of one sentence. He would have to take advice from a colleague, but could not do so immediately as the colleague was at that precise moment defending a client in court. A client with more means at his disposal than he had, Richard had thought grimly, and with some justification. Mr Browhouses was a master at stalling him, instead of getting on with his case.

Disgruntled and dismayed, Richard wandered into that area of London where the goldsmiths plied their trade. By coincidence at that same time Sarah was seeking a buyer for her mistress's jewellery.

Richard recognised the girl immediately, though he could not remember her name—just thought of her as Meg's maid. Or, more to the point, the wench who was playing havoc with Alan Crompton's emotions. Never in all the years of his friendship with Alan had Richard known the fellow so forgetful. He'd teased him about being in love and in response had received a moony-eyed smile.

Richard was about to speak to Sarah, then hesitated, for it struck him that her movements were suspicious. He drew back into an alleyway so that he could watch her unobserved. What was the woman up to? She looked about her, peered into doorways and windows, then, after yet another glance around, moved on to another shop. This time, after a brief hesitation and another anxious look over her shoulder, she darted inside.

Richard left his hiding place and sauntered along with a pretence of nonchalance. The shop door stood open and he was able to see inside. Sarah was talking to a wizened little man who was holding a necklace up to the light. Those were no ordinary cheap beads; they sparkled like diamonds and were delicately set in gold.

Money changed hands. Sarah dropped some coins into a drawstring bag that hung from her leather belt. Richard's suspicions deepened, but he decided not to challenge her there and then. He drew back so as to be out of sight when Sarah emerged from the shop. She turned and, walking with the swinging strides of a healthy young countrywoman, set off along the street.

He followed at a discreet distance. Sarah didn't look

back even once. Her mission accomplished, she seemed intent on getting back to Thurton's house as soon as possible. Richard harboured grave suspicions. He must ask Meg if any of her jewellery was missing, tell her what he had witnessed. He was glad to have a positive reason for approaching her, for Meg had been avoiding him ever since that evening, when she had asked the impossible. How could he marry her now? Where could he take her if he did? It would probably be one of the shortest marriages on record anyway! He had no doubt that Meg would be a widow almost as soon as she became a wife. And—apart from his own reluctance to contribute to that state—how could he then be any help to her?

Only when Sarah reached the back entrance of the house did Richard make his presence known. She was about to step inside when he caught hold of her arm. The girl jumped as if she was a mass of nerves. Then she recognised him.

'Oh, Sir Richard! You gave me such a fright! I thought you was a robber.'

'Now why should a robber be after you, I wonder? Are you carrying valuables?'

Colour spread all over the girl's face. He had never seen anyone look more guilty!

'Where have you been?' he asked.

'Just out. Seein' to something for my lady.'

'Something for your mistress?' he queried.

'That's right. An' nothin' a gent needs to know about.' Sarah quickly recovered from her surprise, and tossed her head with something of the cheeky confidence she normally had. 'I gotta go in now, sir. My mistress will be a-wonderin' where I've got to.' She lifted her skirts and ran.

'Tell Lady Margaret I wish to call on her.'

Sarah looked back at him over her shoulder. 'I'm not sure if she's at home, sir.'

He was quite sure that was a lie, but the girl was gone, almost immediately out of sight in the maze of passages at the back of the house.

Richard turned away. He wanted desperately to see Meg, to speak to her, to plead with her yet again to trust him. He could understand why she doubted him. He had been part of the deception played upon her by the Earl. When he had ridden to Norwich to bring her to Bixholm, he had never expected to fall in love with her. If only she'd been someone different, a woman who would be happy to be Queen of England! But then she wouldn't be Meg.

How could he expect her to forgive him—ever? All he could do was continue with the plan he had instigated. Then, he hoped, somehow—if—when—it was successfully concluded, he would be able to win back her trust—and her love.

At least she was safe for the moment. Thurton and Nancy would see that no harm befell her. She was far too valuable for them to take any risks. She would be cosseted and cherished, kept fresh and beautiful ready for those times when she might meet the King. Strangely, she was safe enough in his company also. There was no doubting the lust she awakened in the bawdy old monarch, but, with all his faults, he had never been a rapist. Indeed, many would suggest that it would be impossible for him, for he was, it was rumoured, almost impotent.

Richard gained little comfort from the thought. He could not bear to think of Henry even holding her hand!

He had seen his fat fingers clutch at her knee, and the revulsion Meg had tried to cover had been visible.

He tried to push the picture from his mind and turned away from the house. He strode off at a cracking pace, because movement might help him to keep his sanity and he had one more task to undertake before he set out for the field where, on the next day, he would ride in the Tournament.

He headed for the docks and walked along the wharf, reading the names of the vessels moored alongside. The ship he sought was not to be seen—probably it had not yet arrived from France. He chafed at the delay and prayed that the vessel was safe.

On the day of the Tournament people began to gather soon after dawn, anxious to get the best viewpoints. The atmosphere was excited, noisy and carefree. Gaily striped fair-booths appeared around the field, cheapjacks and fraudsters shouted for punters to try the three-card trick. Vendors arrived with food, hot and cold, ales and beers, fairings, penny ornaments and toys. Strolling musicians and players began to entertain the crowd long before the jousting was due to begin.

Only noblemen and gentlemen of high birth were permitted to ride in the Tournament, but for them it was an essential exercise. Its original purpose had been for the development of skills in horsemanship and fitness for leadership in times of war. Over the centuries it had developed into a sophisticated but still dangerous sport. The King watched from his place of honour in the centre stand, surrounded by courtiers, older knights and their ladies. Meg was seated at his side.

Henry was in the best of moods, living up to his nickname of bluff King Hal. He laughed and chatted with those around him and from time to time turned to address some remark to Meg. This second meeting emphasised even more than the first that he found her fascinating, for he made no attempt to hide his feelings. He grasped her hand and held it, looked deep into her eyes and smiled.

As the Earl and Nancy had escorted Meg to the Tournament they had instructed her how to play her part. Merely smiling was not enough; she was to laugh and flirt openly.

'Try and get him to take you to bed,' her uncle had urged.

'Shouldn't be difficult!' Nancy had chuckled. 'He's as eager as a lad at his first affair.'

'I couldn't do that unless he'd asked me to marry him,' Meg had objected, genuinely shocked.

'Don't you worry about that, my dear. It's not only a wife he's after—the King yearns for sons.'

'He has an heir in Prince Edward,' Meg had pointed out.

'The boy's said to be sickly. He's not growing up into a strapping big lad,' Nancy had told her. 'Henry feels cheated that he's got two daughters and only one son, whereas the Kings of France and Spain have a quiverful.'

'You get with child and your cares will be over,' the Earl had said. 'He'll rush you into marriage quick as lightning.'

'And if I don't produce a son, he'll send me to the block,' Meg had muttered bitterly.

'Don't keep harping on that, you silly girl,' Nancy had said. 'It's not likely to happen again. Not if you behave yourself.'

The conversation had ended there as the Earl had

triumphantly presented Meg to the stewards in charge
of the Royal Pavilion.

'His Majesty has expressed a wish for my niece to
sit at his side.' Thurton's voice had been loud and commanding.

So here she was, playing a part. She had to pretend,
but it was not so difficult as she'd feared. Just as on the
previous occasion, when she'd first met the King, she
found him pleasant, even charming. She would have
been perfectly happy to sit with him and converse with
him if only she had not been expected to marry him.

Richard and Gervase were both riding in the Thurton
colours of primrose and blue. All the knights were encased in armour, which made it difficult to tell one from
the other, except that Gervase wore a favour, a lady's
silk scarf knotted on his helmet.

'De Heigham—have you no lady to ride for?' asked
the King as Richard presented himself before the royal
stand.

'I fear not, Your Majesty. Perhaps on another occasion I shall be in a happier position.' His eyes flickered
for the briefest of moments in Meg's direction.

She regarded him woodenly, unsmiling, hiding her
feelings, for the love that had grown in her could not
be discarded as if it was no more than an old shoe. She
told herself that it was dead, that it had never meant
anything, all affection had gone. He had refused to help
her and now she felt only a deep void inside her. After
that one quick glance Richard kept his eyes fixed upon
the King.

'You shall have something from my new sweetheart,'
Henry said magnanimously, turning to Meg. 'You
danced so delightfully with this knight, surely you will
not let him ride without a favour?'

'Perhaps he does not wish for anything from me,' said Meg.

'Nonsense. Every knight needs someone to fight for, even if it is only for one day. Surely you can spare a scarf or a handkerchief.'

'Very well, if you desire it, Your Majesty.' Meg agreed reluctantly. She had vowed she would have nothing more to do with Richard and felt humiliated yet again by being made to hand him her lace-edged kerchief.

'You are most gracious, Lady Margaret.' He smiled, and there was such warmth in his face that her traitorous heart flipped. He bowed and continued, 'As I am wearing Thurton colours, I shall be riding for you as well as for the Earl.'

She regarded him coldly. 'Sir Richard, your loyalty is to the Earl. There is no difference between you and Gervase Gisbon.'

Her words stung. Richard flinched, then quickly regained his composure. 'But only I have your favour. I shall cherish this token, and trust it to bring me good fortune.'

The King appeared not to notice the undercurrents of emotion that throbbed between Meg and Richard. 'Good fellow! Gallantly spoken!' he said. 'I know of old how skilled you are at the joust. We shall eagerly watch your performance.'

Heralds announced the events and the contestants rode forward. Horses were gaily caparisoned, and knights clad from head to toe in specially adapted armour, the helm reinforced and a grand guard covering the left side of the visor. A lance-rest was fixed to the breast-plate. They should be invincible in such gear, yet somehow the sight of it increased rather than lessened the impression that they were about to participate in a dangerous 'sport'. Even the tiltyard had not prepared Meg for the fear that gripped her when she watched Richard riding in the Tournament.

The long lances were lowered, held under the right arm and directed across the neck of the horse. The combatants charged towards each other at full gallop, each with the central barrier on his left. They rode a straight course with levelled lances, attempting to unseat opponents. It was a trial of skill, necessitating great steadiness of aim. The air was alive with the pounding of horses' feet, the shouts of the crowd, the clash of lance on metal. Richard's daring won the applause of the onlookers, but so frightened Meg that she could scarcely bear to watch.

She closed her eyes when Gervase rode against him. It was quite unreasonable of her to pray that Richard would emerge the victor, but she could not help it. In spite of everything he held her heart. It was excruciating to watch him riding so bravely, with her kerchief fluttering from his helm, and remember so vividly how he had rejected her. She must never again trust him. Never! She had to act on her own to save herself from this hideous farce of a marriage.

'Well done!' The King, at her side, bellowed encouragement. They were all his knights. He had no side to take. But he understood the niceties of the sport in a way that Meg did not.

'This man's worth watching,' Henry said to her. 'He's one of the best. An acknowledged expert—though I unseated him easily a few years back. That was a day, that was! You should have seen me then!'

She tried to understand what was happening, but could not. She was grateful when Richard did well and as far as she could see had escaped injury. She was even more grateful when the jousting was over. Prizes and accolades were bestowed upon the winners, among whom were both Richard and Gervase. There was much trumpeting and playing of fanfares as the ceremony ended in its time-honoured way.

'An excellent performance by almost all the knights,' the King commented. 'Did you find that enjoyable, little Meg?'

'Most certainly it was exciting,' she replied. 'I am not sure if I enjoyed it—I was so afraid someone would be seriously hurt.'

'You are a kind and gentle young lady.' Henry smiled. 'And you are right. Sometimes there are serious injuries, but that is no longer the object. The knights have perfected skills which allow them to avoid such happenings.'

'I know little about jousting,' she admitted. 'But the courage of everyone was clear, even to me.'

'We shall watch more jousts together in the future,' said Henry. 'It has been a pleasure to have your company, sweet Meg.'

With that he prepared to depart, again accompanied by the trumpeters and surrounded by officials and soldiers. Meg rose to her feet and curtsied low.

'It is merely *adieu*, my sweetheart. We shall meet again ere long.'

The Earl and Nancy escorted Meg back to the house. Their excitement was, if possible, even greater than on the previous occasion. Meg said little. She was preoccupied with her plans to escape the following day. She saw Richard distantly, but turned her head away and clenched her fists, determined to forget.

As she had predicted, that evening the feast was even more sumptuous than usual. She took care to avoid moving in Richard's direction, though her wanton body desired it. She formed the impression that he wished to speak to her, but she would have none of it. When he came near to her, she moved away, and would not exchange even a smile with him.

Her heart was breaking to think she would never see him again. She despised herself that it should be so, for she ought to be glad to be leaving him. He had deceived her most shamefully. She would never understand how he could have been so loving to her, yet leave her to this fate, which to her seemed a living death.

Chapter Eleven

Long before daybreak Meg and Sarah were up and dressing in the unfamiliar male garments. They handled them fastidiously, for none of them were new and some not very clean.

'I'm sorry about that, my lady,' Sarah said. 'I'd have washed 'em, but those thick things'd never get dried in time.'

'Just as the stableboys wear them,' commented Meg.

'That's right. It'll make us look more the part.' Sarah wrinkled her nose as she shook straw and dust from a jerkin.

Nervousness made their fingers clumsy. Meg was grateful that the fashion was for padded shoulders, which gave her a false appearance of manliness, and she bloused the tunic out over the wide leather belt. Fortunately it was long enough to cover her rounded hips, though her legs still looked decidedly feminine encased in thick knitted stockings. She looked Sarah over critically. They had cut each other's hair the night before. Meg's short curls gave her a cheeky look, whilst Sarah's, dark, straight and plain, reached to just below

her ears. With a good stretch of imagination it was possible that she could pass as a boy.

'How do I look?' asked Meg.

Sarah grinned. 'You know what, my lady? I reckon
we both look too clean.'

'Even in these clothes?'

'Hands in particular,' Sarah said. 'Takes years to get
that ingrained look, but we'd better have a try.' She
knelt on the floor and scuffed her hands about in the
rushes. 'Good thing they haven't been changed for a
few weeks.'

Meg followed Sarah's example. Even after rubbing
them in dust and broken reeds her hands looked small
and distinctly feminine. She'd keep them out of sight
as much as possible.

'Now rub your face, my lady,' Sarah instructed, and
Meg obeyed. With dirty faces they stood and regarded
each other seriously, for this was no laughing matter.
Giving a wrong impression could mean capture and a
fate that did not bear thinking about.

'You'll pass now, my lady.'

'You must stop calling me that,' Meg said. 'We're a
couple of stable lads. Equals, too. We need boys'
names.'

'I thought of mine last night,' Sarah said. 'I'm going
to be Septimus.'

'So you shall be, dear Septimus,' Meg said. 'I'm going to be Matt.'

'Yes, my—' Sarah began, then stopped herself. 'Yes,
Matt.'

Meg stood for a moment, looking around the room,
checking items in her mind. Money was hidden in the
belts they wore. She had kept back a few jewels, and
these had been sewn into the linings of her ragged gar-

ments. She had bundled up the everyday clothes she had brought with her from the nunnery, taking not even one thing which had been paid for by her uncle.

Sarah packed her favourite skirt and some shoes. 'That'll do for me,' she said. 'Food's more important.' She had secretly taken some victuals from the kitchens and carried these in a rush bag.

Together they pushed things under the bedclothes, so that if anyone peeped into the chamber it would appear that the bed was occupied. Sarah put a chamber-pot on the pillow and pulled the bedspread up over it.

'That'll surprise 'em, if they start pokin' about,' she grinned.

Meg was not sorry to be leaving either the room or the house, but her heart was heavy at the thought that she would never again see Richard. If only he had agreed to come with her! If they could have run away together, she would not have minded if they'd had to live in a hovel. She'd never been afraid of hard work. She had often assisted the nuns with household tasks at the nunnery, the baking and cleaning, even the growing of vegetables and herbs.

Angry tears started into her eyes. She found it impossible to understand how Richard could have acted so lovingly towards her, kissed and caressed her so tenderly, whispered that she meant more to him than anyone in the world—and then refused to marry her.

She could have faced anything if they had been setting out to seek a new life together. As a married woman, she would have been protected from the King's advances. They would have risked the wrath of Thurton and Nancy, but surely they could have found somewhere to live, made a home together far, far away? Yet even as that dream entered her mind she knew her uncle's rage would have been quite terrible. He might have been so enraged at having his plans thwarted that he would have hunted them down. That could be the case even now. She trembled as she recalled Sarah's words—*'You'll be caught. All you'll get for your pains is a beating.'* With an effort she pushed all those fears to the back of her head.

'Are you ready, Septimus?' she whispered.

'Aye, Matt. God go with us,' Sarah prayed softly.

'Amen to that,' agreed Meg.

The sound of snoring came from the Earl's room as they crept along the passageway. A glance into the Great Hall revealed bodies sprawled over and under the tables, a general mess of overturned flagons and leaking barrel bungs, the rancid smell of stale food and ale. One dog lifted its head, but it only yawned, as replete as its master, having fed well on scraps and spillages.

The stables were at the back of the mansion. Not only had Sarah managed to get clothes from one of the stablehands, she had bribed him to have horses ready.

'Dugald,' she called softly.

They waited anxiously.

'He promised to be here, waiting for us,' she muttered. A horse scraped its foot.

'Dugald,' she called again. 'It's me, Sarah.'

Then a lad stepped forward, leading two horses saddled and ready. He grinned at the sight of them. 'Didn't recognise you, Sarah.'

Meg was heartened to hear him say that. It meant that their disguise was passable—at least in the half-light of dawn.

They wasted no more time, mounted quickly, and with a brief word of thanks rode out of the stableyard. To Meg's ears the clatter of hooves sounded loud enough to waken the entire household as they rode through the wide gateway and out into the street.

Even at that early hour there were people about: workmen carting away rubbish, beggars sleeping in corners, scavengers looking for scraps. The stench was worse than during the day.

Meg recalled the direction from which they had arrived, and knew they needed to head north-eastwards. They walked the horses at first, then trotted on a little faster. She breathed a sigh of relief when they passed through Bishopgate without being challenged. Some time later, when they reached wider tracks and the city had been left behind, they spurred the horses into a canter.

'Are you sure we're on the right road, my lady?' asked Sarah.

'Matt, if you please, Septimus,' Meg corrected her.

'Sorry, Matt. It just don't sound right,' Sarah protested.

'It doesn't matter how it sounds; it's a matter of safety,' Meg reminded her sternly. 'You'll get used to it, Septimus. As to whether we are going in the right direction, I confess I cannot be absolutely sure, but I think this is the way we came.'

Right or wrong, there could be no turning back. By mid-morning they were well away from the city of London, following rough and rutted tracks through open countryside. They dismounted by a small stream to rest and water the horses. Sarah delved into the rush basket and produced bread and cheese and a leather flask of ale. They sat beside the gurgling water to share their meal, whilst the horses cropped the grass.

The short break had been welcome, but they dared not tarry. Then they were in the saddle again, riding as fast as their mounts could take them, mindful that they must try and reach the shelter of a hostelry or monastery before nightfall. Robbers lurked in the woods and would be more likely to strike after dark, though one had to take care at all times. Two lads would be easy targets for attack.

Peasants were at work in the open fields, oxen pulling ploughs and carts. They passed through hamlets that were no more than a cluster of seven or eight clay-lump thatched hovels. On and on, until the sun was dipping low in the west and casting a golden red light over the landscape.

'Matt—it's time we found somewhere for the night,' Sarah said.

'I agree, Septimus.' Meg had been thinking that for some time. It was more than an hour since they had passed any place where they could have stayed, and that had been a particularly disreputable-looking ale-house. She would rather sleep under a hedge than there!

Again they stopped, this time at a crossroads, beside which was a pond where the horses could drink. They had ridden hard and were all in need of a rest. Sarah opened her rush bag and brought out the bread and cheese and ale.

'Better keep some for later,' she said. 'In case we don't find nowhere to stay.'

Meg agreed. She looked around. There was no habitation within sight. A milestone had the word 'WARE' engraved on it, and below it 'XX miles'. Meg sighed.

'We're on the right road, anyways,' commented Sarah.

'But it's twenty miles to Ware,' Meg said despondently. 'We'll never get there before dark.'

'Someone a-comin',' said Sarah.

Two monks were walking towards them. Meg stood up, pulled her hat lower on her forehead to hide her face and hoped their disguise would not be broken. The monks' cowled heads were bent. They wore black habits—Dominicans, she assumed. As was customary, they had Bibles tucked inside the folds of their dark woollen clothes. This left their hands free to carry staffs.

'God be with you, young men,' said one of the monks.

'And with you, Brother,' said Meg. She spoke gruffly, but something in the timbre of her voice must have struck him for he peered closer into her face. She drew back, and as he did so she recognised him. He was one of the brothers who had in the past sometimes visited the nunnery.

'Will you spare a crust for a Religious?' he asked.

The whining voice confirmed her suspicions; she had heard it before. She glanced at Sarah and saw horror on her maid's face, fear in her eyes. She too had recognised the man. Father Bernard had been cast out of the order in Norwich because of his lewd ways and because he had fathered a child, taking advantage of a girl who had been ill-treated at home and had sought sanctuary in the nunnery.

'Give bread to the holy man, Septimus,' said Meg.

She hoped that would satisfy the mendicant, but he ignored Sarah's offering, continuing to stare at her. Meanwhile the second man had his eyes fixed on the horses. Meg moved in that direction, but he moved faster. Before she could reach them, he took the reins into his own hands. He fielded her off. He was strong—he pushed her away. She managed to dodge the worst of the blows he threw at her.

'Nice animals, Bernard,' he said. 'We've walked far enough for one day.'

'Too good for these louts,' the other monk agreed. 'The good Lord must've sent these specially for us.'

'Don't touch those horses,' Meg snapped. She tried to grab the reins.

The man laughed at her and caught her hand in his. His grip was powerful; it felt strong enough to crush her bones. Then suddenly he opened his fingers. She tried to draw her hand away, but he caught her by the wrist.

'Hey, Bernard—look at this.'

He held out Meg's hand and at the same time tore open her jerkin. The shape of her breasts was clearly visible beneath the fine linen shirt. She kicked and fought. She tried to bring her knee up into the assassin's groin. But he held her at arm's length. Suddenly Meg was grasped from behind.

'Well, well!' Bernard's voice was gloating. 'A couple of wenches! And would you believe it, Marcus? I think I know who they are.'

'Good for a night's fun, anyway.' Marcus grinned. His expression made his evil intent revoltingly clear. He released his hold on Meg's wrist and stepped back. No remnants of the holiness they had once professed remained with them.

Whilst they were both occupied with Meg, Sarah seized the opportunity and leapt up into the saddle of her horse. She wheeled it sharply and with a hard kick rode straight at Marcus. He turned to run away, but fell over and was struck by the horse's hoof. There was a loud crack. He cried out in pain. Sarah ignored him. She turned her horse, preparing to ride back.

'Let her go,' she yelled to Bernard. 'Or I'll ride you down as well.'

'Try it. Just you try it.' Bernard grabbed Meg round the waist and pulled her in front of him, making her into a human shield.

Meg struggled, kicked and tried to turn her head to bite her attacker, but he held her in a vice-like grip. She was furious, but powerless. Sarah reined in her horse; she turned it to face towards Marcus. He was lying on the ground where he had fallen, moaning but undoubtedly alive.

'Let her go, or I'll ride over him again,' she shouted.

'No. No, stop her!' screamed Marcus. 'My leg's broken.'

'You can trample him to death for all I care,' Bernard challenged her.

'Help me—Bernard, you've got to help me.' Marcus yelled and screamed.

'Stop snivelling, man,' commanded Bernard. Then to Sarah he shouted, 'I remember you, Sarah Wilgress. You told tales on me when I stayed at the nunnery.'

'Only the truth,' Sarah said coldly. 'I'll inform on you again, if you—'

'What can you do?' he jeered. 'I know who this is too! This tasty morsel I'm holding in my arms is Lady Margaret Thurton.' He sneered as he spoke her name.

Sarah's horse danced about. She was having difficulty in holding it. 'Let my lady go,' she yelled.

'Never,' he said scornfully. 'She's far too valuable a property. Her uncle will be exceedingly grateful to have her returned to him. I'll make a fortune out of this!'

He was so pleased with himself that he relaxed his hold—only slightly, but it was enough for Meg. She threw back her head, her teeth closed on his ear and she bit with all her might. His yell rang through the still summer air. He jerked his head aside and raised one hand to the bleeding lobe. Meg struggled harder; she twisted and pulled, but it was useless. He did not let go of her for a moment—his grip tightened.

His determination to hold her increased. With his blood-stained hand he pulled her hat forward, covering her eyes, and entwined his other hand in her hair. He forced her down to her knees and held her there, kneeling and helpless, under his control. Any movement was excruciatingly painful. Sarah could do nothing, for he made sure Meg was always between him and that snorting animal she was mounted upon.

'Get up,' he growled, jerking at her hair. The pain brought tears streaming from her eyes. She reached up and tried to move his hands, but it was a useless gesture. She had no option but to do as he said. He pulled her over to where her horse was contentedly cropping the grass. He grabbed its reins.

'Mount,' he commanded.

Hope flared momentarily in Meg's heart. She obeyed with a false show of humility, but as she settled in the saddle she kicked out. She aimed her foot at Bernard's head, but he had anticipated trouble and easily dodged away.

'You'll pay for that,' he threatened.

The horse, aware that all was not well, whinnied and wheeled and threw up its head.

'Whoa, you devil.' He pulled it down roughly, and hit it hard. The horse bared its teeth, but submitted.

Bernard brought a length of rope from the folds of his habit. He flung it round Meg, and before she realised what was happening her arms were pinioned to her sides. Bernard heaved himself up into the saddle, pushed her forward and settled in behind her. A kick sent the restive animal charging away.

'Bernard—don't leave me.' Marcus's voice screamed after them. He tried to struggle to his feet, but fell back. He lifted his hands in supplication. Bernard ignored him. He screamed louder as he saw Sarah, determined to keep up with Bernard, riding straight at him. He crouched and covered his head with his arms, clutching his rosary beads. Sarah jumped over him as he fainted. She did not even look behind.

Meg was terrified and helpless. Every movement of the horse jolted her. She was held awkwardly upright, and the rope cut into her flesh. She was being taken back to London with all possible speed. Back to her uncle. Back to the King.

Sarah followed, riding faster than she had ever done in her life, taking risks she would never have contemplated in normal circumstances. Having only one rider, her horse could cover the ground faster than Bernard's. But what could she do when she caught up with him? She cursed her lack of strength, her limited expertise in riding. She had some vague idea of trying to grab the reins from Bernard and pull the galloping animal to a standstill. Even as she thought of it she dismissed the idea as impractical, and concentrated on following him. It took all her courage and concentration to stay on the galloping beast and keep up.

The rough road turned sharply around the wall of a barn and momentarily they were out of sight. Sarah followed as fast as she was able. Shouts rang out somewhere ahead. Men's voices, angry voices, and one of them sounded wondrously familiar. She couldn't believe it! Her ears must be deceiving her! She prepared herself for disappointment as she rode round the corner—but it was true!

She almost fainted with relief. Alan Crompton and Sir Richard were there, miraculously face to face with Bernard and Meg. His horse had risen on its hind legs and Bernard was striving to control it, yelling at the oncoming riders.

'Out of my way. The boy's had a fit. I have to get him to a physician immediately.'

Meg was making muffled sounds. Bernard was almost smothering her, holding her close to his chest, his wide-sleeved, rough woollen habit hiding the rope with which she was bound.

'Hush, lad. I'll take good care of you.' Bernard's voice was smooth and caring as he tried to bluff his way past the oncoming riders.

'What ails the lad?' asked Alan.

'He's been cursed by a witch. She's made him ill and he's turned against all his friends. He needs help—'

'Poor young man.'

Richard and Alan drew their horses aside. 'God help you on your way,' said Richard.

'Alan,' Sarah shouted. 'Stop him.'

They stared at her without recognition. Wild-faced, in boy's clothes, hair cut short, her hat blown off long since.

'It's me. Sarah,' she screamed.

'That's her. That's the witch.' Bernard dug his heels into his horse's flanks. It sprang forward, passing the bewildered Richard and Alan.

'He's kidnapped my lady,' Sarah shouted.

Richard reacted immediately. He set off at full gallop, chasing after the monk.

'Sarah!' Alan was horrified. 'What's happened? Are you all right?'

'I'm all right,' she shouted. 'Don't let that bastard get away—'

The swear word slipped out. Alan took one long hard look at Sarah, then, obeying her wish, spurred his horse. It leapt forward at full gallop. Sarah followed.

Bernard glanced over his shoulder. His pursuers were coming up fast. The gap between them narrowed with every minute. He knew he'd never get away and decided to save his own skin. He loosened his hold on Meg, gave her a shove and flung her off the horse.

It had the desired effect. All three riders halted where Meg had fallen. She lay frighteningly still. Trussed by the rope, she had been unable to do anything to save herself. She'd fallen hard, but fortunately on to soft muddy ground.

'Meg. Oh, my darling—speak to me,' Richard implored her.

Her eyes were closed. Sarah knelt beside her. 'She's alive,' she said. 'She's breathing.'

Richard used his dagger to cut the ropes that bound her. Sarah took her mistress's hand and chafed it between her own, seeking to assist the blood flow. Meg remained unconscious. Richard took off his cape and wrapped it around her.

'Please God, don't let her die,' Richard prayed.

'My lady needs rest, and a physician to look to her injuries,' said Sarah.

'I'll take her to Leet Castle,' said Richard. 'It's not far from here.'

'Will she be safe there?' asked Sarah.

'I shall guard her with my life and she will be attended by one of the best physicians in the land. I know nowhere else she can get the attention she requires.'

Tenderly he lifted Meg, wrapped in the cloak. 'Hold her for me, Alan, whilst I mount.'

Both men were strong; they had no difficulty in holding the inert body. Alan lifted Meg, very, very carefully, and handed her up to Richard. He placed her in front of him, tucked close to his own body, held by one strong arm as he rode at a steady walking pace.

Alan swept Sarah into his arms and kissed her long and hard. 'I've been so worried about you, my love,' he said. 'Why on earth did you dash off like that, without a word to anyone?'

'My lady was in danger; you know that, Alan.' Sarah regarded him witheringly.

'You should have told me.'

'We were afraid to let anyone know. You'd probably have forbidden us even to try and get away.'

'You're right!' Alan helped Sarah up into the saddle, then leapt up on to his own horse. As they followed a short distance behind Richard he added, 'Now you see what a foolish escapade it was.'

'What else could we do?' Sarah challenged. 'My lady said she'd rather face death than marry the King. She'd have gone on her own, but there was no way I'd have let her do that, so don't you suggest it.'

A little later, with a touch of her old mischievous smile returning, she asked, 'Was there a great to-do in the house when it was discovered we was missing?'

'There probably is now. We didn't even know you'd gone until mid-morning, when Richard went to look for Lady Margaret. He knocked on the door of her chamber and there was no answer, so he looked inside. You were not there, and a dummy with a chamber-pot for its head was lying in the bed.'

Sarah chuckled.

'It wasn't funny,' Alan said. 'Richard was frantic. He expected me to know what you were up to and accused me of helping you. We were both nearly out of our minds when we went out to the stables and realised you two had ridden off alone.'

'I wanted to tell you, Alan. Honest I did. I'm sorry you was so upset. We didn't dare tell anyone. So how did you know which way we'd gone?'

'I remembered the stable boy you'd befriended. I made him tell me what he knew.'

'You didn't beat him?' Sarah asked anxiously.

'I felt like taking a whip to him,' Alan said grimly. 'But we bribed him instead, just as you did. He didn't know where you were going, but Richard felt you might have been heading back to Norwich.'

'Thank goodness you did,' breathed Sarah.

Leet Castle stood on the bank of a slow-flowing river. Some clay-lump thatched hovels were clustered around the outer walls of the tall-towered castle. The last rays of the setting sun twinkled on its windows as they approached.

Sarah was suddenly very tired. She had never before ridden so far or so fast, and she was desperately worried about the state of her mistress. Richard had moved steadily on and Sarah and Alan had followed, talking in low voices.

At walking pace they approached the entrance to the castle, where they were confronted by the joists of the underside of the drawbridge, uplifted and unwelcoming.

'Open up,' Richard called. 'Tell your officer of the

watch that Sir Richard de Heigham is here and requires immediate assistance.'

Within minutes a tall, grey-haired man came forward. He looked up and a smile spread over his face.

'Sir Richard! How good to see you.' He turned to the guards. 'Lower the drawbridge—and quick about it.'

As soon as they were inside the courtyard, Alan and Sarah dismounted. They hurried over to Sir Richard. Meg was carefully lowered into the waiting arms of Alan Crompton whilst Sarah gazed anxiously at the waxen face of her mistress. There was still no sign of life.

Chapter Twelve

Meg had no recollection of what had happened after Bernard had flung her from the horse. When she came to she tried to move and found that her whole body ached. Clad only in her shift, she was lying on a large four-poster bed, the heavy curtains closed, making it into a rich tapestry box. Suddenly she remembered that Bernard had been carrying her back to London. Was that where she was now? She shivered with fear at the thought.

She stretched out one arm, moving with care, for even reaching to draw back one of the curtains was painful. The room was strange to her. There was a window through which the morning sun streamed cheerfully. Rushes were spread on the floor. She heard a door open and a moment later gasped with relief.

Sarah was there, beaming at her. 'Oh, praise God, my lady! You're awake'

She hurried across the room and dropped to her knees at the bedside. She would have clasped Meg in her arms, but quickly realised that would hurt her mistress.

'We're not back in London, are we?' Meg asked.

'Gracious, no! Away in the back of beyond, this is.'

'Did Bernard bring us here?' Meg whispered.

'Don't you remember, my lady? He threw you off the horse and rushed away as if the devil himself was after him, as well he might be. Wicked old man. It was Sir Richard who brought you here.'

'I remember Richard was there, but—'

'Thank God he was!' said Sarah. 'He brought us to this old castle. He's known here. The Captain of the Guard let us in straight away an' he sent for the physician.'

'The physician?' asked Meg. 'I don't remember—'

'You was unconscious, my lady. He looked at you last night, an' said as how no bones had been broken an' it was just bruises and shock—an' that with rest you'd get over it—an' Sir Richard and me have sat with you for most of the night—'

'Richard? Here?'

'Yes, an' that reminds me. I must go and tell him that you've woke up. He didn't want to leave you, but I said as how he'd got to keep up his strength and he'd better go an' get something to eat. He's with Alan now.'

'Alan's here, too? Your Alan?'

'That's right, my lady.'

'How did they find us?'

'Never mind about that now. The important thing is they did, an' I can't bear to think what would've happened if they hadn't. That wicked old Bernard, posing as a holy man! An' that Marcus, too. I'm glad I broke his leg for him. It's no more than he deserved. I'd have killed him if I'd got the chance.'

'Dear Sarah.' Meg gave a wry smile, recalling that in fact Sarah had jumped her horse over the fallen man.

'There! I've made you smile! An' here's me rambling on and I've never asked you how you're feelin'.'

'A bit sore,' Meg said with a grimace. 'But I'm sure I'll survive—at least I would if I could get washed and then have something to eat.'

'Hungry, are you?' Sarah clapped her hands together with joy. 'That's good to hear. As for washing, I brought up a jug of hot water. I left it over by the door. I'll fetch it—'

'Help me out of bed first, please, Sarah.'

Shakily, holding on to Sarah for support, Meg managed to stand on her feet. The physician had been correct. She had no broken bones, but every movement was painful. It took ages to complete her toilette and to get dressed. Sarah had washed Meg's everyday gown when they had arrived at Bixholm.

'It got a bit creased on the journey,' Sarah fretted, shaking it vigorously.

'I'm not worried about that.' Meg smiled.

Sarah laced her bodice, with tender careful fingers, quite loosely, mindful of the bruises that coloured her mistress's body. Her arms were yellowish, black and green where the cord had been lashed around her. Her shoulder was swollen and bruised where it had hit the ground, likewise her hip and ankle. Sarah tut-tutted over the state Meg was in.

'If I could get my hands on that brute!' she exclaimed more than once.

'But I'm alive. And you're here to help me,' Meg said. 'I can't thank you enough, Sarah, for coming with me.'

'Yeah. We've been through a lot together, ain't we? But never anything as bad as yesterday, an' I hope to goodness we never ever have to do anything like that again.'

'Amen,' agreed Meg.

Sarah brushed her hair, which didn't take long, for it was just a golden glow of curls around her face.

'There, my lady! You look more like your old self—a bit pale, but lovely all the same. Now, you sit in that chair by the window and I'll fetch something for you to eat.'

She hurried away to the kitchen and very soon returned bearing a laden tray, which she placed on a small table in front of Meg. She stood with arms akimbo, watching, until she was satisfied there was nothing more she could do at that moment. Then quietly she left the chamber.

Meg willingly tackled the appetising food and sipped the tankard of small beer. The window by which she sat looked down upon a relic of a formal garden. It must once have been lovely, but had been sadly neglected, the little boxwood borders overgrown, and more weeds than useful herbs in the beds. Nevertheless it was a pleasant outlook.

Suddenly Sarah came into view, walking hand in hand with Alan Crompton. Their pleasure at being together was obvious, open for all to see. Even as Meg watched, Alan took Sarah into his arms and kissed her, whilst she twined her arms around his neck, holding his head down to hers as if she never wished to let him go. She ran a finger over the scar on his face, a gesture that expressed her wholehearted love, despite the blemish which gashed his fine, honest face.

It stirred the ever-present ache in Meg's heart. Her own love was every bit as strong as was Sarah's, but Richard's response was never as clear and unfettered. A few moments later, Alan took hold of Sarah's shoulders and stepped away from her. He held her for a moment at arm's length, then turned and strode away.

Sarah attempted to run towards him, but he waved her back. A groom brought forward a horse and held it for Alan to mount. With one last wave of farewell, he rode swiftly away. Sarah stood watching until he was out of sight, then with drooping shoulders she turned and walked into the castle.

Her sorrow seeped into Meg's soul. Puzzled and unhappy, she pushed the tray away. She wanted nothing more to eat or drink. She had a premonition that all was not well at Leet Castle. She sat still, with her gaze fixed on the scene outside, and shivered involuntarily.

Richard stood at the open door of the chamber. Meg was unaware of his presence and for several minutes he stayed there, quite still, gazing at her.

He found it pleasing that she was dressed again in those simple garments she had worn when he had first encountered her in Norwich. They were so plain as to be almost puritanical, but how sweet and innocent she looked. He cursed the wickedness of Thurton, hell-bent on driving her into Henry's lustful arms.

He had discovered quite early yesterday morning that she had left Thurton's London house. Then Alan had told him that Sarah was also missing. Richard had recalled Meg's anger and despair when he had been with her in the garden, and he had plunged into an abyss of fear and worry. He'd searched the whole house, opening doors, peering inside, regardless of who was there or what embarrassing situation he came upon. He had been too maddened to care. She had gone! Vanished.

He had cursed himself for not agreeing to her suggestion that he should marry her, but that would have placed her in greater danger. He didn't trust Thurton or Nancy. Meg was so honest and outspoken that they might have tricked her into revealing the plan. He'd remained convinced that he was right in his reasoning, and he'd also believed that because she was being courted by Henry she had not been in immediate danger. Now he could see that he should have told her that he was trying to make arrangements to take her to France. He'd cursed himself again, but it had been too late for recriminations. The only thing that had mattered was to find her.

Alan had questioned the lads at the stable. He'd sought out Dugald, knowing Sarah had made a special friend of the lad. At first Dugald had angrily denied any knowledge of missing horses or anything else. Not until Alan had persuaded him that his concern was entirely for the safety of Sarah and Meg, and had given his solemn word that he would tell no other person of his part in their escape, had Dugald spoken.

'Are they in danger?' he'd asked.

'Sir Richard and I both think so. For the love of God, Dugald, tell me—did they ride away together?'

Dugald had nodded.

'Which direction did they take?'

'The lady spoke of Bishopgate,' he'd muttered. 'An' that's all I know.'

'They'll be heading back to Norwich,' Richard had said. 'Let's go that way and look for them.'

They had ridden hard all day. Once or twice they had questioned travellers coming in the opposite direction, but no one had seen them. Two young ladies riding alone would have been so unusual that they would surely have been noticed. Richard had begun to think they must have taken a different direction, but where else would they go?

He had begun to despair of catching up with them when he had encountered the monk. Richard groaned

at the memory. He couldn't believe that he hadn't recognised Meg, even dressed as a boy and clutched inside
Bernard's rough woollen habit. But for Sarah's warning
shouts Bernard would have succeeded in carrying her
off.

He uttered a silent prayer of thanksgiving that he had
been able to rescue her. It wrenched at his heart to see
Meg, sitting by the window, for she was looking out
with a lonely, forlorn expression on her face. How pale
she was, too! He moved a step towards her, intention-
ally making a sound so that she would hear. Slowly she
turned towards him, then rose to her feet rather shakily.
She did not smile, and as her eyes met his he saw tears
in them.

'Meg.' He breathed her name reverently.

With long, urgent strides he crossed the room and
would have taken her into his arms, but she held her
hands out to prevent him. 'Please don't touch me.'

He stood stock-still. Gently, with understanding, he
asked, 'How are you, my dear one?'

'Bruised and sore.'

Even as Meg warned him away, delight at the sight
of him engulfed her. She had tried to resign herself to
the sadness of never seeing him again, but had missed
him every minute. Their relationship was so tenuous, so
fragile, yet to her more powerful than any emotion she
had ever experienced. No other man would ever awaken
such strong feelings in her, of that she was convinced.
It was madness when there was so much she doubted
about Richard. Yet in that moment of meeting, after she
had expected to die, or to be taken inexorably back to
London and her evil relative, she moved towards him.

It was her body, not her mind, that was in control.
She lifted her face for his kiss. His lips closed over hers,

gently but possessively, awakening excited pulses which quivered from her head to her feet. Love enveloped her. Richard's arms encircled her, but gently, so gently. He touched her with care, his hands exploring, always watching her reaction.

'I'm so afraid of hurting you, my dearest,' he whispered.

'The pain seems less when you kiss me,' she murmured.

'Then I shall keep kissing you until you are fully restored,' he volunteered.

With the utmost tenderness he kissed her forehead and the tip of her nose, then turned his attention to her lips. He drew her closer into his arms—and pain shot through her ribs. He loosened his hold at once.

'I'm hurting you.'

She didn't want him to stop. 'It's all right. It will go away. Kiss me again.'

He did so willingly, a long, lingering kiss that, despite her bruises, throbbed deliciously through her. It brought a rush of desire, transporting her from the everyday world. A few moments previously she had looked out of the window and, seeing Sarah with Alan, had felt envious. Now the sun was shining in through the glass at her side, Richard kissed her again and again, and her world was alight with joy.

But she was still far from well and the aches and pains returned. Richard noticed. 'You should be resting,' he said solicitously. 'Shall I carry you?'

'No,' she gasped. 'Just let me take your arm—'

As if she had been waiting for just this moment Sarah knocked on the door. 'The physician said you'd to rest, my lady,' she said sternly.

He stayed with Meg until she fell asleep. His eyes

never left her face and he cursed the day he had been
forced by Thurton to swear that oath on the Bible. He
would keep it. His honour demanded no less. But he
knew that vow would try him harder than any other
thing in his life.

The physician's prognosis proved to be correct.
Meg's recovery took its natural course; she was young
and healthy and within a few days was able to walk
unaided. Despite her disability they were happy days,
spent mostly in Richard's company—and indeed, for
many hours, in his arms.

Ever solicitous, considerate, clearly he was happy to
be with her. The feeling that throbbed between them
was real and strong; it had nothing to do with courtly
love. To her it seemed that they were made for each
other. Every day she expected him to speak of marriage,
but though they talked a great deal that was never mentioned.

He kissed her, caressed her and enfolded her in loving embraces until she almost swooned in his arms. She
yearned to be his entirely, and she could tell that his
arousal matched hers, but he never actually made love
to her. Always, just when she wanted more than anything in the world to be seduced by him, to give herself
to him entirely, he drew back. He would pull away from
their embrace, tear himself from her arms, murmuring
of some important engagement which he had to attend.

Why was it not as frustrating for him as it was for
her? She had no doubt that their desire was mutual, even
if for him it was not true love. In the past when he had
spoken of courtly love he had warned her that a gentleman would carry the affair as far as the lady was willing. Sometimes she wondered if there was some other

lady to whom he was attached or even betrothed. She had seen him talking teasingly to some who had been ladies-in-waiting to Queen Jane. Perhaps, although he dallied with her, it meant nothing to him, and there was another he wished to marry.

She sighed. She could not speak of it. That would have been far too bold for a lady brought up as she had been. Sometimes she regretted her early years in the nunnery, which had imprinted such deeply held moral restrictions upon her. It made her ashamed of the intensity of her feelings. Her only recourse was to hide those emotions that could so easily consume her. She fought against the wild wantonness that Richard caused, which flared up in her and threatened to engulf her whole being. If he truly loved her, surely he would behave more warmly towards her.

Doubts festered just below the surface of her mind, as they had done ever since their first encounter. She would have avoided all contact with him, but that was not within her power. Her love for him was too great, the pleasure of being with him so sweet. Yet, as she recovered from her injuries, questions that had been at the back of her mind thrust themselves forward.

'Sarah, where is Alan? I saw you with him the first morning we were here. But that's several days ago and I haven't yet had an opportunity to thank him for his part in our rescue.'

'He's gone to London, my lady.'

'To London? Why should he wish to go there?'

'Sir Richard sent him on a mission.'

'What sort of mission?' Meg asked suspiciously.

'That's all I know, my lady. He wouldn't tell me anything more.'

'I see,' Meg said, though in truth she was no wiser than before and, in fact, was more troubled.

For the first few days she had taken all meals in her chamber; now she declared herself sufficiently fit to join the others in the Great Hall. It was a good-sized room, though not so lofty or spacious as that at Bixholm. Fewer people sat at the trestles and it was altogether a much more subdued affair than that over which Thurton presided. A small group of musicians in the gallery livened the evening with a selection of popular melodies.

She was a little surprised to find Richard in the seat of honour at the top table, but, because of that, it seemed natural for her to be placed upon his right. A priest intoned grace, after which the first courses were served. Roast mutton with a sharp mint sauce, pigeon pie, wheat and rye bread and cheese. It was all well cooked and tasty.

'Eat well, my dear.' Richard smiled at her. 'For it will help you to regain your strength.'

She nodded, accepting another slice of the pie. 'It is delicious,' she said. 'The kitchen is obviously very well ordered. But I still do not know to whom this castle belongs.'

'Ownership is a moot point,' he replied. 'It is my belief that it is mine. But there are others who dispute that.'

'Then where are they, these "others"?'

'In London, to the best of my knowledge.'

'Suppose they come here—will they not object to our presence?'

'I don't expect them,' he said with a confident shrug. 'Leet is seldom occupied; you've seen how neglected it is. The Captain of the Guard believes, as I do, that I am the rightful owner. He is loyal to me. I've instructed him what action to take in the event of any hostile approach.'

'You think there will be trouble?'

'It's just a precaution. Nothing for you to worry about.' Then, changing the subject, he said, 'It is delightful to see you here at table. Are you really feeling better?'

'Much better, thank you, and it is pleasant to be here.' She ate in silence for a short time, trying to quell her curiosity, but found it impossible.

'How was it that Leet was taken from you?' she asked.

'It's a not uncommon story. Both my parents died of the sweating sickness when I was but eight years old. My little sister died too. I was fortunate to be spared.'

'Oh, how sad!' Meg's heart was touched, her sympathy sincere and immediate. She could visualise all too vividly the grief of that great loss at such an early age.

'It was. I don't like to think back on it. But it's a long time ago. I was sent to live in the house of another nobleman, a friend of my father's. It had already been planned that I should be brought up there, as is customary.'

'What happened to Leet?'

'It fell to a roaming band of brigands who were rampaging around the country. They were lawless times. I was too young to defend my rights and the gentleman in whose house I lived had no spare men to send here. Had he done so, he might have lost his own estates. Those brigands were well armed. Mercenaries, under the command of some of the greatest landowners. Leet was easy prey to them.'

'As my mama was driven out of Bixholm,' she said.

'Aye. A similar dastardly act,' he agreed. 'I've

lodged my claim with lawyers in London, but you know what they say: possession is nine-tenths of the law. I have papers to prove my ownership, but without financial backing it isn't easy.'

'I know,' she said, mindful that her mother had had to accept the loss of Bixholm and that it would never be hers. 'Life has not treated you well.'

He shrugged. 'There are others who have fared worse. I've had to fend for myself from boyhood, but I've managed. My foster-parents were good to me.'

'Do they live near here?'

'Unfortunately they have both died, and their estates are in the North of England. They have sons who have taken over. As soon as I grew up I felt I must make my own living. I rode south and hired out my services to gentlemen and ladies who were in need of protection.'

'Was that how you came to be with my uncle?'

'That was one of the reasons,' he said. 'But enough about me. Let us just be grateful that we were close to Leet when you were so badly injured.'

Meg wished he did not always change the conversation, but felt she had quizzed him long enough that evening.

Dessert was served. Pastries, figs and wild strawberries and cream. She declined Richard's suggestion that they should dance. She did not feel quite fit enough for that, especially if he had the lavolta in mind.

As it was a warm evening they walked in the gardens for a short time. Richard placed an arm around her waist and she leaned her head upon his shoulder, as affectionately as any couple could wish—except that they were not officially so. The night was still; the birds had finished their frantic feeding and settled for the night. Only an owl hooted in the distance. Meg stood still, listening. Was it an owl? She heard it again and was satisfied. Then something else caught her attention. A man was standing beneath some trees. Something about him was familiar.

'Richard—someone is watching us,' she said.

'I do not care if the whole world is watching,' he said, and kissed her.

His attitude was so untroubled she felt foolish for being concerned about it, but, disturbed by the thought that they were being spied upon, she turned her head away from him.

'It will only be one of the servants,' he said. 'Where is he?'

'Over there—' She pointed. She could see nothing.

Richard walked to where she pointed. 'Nobody here,' he said.

She shivered, suddenly feeling cold.

Richard noticed. 'I'd better take you in,' he said.

He escorted her to her chamber, solicitous of her well-being. Sarah was waiting to assist her to prepare for bed. She was almost drifting off to sleep when that figure sprang into her mind again.

It had been Gervase Gisbon! She shook her head in disbelief. It must have been a trick of the light, a memory of that previous night in the garden in London. How foolish of her even to think of it! It was impossible— and yet she was unable to shake her mind free of the thought.

Fear, premonitions of disaster and her bruises, painful if she turned the wrong way in bed, had developed in Meg the habit of waking early. So it was that two days later, shortly after dawn, with sunlight streaming through the window, she slipped quietly out of bed. She had left the casement open and padded softly across the room, careful not to disturb Sarah, who was sleeping on the truckle bed at the foot of her big four-poster.

In the days she had been at Leet Castle she had come to love the view. Below was the formal garden which, though neglected, was a haven of wildlife. Birds were seeking tasty morsels for their young, flitting with filled beaks to nests in bushes and trees all around. Among the weeds she had been pleased to discover some of the herbs with which she was familiar, and she planned to find a lad to assist her to clear the ground around them.

Peace dominated the land. Meg stretched, yawned— then stood, transfixed, her attention caught by movements just beyond the perimeter of the castle. A group of horsemen were approaching fast. She was surprised to see that, even at this early hour, the drawbridge had been lowered. Standing close by was Gervase Gisbon.

A guard stepped forward as if he intended to challenge the visitors. She gasped as Gisbon swung a heavy cudgel and felled the man with a single mighty blow. He dropped to the ground, where he lay silent and stunned. There was no other opposition as the horsemen cantered into the castle forecourt.

With horror Meg recognised the leader of the company. It was Thurton! He reined in his horse and raised one triumphantly aggressive arm. She heard his words clearly.

'I am the rightful owner of Leet. Any man who challenges my right to be here will be severely dealt with.'

Gisbon called a man to hold Thurton's horse as he dismounted. 'Where is that usurper Richard de Heigham?' he shouted.

His presence and his words, aggressive and commanding, struck terror in Meg's soul. Dreams of safety and peace were shattered. Panic seized her.

'Sarah,' she hissed. 'Wake up.'

'What is it?' Sarah was alert almost immediately. In two seconds she was out of bed. She ran to Meg's side.

'God help us!' she prayed.

'He's come to take possession of the castle,' Meg said grimly. 'He'll go mad when he finds us here. What can we do?'

'For a start we'd best get dressed,' Sarah said, with her usual practicality. 'Quick as we can. Don't waste time changing your shift, my lady. I'll help you to put your kirtle on over it.'

It was sound advice. She had never dressed quicker.

Then Richard's voice rang out loud and clear. 'I am no usurper.'

Meg hurried to the window again, though she stood back from it, not wishing to be seen by those below. Boldly Richard was striding out of the castle. He had hurriedly pulled on his nether garments over his wide-sleeved nightshirt and had belted on his sword. 'Leet Castle is mine by right of birth. And so I shall prove one day.'

'If you live that long,' snarled Thurton.

'Do you want to make an issue of it?' demanded Richard. His hand was on his sword.

'You wouldn't stand a chance. Reinforcements are following me,' Thurton told him. 'But I have no desire to fight. In fact, if you co-operate, I may consider handing the place over to you. I want as little trouble as possible so that we may prepare for the impending visit of the King.'

Meg's fear deepened. Sarah gasped. They clung to

each other for comfort and strained their ears to the voices from below.

'I must, of course, feel honoured to expect a visit from His Majesty,' said Richard. 'But why should he deign to come here?'

'Not to see you, de Heigham,' sneered Thurton. 'The King wishes to renew his acquaintance with the lovely Lady Margaret. You know he has taken a great fancy to her.'

'Lady Margaret is not here,' declared Richard.

'Really? The good monk Father Bernard told us otherwise. He says that you kidnapped the lady and carried her off against her will from my house in London.'

'That is a lie,' Richard declared. 'You will not find the lady here.'

What foolishness was that? thought Meg. They would search and she would soon be discovered.

'Oh, my lady—what shall we do?'

At that moment the door of Meg's chamber was flung open. The Captain of the Guard stood on the threshold. He was clearly in a great hurry, and his eyes had a wild look, but he bowed politely.

Meg drew back in alarm. This was the man of whom Richard had spoken so trustingly.

'My apologies, my lady. You have seen what is happening below. Sir Richard is holding Thurton and his men at bay, but he cannot do so for long. You are to come with me, and I will lead you to safety through an underground passage. They must not find you here.'

Chapter Thirteen

Captain Bennington delivered the order so positively that Meg instinctively prepared to obey. She was eager to go and there was little time to think. The very idea of being caught again in the clutches of her uncle and Nancy made her flesh creep. Certainly it seemed sensible, and safer, both for her and for Richard, that she should get away from Leet. And yet—was it the right action to take? She hesitated.

The voice of Gervase Gisbon, shouting accusingly, floated up clearly through the open window.

'De Heigham is lying. It is as the holy friar said. He abducted the lady for his own evil desires. I have seen them often together. They are lovers!'

'You lie,' Richard yelled.

The Captain seized Meg's arm. 'For the love of God, my lady, come with me as quick as you can.'

'No.'

'You must get away. Did you not hear that the King is coming?'

'I did. And he will be told that I was abducted by Sir Richard. He is being falsely accused of conduct that could be deemed treason,' she said. 'Only I can refute that charge.'

'Sir Richard is well able to look after himself,' said the Captain. 'He will get out of this scrape, as he has escaped from many others. When I have led you to safety, I will return and assist him—'

Gervase was shouting again. 'That's Lady Margaret's chamber, my lord. The one with the open window.'

'Do let's get out of here,' pleaded Sarah. 'What good can it do to be caught by that brute?' She took hold of Meg's other arm and used her considerable strength to make Meg move. 'Believe me, my lady, it will be best for everyone. Which way, Captain?'

'Through the Great Hall. There's a secret door in the panelling beside the fireplace. It opens into a passage—'

Despite her objections, Meg found herself being hustled in that direction. She could no longer hear what was happening in the courtyard, but her imagination was running riot. Her uncle would be furious if she could not be found. Richard was already in his power. She could not leave him. She had to speak in his favour.

'You're hurting me,' she complained to her captors.

That was the last thing they wanted to do, so the Captain loosened his hold slightly, but not sufficiently for her to escape. They hustled her along passageways and into the Great Hall. The smell of last night's ale and food lingered. Two of the dogs barked, then, realising that they were not strangers, flopped back and closed their eyes. Meg was impelled over to the huge fireplace at the far end of the room. It was warm, with half a tree trunk smouldering among dusty grey ashes. With one hand tightly encircling Meg's wrist, Captain Bennington felt along the side of a carved oak panel.

He pressed one particular ridge and the panel began to move.

'Cor, I never knew that was there,' exclaimed Sarah.

Slowly the door swung open to reveal steps leading down into the darkness below. Both the Captain and Sarah relaxed slightly, their eyes fixed upon the opening, and in that moment, with fevered determination, Meg pulled herself away. She had the advantage of taking her friendly captors by surprise.

She leapt beyond their reach with a sudden return of strength. Picking up her skirts, she ran as if the devil himself was after her. She forced herself to ignore the pain that shot through her limbs. She dodged trestles and upturned benches, the uncleared residue of the previous evening's meal, driven by the need to assist Richard. Never had the Great Hall seemed so long.

Captain Bennington and Sarah were in pursuit of her. They were her friends, but she had to escape from them. She rushed out of a door and blessed the fact that it was half open. One of the dogs decided it was a game, and raced and leapt beside her as she ran across the wide foyer and through the outer door.

She emerged at the top of the wide steps that led to the courtyard. Faces looked up at her, startled, silent, so many of them! Richard, clean-shaven, bare-headed, that arrestingly rugged face which she knew and loved. Thurton, bearded, florid, with small eyes and an oversized bulbous nose. She hated him with a malevolence that almost frightened her. Gervase Gisbon, duplicitous, whose blond and handsome features, always icy-cold, struck fear into her heart. Other members of the Earl's company were gathered around him, awaiting orders. She recognised a few of those closest to him. The servants stood back as far as possible from the central group. Those who lived at the castle were plainly bewildered, unsure to whom they owed allegiance.

Richard was the first to move. He sprang forward, dashed headlong toward her, up the steps two at a time. 'What are you doing here? Go. Go! Get away while you can.' He glanced over Meg's shoulder and saw Captain Bennington.

'I gave you orders to take her—'

'It is not the Captain's fault, Richard,' Meg said. 'I heard those false accusations—I had to come and prove them untrue.'

'Never mind that! I can look after myself,' Richard hissed at her. 'Go—'

'I will not—'

She stepped past Richard. He tried to grasp her arm, but she moved aside. 'I will not be silenced,' she said. 'I want everyone to know that Sir Richard had no part in my leaving the Earl's house in London. I went of my own free will, accompanied only by my maid. It was Sir Richard who saved us both from those evil monks, Bernard and Marcus. As for the other charges—' she began but was interrupted.

'There is no need to discuss that at this moment,' said Thurton. 'We will sort that out later. For the moment my only wish is to be reunited with my dear niece.'

He moved heavily and clumsily up the steps. His mouth smiled, but his eyes were hard. She stepped back, her distrust of him as trenchant as ever.

'Give your uncle a kiss, wench, to show there are no ill feelings.'

His hands reached out and clasped hers, pulling her closer. With reluctance she deposited a peck on his bristly cheek.

'Now, let us go inside and take refreshment.' He clapped his hands, summoning the servants. 'Fetch the best food and wine you have in the house and send the butler and the cooks to me.'

Thurton used his authority positively. He dismissed Richard and Captain Bennington. 'No need for you to follow. I will deal with you both later. I wish to speak to my niece privately.'

She saw the flash of anger in Richard's eyes. He opened his mouth to protest. She shook her head in warning, for he could neither do nor say anything that would help.

'See to the quartering of my men,' the Earl thundered on. 'Have the best chambers thoroughly cleaned and prepared for the King, and for myself and Nancy.'

He was taking control of everything, including Meg. He held her arm in a grip that pinched as side by side they entered Leet.

'Richard de Heigham has designs on this estate. Scant hope he has of taking it from me. *"What is mine I hold."* That is my motto.' Inside the castle he stood still, looking around, half smiling. 'I haven't been here for years. It's a pretty property, is it not, Meg?'

She controlled her dislike of the man. For the moment she was powerless and she knew it. Her common-sense told her that a pretence of quiet acceptance was the least likely to inflame the situation. For the moment the Earl, undoubtedly for his own reasons, was holding out an olive branch to her. It was in her interest and, she hoped, Richard's also that she took it.

'I like it very well,' she said. 'I could happily live here.'

'Ah, but we have better things in store for you, my dear. You know that, don't you?'

She made no reply. They entered a side-chamber. The Earl flung himself down in a chair and indicated that Meg should be seated nearby. Undeterred by her silence, he carried on, using a creepily gentle voice. 'You have completely captured the King's heart, my dear. When he sent for you and we searched everywhere and you were not to be found, Nancy and I found it very difficult to find a reason for your absence.'

'I am sure you know why I left London.'

'I neither know nor understand, but that is beside the point. On this occasion I forgive you, but I shall not be so lenient if you cross me again. Do you understand?'

She nodded.

'Good. Then I will say no more about it. We are reunited; that is all I care about—at the moment!' His expression of repressed fury emphasised exactly what he meant by that. 'I shall not berate you for all the trouble you caused. I had to explain to His Majesty that you had expressed a wish to go into retreat, and therefore I had allowed you to come here to my Castle of Leet. You will remember that when the King arrives, won't you, dear niece?' His tone held an unmistakable threat.

Servants came in with laden trays, flagons of ale, wine, dishes of porage, fruit and steaming, freshly baked rolls. They hovered, ready to serve the Earl, but he waved them away.

'I'll see to myself. Go. All of you.'

Meg could feel the webs of deception gathering around. She was trapped again. She clenched her fists, but this was not the time for open defiance.

'You know what you must say to the King, don't you? You must explain that you were troubled in your mind. That you doubted you were worthy of the attention he was so graciously bestowing upon you and you felt you needed time for quiet reflection, for the regeneration of your soul.'

She listened with astonishment, but what could she do? Meekly she nodded.

'You will assure the King that you were not seeking to be separated from him, and welcome him wholeheartedly when he arrives. Have I made myself clear?'

'Perfectly.' It was only a whisper.

'That's a good wench.' Thurton smirked with satisfaction. 'You see, Nancy whispered to Henry that you were such a shy young lady you simply could not believe that such a great man as he could really fall in love with a girl such as you. It was an excellent ploy. It couldn't have worked out better, for His Majesty was most touched. Of course, Nancy was quick to point out that you are indisputably of royal descent and, even though you were brought up in a nunnery, it was in a very genteel manner.'

The Earl paused and chuckled. 'I have to say that Nancy spoke your case most eloquently, and, far from cooling the royal ardour, her words seemed only to increase the affection and esteem in which His Majesty holds you.'

'I am sure I do not deserve it,' murmured Meg.

'On that I agree with you,' Thurton said tartly. He took a long draught of ale, bit into a roll, and stuffed a slice of ham into his mouth with his fingers. A broad grin spread over his fat red face. 'But thankfully we do not always get what we deserve.' He spoke with his mouth full. 'You will have to reconcile yourself to that fact. You wouldn't believe the joy you brought to His Majesty when we told him that you were here, safe and sound, at Leet. He demanded to be brought to you immediately, so that he might personally declare his attachment to you.'

Meg hung her head, miserable and dispirited. She could think of no way out. She was sorry if she had indeed awakened in the King this devotion that was pleasing her uncle so mightily. She had no wish to hurt or harm him.

'That was a clever move of yours, my Meg. Your absence has certainly made the King's heart grow fonder,' the Earl crowed.

'That was not the reason I—'

'Do not say another word on the subject, my dear niece.'

'But, Uncle—'

'Not another word,' he thundered. 'Have something to eat.'

'I am not hungry, thank you.'

He shrugged.

'May I have permission to leave the room, Uncle?'

He ignored her and stuffed more food into his mouth. She stood up and moved quietly away. As soon as she was outside the room she hurried through the castle and out into the courtyard, seeking Richard.

She found him in the stables with the head groom. Together they were examining one of the Earl's horses, which appeared to have been lamed.

'Richard—'

He swung round at the sound of her voice. 'Meg!' His eyes studied her face. 'Are you all right? He didn't—?'

'My uncle spoke kindly to me,' she said. 'But you—?'

He smiled. His face relaxed. He turned to the groom and instructed him to carry on with the treatment. Then, taking Meg's arm, he led her away from the busy stable block.

'Shall we walk in the herb garden?' he suggested.

She turned her steps in that direction. They walked side by side, but without physical contact. She told him all that the Earl had said to her and how she was expected to act when Henry arrived. 'You were wise to pretend obedience,' Richard said. 'And you are safe because it is not in Thurton's interest for you to be harmed in any way.'

'But what can I do? Can we not escape together through that secret passage?'

'Perhaps. But the time is not yet right—'

'Ah, the young lovers!' a nasal voice purred.

Meg started. Gervase Gisbon had crept up behind them. How long had he been there? How much had he heard?

'A message from his lordship, de Heigham. He wishes you to attend on him immediately. I believe he fancies a day's hunting tomorrow.'

'Then I must bid you farewell for now,' said Richard, bowing to Meg.

'Ah, so sad,' breathed Gervase. 'Soon it will be farewell for ever, I trow.'

Meg did not wait to hear more. She walked smartly away from both of them. For the present it appeared that both she and Richard were safe, and would be so long as they were useful to the Earl. She quailed at the prospect of the King's arrival and the deceit she was expected to enter into. Again there seemed to be no way out—and even now Richard had shown no enthusiasm when she'd spoken about escaping together.

Nancy arrived the following day. With her came several packhorses and a cart loaded with a variety of domestic items: special bedding for the King and tapestries to beautify the rooms he would occupy, vast quantities of preserves and pickles, hams, jams, other meats and all manner of things beside.

'Is there anything left in the London house?' the Earl enquired. 'You seem to have brought just about everything with you.'

Meg, with Sarah at her side, watched and listened to this altercation with considerable amusement from her chamber overlooking the entrance to the castle.

Nancy stood with arms akimbo, plump hands on her non-existent waist. 'Have you any idea what it takes to run a household of this size? Let alone make the place fit for a king? You said this so-called castle hasn't been lived in, not properly, not by the gentry, probably not since Domesday! And I can see that's not a word of a lie,' Nancy snapped.

She was tired from the journey and felt she deserved a better welcome after all the trouble she had taken.

'All right. All right, Nancy, my love. I didn't mean anything by that remark.'

Nancy was a little mollified, but continued to regard him scathingly. 'You'd be the first to complain if I couldn't arrange to have the King decently housed and well fed! Now get out of my way and let me look about and see what needs to be done.'

'Is the King on his way?' the Earl asked.

'He is. But he's making a progress of it. Travelling with all the usual panoply of courtiers and hangers-on. He should be here in about two days' time.'

'There's time for me to go a-hunting, then.'

'Hunting!' Nancy's voice rose to a scream. 'That's right, Edmund! You go off and enjoy yourself! Never mind all the work and preparations that have to be seen to here.'

'Well, what can I do?' Thurton asked, with surprising humility.

'Oh, nothing at all,' Nancy said sarcastically. 'Except oversee the outside clearing and look to the stables. Make sure they're fit to receive the King's horses and his carriage. And wouldn't it be a good idea to send men out to meet him on the road and return with news, so that you can be sure to be here to greet His Majesty, and not out hunting when he arrives?'

'Proper fishwife, isn't she?' remarked Sarah. 'Strange, though, isn't it? I mean, have you noticed how women always have so many things that really have to be attended to, no matter who they are?'

'It's because women have to provide the food and men are always hungry,' Meg said philosophically.

'She's certainly intending to put on some good feasts,' Sarah remarked, licking her lips at the prospect.

'Nancy is a clever woman,' Meg said. 'And very wise to bring wholesome food from London. The kitchens here are not well stocked, and there are few pot-herbs in the gardens to flavour the dishes.'

Nancy wasted no time as she set to, stirring things up in the household, sending servants hither and thither to fetch sheep, pigs and geese for slaughter. Doves were culled from the dovehouse, fish caught in the stew ponds, sacks of fresh milled flour were carted in. She had others hurrying in and out, clearing away the rushes that had lain on the floors too long and replacing them with sweeter-smelling ones. Scrubbing and cleaning went on apace.

'Good thing it ain't our business to get involved,' said Sarah.

Meg smiled at her in complete agreement. She found it entertaining and droll to watch the unloading of the carts and the unpacking and carrying away of panniers from the packhorses—until the door of her chamber was thrown open.

Nancy stood on the threshold. Her eyes swept around the chamber. She glared at Meg, but kept her lips tightly compressed, making it clear that this was not a friendly visit. She was followed by half a dozen servants who were all silent, cringingly obedient. Among them they carried the entire collection of clothes which had been made for Meg.

'Put them down carefully,' Nancy instructed. 'Then get out.'

Her servants did as they were bidden. Sarah stayed.

'That goes for you too,' snapped Nancy.

Sarah shot a startled glance at Meg, who nodded. 'Do as Mistress Nancy says, Sarah.'

When the door was closed and they were alone, Nancy faced Meg. The fury in her eyes had intensified.

'The trouble you've caused! I'll never forgive you for this. Your behaviour is quite beyond belief. You have the world at your feet, riches far above any woman's wildest dreams, the opportunity to become Queen of England. All that on offer to you. You didn't have to lift a finger to help yourself! And you run away! I'd beat you black and blue if I had my way!'

Meg stood with her head held high and her hands neatly at her sides. 'I'm sure you would,' she said quietly.

'Have no doubt about it,' snapped Nancy. Meg's quiet attitude was fanning her anger. 'And I will. I'll do it myself, personally, if you ever try anything like that again. Edmund's too soft. I believe he's even told you he's forgiven you, fool that he is.'

'I didn't believe him,' Meg said coolly.

'Good. Then you understand. And I'll be watching you like a hawk from now on.'

Nancy moved closer to her. She was tall as well as broad, a powerful woman. Against her size and fury Meg felt frail and insignificant. She clenched her fists and faced up to her without wavering an inch.

'One more thing,' said Nancy. 'What's this about you and Richard becoming lovers?'

She grasped Meg by the shoulders, as if she would shake the truth out of her.

'That is also a lie,' Meg said.

Nancy narrowed her eyes until they were accusing slits in her puckered face. 'Are you a virgin?'

'Why should I answer that?'

'Because we must know. The King will demand no less. I can have the physician examine you if you will not answer me.'

Rather than face such humiliation, Meg said, 'There is no need for that. You have my word on it.'

Nancy stared at her a few moments longer, as if she was debating with herself whether to believe it or not. Then she said, 'You will accompany me to the chapel and swear on the Bible to the truth of that.'

Meg had no difficulty in complying, though she detested the bullying manner in which she was being treated.

When it was done, Nancy issued another order. 'Now you will return to your chamber and change out of that dreadful dress. It makes you look like a kitchen-maid. For this evening you may wear any of the gowns we have had made for you. When the King arrives I shall oversee your toilette.'

Having dismissed Meg, Nancy went in search of Thurton. He had returned to the room in which he had spoken to Meg and was sitting at ease, with a pot of ale on a small table at his elbow.

He started up guiltily when Nancy burst in upon him. 'Nancy, sweetheart, I've been on my feet all day and I've only just sat down. I've instructed the servants to air the bed for Henry, just as you suggested, and—' He broke off when he noticed the expression on her face. 'What have you been up to, my love? You look exceedingly pleased with yourself.'

Nancy smiled, sat down on the bench beside him and helped herself to a swig from his pot of ale.

'I've spent some time with our stupid little rebel and I believe all will be well.' She smirked, and drank more ale. 'Have you spoken to Richard?'

'I have, and he assures me he has kept his vow. I've also questioned Gisbon more closely. He observed them together, but admits that he never actually witnessed anything more than a few kisses between them.'

'Good,' purred Nancy. 'I'm sure that's true. And I've come to realise something else, my lord.'

'Something else? Don't play games with me, Nan. What is it?'

'Your sweet, innocent young niece, Lady Margaret, is in love.'

'In love? With whom? I'll soon put a stop to her nonsense—'

'Hush, my dear. We can use this to our advantage. You see—it is Richard upon whom she dotes.'

'Richard! How dare he—?'

'I don't think it is a matter of daring, Edmund. It has happened, as these things have a way of doing. But I believe it will serve us well.'

Thurton eyed her suspiciously. 'Don't talk in riddles, woman. Meg's supposed to fall in love with the King.'

'Don't be a complete fool, my sweet. How could any woman fall in love with Henry as he is now! Ten years ago it would have been quite different—not now! Don't make me laugh.'

'So?'

'I believe she is so smitten that she will do anything for Richard's sake.' Nancy paused meaningly.

'Even accept the King as her lover?' The Earl spoke thoughtfully.

Nancy nodded. 'If we play our cards carefully.'

'Is Richard in love with her? Seriously in love, I mean? He's very protective towards her, I know, and he's kept his vow because he believes that's the right and honourable thing to do.'

'Just as Meg has now sworn on the Bible that she remains a maid,' said Nancy.

'I don't see where this is getting us,' grumbled Thurton.

'Well, my sweet. Let us suppose that something happens that puts Richard in danger.' She paused. 'Perhaps under threat of some sort? For dallying with the King's sweetheart, shall we say?'

An evil grin widened the Earl's mouth. His small eyes almost vanished beneath his beetling brows. 'Treason. That's what that would be. He should be sent to the Tower—'

'Eventually, I agree. But first he must be imprisoned here, Edmund. Kept under lock and key in the dungeon,' Nancy said.

'In chains,' Thurton added maliciously.

'Exactly. You'll see to it immediately?'

'Well…' The Earl hesitated. 'There's no need for it to be done today, is there?'

'Why not today?'

'I need the man. He's so good at everything. I was planning to reconnoitre another route on which to take the King hunting.'

'Hunting! That's all you think about.'

'You know that's not true, Nan. I've got plenty of other things on my mind. At the moment I have to make sure Henry has plenty of sport when he's here. And it's not just the hunting. Richard's better than any man I know at organising the entertainment, the musicians, and putting on a bit of pageantry.'

Nancy was obliged to agree. Richard had his uses. 'Very well, Edmund. You shall have one more day's hunting before you have him locked away.'

'I'll advise Gisbon that I shall have work for him when we return.'

'An assignment he will not be averse to carrying out,' Nancy remarked with satisfaction.

Two evenings later it was Gervase Gisbon who called at Meg's chamber to escort her to the Great Hall for the evening meal.

Thurton was at the head of the tables, in the place that had previously been reserved for Richard. Meg was seated on the Earl's left. The musicians had accompanied Nancy from London, together with some of the entertainers. They ate and drank, the music was pleasing and the merriment produced howls of laughter. Nancy seemed to recover some of her sharp humour, and the Earl was at ease.

Meg wondered why Richard was not there. She hesitated to ask. His absence did not matter to her, she told herself, but she missed his comforting presence.

Chapter Fourteen

'The King is on his way.'

Meg heard the shout of the messenger but chose to ignore him. He came galloping into the castle courtyard and his foaming charger slithered to a halt. She slipped away, unnoticed amid the hustle and bustle that stirred all within the castle—except her.

She felt only dread at the prospect of this royal visit. Her attempt to escape had been thwarted—what hope was now left? She felt sick at the thought of the lies Nancy and her uncle had fed to the King. Saying she was so overcome at the great honour! And that her absence had made his heart grow fonder!

She felt more alone than ever before. Evidently Richard had totally abandoned her now. She had forced herself to accept the fact that he did not love her, and never would, but how she missed his reassuring company. There was no one else to whom she could talk so freely—except for Sarah, of course. But, wise and practical though her maid was, she knew nothing about the ways of the Court.

Meg wandered away, following a towpath beside the slow-flowing river. Richard had taught her so much.

They'd been together for some part of every day since she'd left the nunnery. She'd thought of a question to ask him, as an excuse for her search, and had wandered all over the castle. She'd looked in every place she could think of where there was even the remotest hope of finding him but it was as if he'd just disappeared. She was hurt and puzzled and increasingly anxious. Even though there was a rift between them, she couldn't believe he would have left without telling her, without a word of farewell.

She walked on until she was beyond earshot of the hustle and bustle from the castle. She hoped the peaceful prettiness of the river, flowing gently, stroking the weeds in its depths, would calm her. But she was far too disturbed. Again she would be expected to face up to the King's eager courtship. Deeply disturbed, she sat on a log and wrestled with the problem.

She would never agree to marry him—nor to become his mistress. Either situation would be anathema to her. She would have to speak privately to His Majesty, tell him gently and as soon as possible that although she admired and honoured him, she did not love him. And that she never could. She tried to imagine a situation where this might be possible but her mind simply went blank. How could she? What would his reaction be? He could take a terrible revenge—even have her imprisoned. Would she be strong enough to go bravely to the block, as it was said Anne Boleyn had?

'My lady—'

Sarah's breathless voice broke the silence. With skirts lifted to her knees she was running along the rough path, jumping over obstacles, an expression of concern on her face.

'My lady, you must come back. They say the King will be here in less than an hour.'

Meg gave a wan smile. 'I saw the messenger arrive. I've no wish to go back.'

'I know how you feel,' Sarah said. 'But I thought I'd better warn you.'

Meg nodded gratefully. 'I'm glad you did. Are they looking for me?'

'Not yet.' Sarah dropped down on the ground, her legs sprawled out, panting from her exertion. 'With all the fuss that's been goin' on since that Nancy got here, you'd have thought there'd be nothin' more to do. But they're all a-rushing about like hens in a barnyard when there's a fox about.'

Idly Meg watched the water gurgling past, swirling twigs and leaves away to the distant sea.

'Have you seen Sir Richard today?' she asked.

'No. I haven't. Would you like me to ask in the stables, to see if he's ridden off somewhere?'

'I've looked,' Meg said. 'His horse is there.'

'He might have taken another.'

'I don't think so.'

'Just gone. Like my Alan did,' said Sarah dolefully.

'You must miss him.' It wasn't a question. She knew how Sarah felt about Alan, and, despite everything, she felt the same about Richard.

'I haven't seen Captain Bennington either,' Meg said thoughtfully.

'No. Nor any of the men that favoured Sir Richard,' said Sarah. 'In fact it's been whispered to me that Sir Richard ordered them all to leave Leet the day after Thurton arrived, for their own safety. He feared fighting might break out among them.'

'Do you know where they went?'

'I don't. It's been kept secret.'

'Perhaps Richard went with them.' Even as she voiced the supposition, Meg doubted it. They sat for a few minutes, alone with their troubled thoughts.

It was Sarah who broke the silence. 'You ought to go back, my lady. It'll only make them madder if they can't find you.'

She was right, as always. Reluctantly Meg stood up and together they wandered back to the castle.

Nancy pounced upon her the moment she set foot inside the courtyard. 'Where on earth have you been? I've been searching the whole place for you. Get up to your room straight away. I've laid out the gown you're to wear to receive the King—'

'I will do as you say, Nancy, but I have to tell you I've made up my mind. I do not wish to marry the King.'

'I don't want to hear about your wishes. You will do as you're told.'

'I will not—'

'Not another word. Come with me. I'll make you change your mind.'

Meg hesitated. Nancy's mood was frightening. She grabbed hold of Meg's wrist and pulled her along. She was leading her towards a grille set in a wall of the gatehouse. She shouted for the guard.

'Open up.'

The guards were all Thurton's men. The Earl had arrived with a large advance party, and a great many more had followed him. They unlocked the heavy iron door and swung it open. Old, irregular stone steps led down. Nancy gave Meg a shove.

Meg braced herself. 'I'm not going in there,' she protested.

Nancy shrugged. 'You will,' she said. There was cold certainty in her voice.

'Lock me up, if that's what you want, but I'm not a criminal and I won't go in there—not willingly. Nor will I entertain the King,' she continued to protest.

'I'm not going to lock you up,' Nancy said. 'I'm inviting you to pay a visit to a friend of yours.'

Her guttural voice held a triumphant note. Meg turned sharply. The evil smile on the other woman's face awakened a dreadful presentiment.

'What—friend?'

'You don't need me to tell you, do you?' She paused meaningly. 'I've seen you looking around for him. You've been wondering where he is, haven't you? If you'd asked your uncle or me, we could have told you.'

'Richard!'

Nancy chuckled.

A gasp of fear made her turn around. Sarah had followed her mistress at a distance. She had heard and was echoing Meg's distress.

'Go.' Nancy pointed towards the castle. 'Your mistress will need your assistance to robe her; look to her gowns.'

Sarah bobbed the briefest of curtsies and cast a sympathetic look at Meg before obeying.

Meg's dread deepened. She stared in horror down the uneven, moss-covered steps. She knew they led to the dungeon, though she had never before looked inside. Her knees began to shake. It took all her self-control to force herself to move forward. One of the guards put a hand on her elbow; without his assistance she would have fallen. Step by step she went down.

At the bottom was the guardroom. It would have been in pitch-darkness but for a couple of blazing brands.

Two other guards were lounging on wooden benches; a dog lay at their feet. They stood up as the ladies entered.

'Bring out the prisoner,' Nancy ordered.

A mighty lock was turned with a huge iron key. The two men went out, carrying one of the torches. It revealed a low, narrow passageway, deep underground, built of stone. At the end was a heavy wooden door. The guards passed through and the light of the torch disappeared.

'Prisoner's chained to the wall,' said the remaining guard cheerfully. 'It'll take them a few minutes to unlock him. Will you take a seat?'

Neither of them answered. Meg remained standing in the centre of the room. Her eyes were fixed, her face drawn, waiting for the first sight of the man she loved so much. She shivered. It was cool, even though a fire blazed in a grate set in one of the walls. She could guess how cold it must be below. Nancy moved across the room, held her hands out to the blaze and even so pulled her shawl closer around herself. There was little warmth in the fine linen of Meg's summer morning gown. She was chilled inside and out, empty and cold. What did it matter that her flesh was goose-pimpled? She waited and agonised.

He stumbled as he walked, dragging his feet. The guards, one on either side of him, held tightly to his arms. He blinked as they pushed him into the room. A smell of dankness and mildew emanated from his clothing.

'Richard.' Meg started forward, reaching out her hands to him.

He stared at her. For an unbelievable moment she thought he didn't recognise her, then she realised his eyes were having to accustom themselves to the light.

'It's me—Meg.' She was pleading for a sign, a word, some reassurance, for he had a wild, almost savage look. His mouth moved as if his tongue was dry.

There was an impatient note in his voice when at last he answered, 'I know who you are, Lady Margaret.'

She thrilled to hear his voice, a little husky, but with that vibrant note that had first attracted her to him. She reached towards him, wanting to grasp his hands, to fling herself into his arms. Chains rattled as he held up his hands, for they were still manacled. So too were his ankles. He was warning her to keep away. No wonder he had walked with such difficulty. He was bare-headed, his dark hair matted, two days' growth of beard stubbled his face and his clothes were dirty.

Meg was shocked and emotionally disturbed. She could see no reason why Richard should be treated like this. Since he could not hold her, she opened her arms in invitation, regardless of the watching eyes of Nancy and the guards. For one magical moment she saw a flash of spirit in his dark gold-flecked eyes. Richard was still there, somewhere within the ill-treated body. She yearned to hold him close but he stepped back. He lifted his handsome head and stood looking at some point behind and above her.

She refused to accept his rejection, ignored the awfulness of the smell that had seeped into his grubby garments. She was overwhelmed by an immense tenderness towards him. What had they done to him that he should be in this state? He could only have been imprisoned for a couple of days. She reached up, wanting to pull his head down to hers. He resisted.

'Dear Richard—I am so sorry—I can't bear to see you like this—'

'Keep your pity—I don't need it.'

'So brave. Quite touching,' sneered Nancy.

'Ah, Mistress Nancy,' he said. 'I take it you've come here to gloat.'

'The situation is quite pleasing to me.' Nancy smiled.

Meg ignored that interplay of words. 'What can I do?' she whispered.

'Nothing. Leave me alone and look to yourself.' Richard had never spoken to her so harshly before.

She dropped her hands and took a step back from him. She was hurt by the tone of his voice, by the glowering anger in his eyes. She felt it was directed against her as much as against Nancy and the Earl. But for her he would not be in this predicament. It was her fault because she had rebelled against her uncle's will. She had refused to accept the King's attentions and had run away from her home and guardian. According to custom, and even to the law, she was at fault.

She faced Nancy. 'I am the one who has angered the Earl. Sir Richard had no part in my rebellious behaviour. So why is he imprisoned?'

Nancy looked so pleased with herself that Meg longed to strike her.

'I could say it's because he's a fraudster.' The woman sounded amused. 'Usurped his lordship's place. Set himself up as owner of Leet Castle when he knows full well it is not and never has been his.'

'Leet is mine,' Richard growled. 'I shall prove it one day.'

'If you live so long,' snapped Nancy.

His lips clamped together. He said nothing.

'I suppose you've heard the King is about to arrive?' Nancy continued to taunt him.

'You will appreciate that I've received very little news in the past day or two. You may present my com-

pliments to His Majesty.' He spoke coldly, unemotion-
ally, and his haughty, remote attitude was beginning to
needle Nancy.

'There are, of course, other reasons why this prisoner
is being held, as I am sure he knows,' Nancy said. 'Take
him below. We've seen enough.'

'No. No!' Meg cried in anguish. She tried to hold on
to him, but Richard pushed her away.

'Now I know it must be true love!' Nancy said. 'How
can you bear to touch him, let alone cling to him, stink-
ing as he is?'

'It's the rats,' he said. 'The dungeons have not been
used for years. I never incarcerated anyone down there,
no matter what their crime.'

'It is inhuman to hold anyone in such dreadful conditions!' Meg pleaded.

Nancy shrugged. 'Why should I care? His fate is in
your hands.'

'Pay no heed to her,' he said. 'Forget me, Meg. Look
to yourself.'

The guards took up their positions, on either side of
the prisoner. They wrenched him away from Meg's
clinging hands.

Richard attempted to bow but was restricted by the
guards and the chains. Nevertheless he moved with dignity, and without another word or look he was taken
back to the dungeon. Meg stared after him, into the
empty passageway, standing, too horrified to move until
Nancy jerked at her arm.

'Let's get out of this place. We've wasted too much
time already,' she said brusquely.

Meg obeyed, turned and stumbled up the steps. She
was in a state of shock. The good fresh air outside
helped to revive her. The sweetness of it and the warmth

of the sun on her face and hands increased the agony she felt for Richard, forced back to the dark stench of the dungeon. The iron grille clanged to behind them; the guard locked it.

'What did you mean when you said his fate is in my hands?'

'Don't pretend you don't understand! You're no fool. You know why you've been brought from the nunnery and treated like royalty.'

'Because you wish me to marry the King.'

'Exactly. It would be so easy for you, wouldn't it?' she said. 'So easy, Meg. So wonderful for you if you were to become Queen of England. Wouldn't you like that?'

Meg gazed at her mesmerised. Nancy was enjoying her power, watching the effect of her softly spoken words. The trap had been carefully laid.

'If you were Henry's much loved Queen, you'd be in a position to bestow other, much grander palaces upon your loving uncle. He would sign Leet over to Richard immediately. It's entirely in your hands, Meg. Behave properly, do as your uncle requests, encourage the attentions of the King and immediately conditions in the dungeons will be improved.'

'And Richard will be freed?'

'Of course. Come. The Earl is waiting. He will want to hear your promise of obedience for himself.'

Nancy grabbed Meg by the wrist, hurried her into the castle and along the passages to the room in which the Earl awaited them. He lounged at ease as they entered and did not trouble to rise.

'Ah! I take it you've taken her to visit the prisoner? She looks quite pale.'

'It was not a pretty sight.'

'Good. It wasn't intended to be.'

'You'll find your niece is in a much more receptive mood, Edmund.'

'Well, Meg. What do you say now? Are you prepared to give Henry a warm welcome, as befits the King of England?'

'I have always greeted the King with respect and will continue to do so,' said Meg.

'Don't prevaricate with me, wench! You know what he wants from you. You've awakened memories of his lusty youth, Meg, rejuvenated him—you should be pleased and proud. All I want is your promise that you will agree to anything and everything he wishes.'

Meg hesitated, but only briefly. Marriage to Henry was a terrible price to pay—but not for the release of Richard. She could not bear to think of him being held in those terrible conditions for a moment longer—perhaps kept there until he died.

The Earl watched her with shrewd eyes. He knew that at last he had her completely in his power. 'I take it Nancy has explained to you the ills that could befall de Heigham?'

'I will do as you say.' Meg spoke softly. 'But on one condition. You must immediately improve the conditions under which Richard is being held.'

'You're in no position to impose conditions, wench.'

'I think I am, for he looks so ill already that I fear if he is not better housed and fed he will die before any marriage settlements can be arranged.'

'What think you, Nancy? Is there any truth in this?'

'Not immediately. He's young and strong.'

'There are rats in the dungeon,' snapped Meg. 'It is known that they carry disease.' She paused significantly. 'If he died, I would kill myself.'

The Earl and Nancy exchanged glances.

'I'll order the dungeon to be cleaned,' said Thurton.

'I shall need to visit the prisoner every day,' Meg continued.

'No,' thundered the Earl. 'You go too far.'

'How otherwise will I know if he is still alive?' said Meg.

'I will allow no contact between you and the prisoner. Your time must be completely at the command of the King, at any hour of the day or night.'

'Let her maid visit the dungeon,' suggested Nancy.

'Very well.'

'I will accept that,' Meg agreed.

'Now, up to your chamber, get changed and stay there until I send for you,' said Nancy.

'I shall be watching you, Meg,' said the Earl. 'And you will smile. Do you hear me? Dance and sing and smile. If you fail to please His Majesty I will have nothing to lose by having de Heigham put to death. And I shall not care if you choose to follow him.'

Meg nodded her acceptance.

It was early afternoon when the King arrived with his entourage. He was riding high on a huge white charger. The brilliance of his riding cloak glittered in the sun, and his black befeathered hat slanted jauntily. It was a scene of splendour. He waved to his subjects, a brilliant figure in the midst of fifty courtiers, a hundred armed guards. A wealth of servants and a multitude of followers stretched back as far as the eye could see. Carriages followed close behind.

The King was outstanding in scarlet and gold, the colours of royalty, majestic and gay. Men, horses, dogs, clothing, harness, banners, hangings, all decorated, opulent—riches and dignity on view to the masses. On those occasions when, for whatever reason, he ventured out of the capital into the shires and provinces, it was essential that he should put on a show. The populace crowded to see him pass by. He was their monarch, he had fought battles for the country, he was the highest and the greatest in the land. To be seen at his most splendid confirmed his superiority and increased the adulation and the esteem which kept him safe on the throne.

Meg was dressed in a very becoming gown of rich blue velvet. It suited her admirably and was one in which she was comfortable, with a fitting bodice and a modestly cut square neckline. Long, loose sleeves were edged with silver lace, and the underskirt, made to be revealed in the front, was of similar costly material. Her short curls were concealed under the gable hood, with long wide ribbons falling down the back in place of her golden hair. A knotted sash emphasised the slenderness of her waist.

Sarah helped her to dress and Meg bitterly explained how Richard was being held in such awful conditions, and that it was no fault of his, but only of hers, because she didn't want to marry the King. Her tears flowed as she talked and Sarah kept a large towel at hand to mop them up, to prevent them staining the delicate velvet of her gown.

'Oh, what ruthless, cruel heathens they are!' Sarah exclaimed. 'How can they treat him so? I can't bear to think about it!'

'They won't allow me even to visit him, and I don't trust them an inch.'

'Wouldn't put anything past them two,' said Sarah.

'Kill their own grandmothers, they would, if they thought there was money in it.'

'I've been forced to act as they say, and it is in their interest to keep Sir Richard alive and in good health,' Meg said. She made no mention of her threat to take her own life should Richard die. That would cause Sarah too much distress and she hoped most sincerely that it would not be necessary. She simply added, 'They have refused to allow me even to see him, but they've agreed that you should go to him every day on my behalf.'

'You know I'll gladly do that, my lady. But what wicked, evil people they are. I'd like to wring their necks, both of 'em.'

'They've promised to keep him in better conditions, Sarah, for the dungeon is in a filthy state, and he says there are rats there too.'

'Ugh! Well, those guards'll have to clean the place up, or they'll hear about it from me. I'll put the fear of death in 'em. For if there's disease around, they'll go down with it too.'

'I do so fear some real disaster will befall him.'

'I'll see they don't do him no harm, my lady. And I can carry messages between you, as well as making sure he has some good food and suchlike. He's a fine, strong young man. I don't want to have to tell him that you're weepin' buckets for him—'

'Oh, no, Sarah. You mustn't do that,' protested Meg. 'And be careful what you say to him. I don't want him to know how much I care.'

Sarah gave her a wry smile. 'Then blow your nose, my lady, and I'll give your face another wash. I reckon they'll want you out of here before long, and you don't want them to know you've been crying either, do you?'

As usual her maid's sensible approach helped Meg to pull herself together. Pride would not permit her to reveal her weakness to anyone else—especially not to Nancy and the Earl.

Ten minutes later Nancy bustled into the chamber. With a great effort of will Meg had composed her mind and controlled her emotions and was able to receive the other woman with a semblance of cool serenity. She obeyed as she was told to turn this way and that whilst her appearance was inspected in detail.

Unable to find any fault, Nancy escorted her out into the courtyard. There Meg was lined up, with the Earl on one side of her and Nancy on the other, to watch the arrival of the King. When he reined in his magnificent white horse the Earl hurried forward to greet his illustrious guest. Henry had to be assisted to dismount, and moved stiffly. The ulcer on his leg was paining him.

'Let us walk forward to meet him,' said Nancy.

She placed Meg's hand in the crook of her arm and together they strolled in the direction of the King. His eyes turned upon her, eyes that were bright and somehow hopeful, and a mass of emotions surged through her. Nancy noticed his attention was caught and held by Meg.

'I wouldn't hesitate for a moment if he cast his eyes upon me as he does upon you,' she said, with more than a hint of jealousy.

'My uncle might not be so pleased about that,' said Meg.

'What a naive young woman you are,' Nancy replied. 'He'd hand me over without another thought.'

She was probably correct too. It also flashed into Meg's mind that it would be more pleasant to be mis-

tress to Henry than to the Earl. The pity was that undoubtedly the King was advancing upon Meg and no
one else.

'Smile,' hissed Nancy. 'Remember—the fate of Sir
Richard depends entirely upon you.'

As if she could, or would, ever forget! Meg lifted the
corners of her mouth. The smile did not quite reach her
eyes, for there was an empty feeling within her, but it
was difficult really to dislike someone who beamed
upon her with such open affection. The King moved
slowly, his gait cumbersome.

'My little Meg!' he exclaimed.

He opened his arms to her, and, knowing what she
had to do, aware it was a matter of life or death for
Richard and for herself, Meg ran forward. She slowed
before she reached him and, mindful of etiquette, lowered herself in a deep curtsey. She stayed in that position until she realised that he had moved closer to her
and was reaching out a plump hand, fingers glittering
with rings.

She placed hers lightly upon it and rose easily, stood
tall and looked up into Henry's face. Already it was
familiar to her: a big head, squarish in shape, the features slightly flattened. People said he had been extremely handsome as a young man, and signs of that
remained, despite his heaviness. She stayed very still,
fearful of hurting him in some way, for despite his huge
bulk she believed him to be in considerable pain. He
drew her towards him and gently she placed herself
within the grasp of those wide-stretched arms.

She looked up into his bearded face and he bent down
and kissed her on the lips. It was not a long kiss, not a
lingering kiss, but there was tenderness in it; it had been

almost fatherly. She drew back a little and was able to smile at him with genuine warmth.

'How pleasant it is to renew our acquaintance, sweetheart,' he said.

'It is my pleasure entirely, Your Majesty,' Meg replied.

'They said that you were a little overcome by my presence. If that is so, I assure you there is no need for it.'

'I was—indeed I am still—conscious of my own unworthiness.'

'I will be judge of that,' Henry declared. 'To me you are one of the most worthy and beautiful of women.'

'You are too kind, sire.'

'I look forward to renewing our acquaintance, sweet lady. But now I have affairs of state to see to. Even when I leave London behind me, they follow with papers for me to sign.'

He continued his progress towards the castle, surrounded by ministers and courtiers. Thurton was among them, showing the way.

Meg stayed behind and watched and shook with fear. She could see no escape from the fate that had been so carefully and hideously planned for her.

Chapter Fifteen

'Which gown will you wear this evening, my lady?' asked Sarah.

Meg sighed. In truth she neither knew nor cared, but of course she had to make a decision.

'You looked lovely in this orange-tawny, with them b'utiful creamy sleeves all slashed-like.' Sarah held up the gown and swayed it about, showing it off.

'Whatever you think,' Meg agreed easily. It was a modestly cut garment and she'd liked it and felt comfortable when they'd fitted it on her.

She'd attended to her toilette, and was about to step into the delicately embroidered underskirt when Nancy rushed into the chamber. She took one look at the gown and snapped an order to Sarah.

'Put that away. Tonight we wish to impress his Majesty. Your mistress is to wear the cloth of gold.'

'No!' exclaimed Meg.

'Yes,' contradicted Nancy. 'The most exciting and the most expensive item in the collection.'

Meg loathed it. The gown which had caused her such embarrassment on that dreadful day when the Earl and Richard had come to watch. Even Mrs Goodley had felt it was immodestly low-cut and had feared it might fall off her shoulders.

Sarah hesitated; she knew how her mistress felt about it.

'Don't stand there gawping, wench. Bring it out and be quick about it.' Nancy's voice rose impatiently.

Obediently, but with her lips pursed in disapproval, Sarah spread the brilliant golden gown on the bed for Nancy's inspection. Nothing had been spared in the making of it. Its expensiveness was evident in the yards of brilliant cloth. Intricate embroidery and tiny pearls decorated and drew attention to the bodice, cut so very immodestly wide and low.

'That's it!' Nancy rhapsodised. 'Your uncle thought you looked absolutely luscious in it. I imagine the King will be of the same opinion, for men do not vary so very much when they look at a woman.' She placed a jewellery box on the chest. 'Here are the necklace and rings you are to wear also. There must be no doubt of the financial standing of your uncle.'

She turned, about to leave, then paused in the doorway to look back and add maliciously, 'I recollect Richard also showed appreciation. What a pity he will not be there to see you tonight.' With that, she flounced out of the chamber.

'What will you do, my lady?' asked Sarah.

'Wear it. I have no option.'

It had become customary, since Richard's imprisonment, for Gervase Gisbon to escort Meg to the Great Hall. She tried to remain calm whilst she waited for him and she was determined to hide her discomfort.

She and Sarah had tried to lift the neckline so that her tightly encased bosom showed less rounded flesh, but it had been in vain. Nor could they alter the line of the shoulders for, as Mistress Goodley had warned, the heavy material of the wide sleeves threatened to drag the garment down much too low. Meg practised standing exceedingly straight and with her arms held slightly outwards to prevent this catastrophe.

The back was cut considerably lower than the front, in a deep vee. This revealed more bare flesh, though Sarah had provided partial cover with additional ribbons to flow from Meg's headdress. The dress was stitched and boned so firmly that it was impossible for them to make any alteration. She felt that the magnificent necklace of diamonds and other precious jewels focused even more deliberately on bare flesh revealed by the gown.

Meg felt constricted and ill at ease. 'Heaven help me,' she moaned. 'I look like a courtesan of the very lowest kind.'

'No, that you do not, my lady,' Sarah replied staunchly. 'What is more, you never could, no matter what they did to you. Your face is too gentle and honest.'

Meg was grateful for the loving response, though she doubted it was true.

A sharp rap on the door announced that Gervase was waiting for her. His eyes, usually narrow and calculating, opened wide at the sight of her. A mocking grin spread over his repugnantly handsome face as he bowed ridiculously low.

'You leave precious little to the imagination this evening, my lady. It is just as well that our revered King is a much married man.'

She could not repress a shudder. His words had been deliberately chosen to evoke all that was base about the

King, reawakening fears that she had no wish to dwell upon.

'It was not my choice,' she said defensively.

'I'm sure it wasn't,' Gervase agreed amiably. 'Its lack of subtlety has the stamp of Nancy and Thurton all over it. What a pity Richard will not be here this evening. But I shall have pleasure in relating this evening's entertainment to him tomorrow.'

'He has already seen this gown,' she said. Then immediately wished she had not spoken.

'All the better. His imagination will run riot. Come, Lady Margaret, let us parade.'

The place of honour where Richard had sat when she first arrived, and which all too soon had been taken over by Thurton, was now prepared to receive the King. A great canopy dominated the end of the hall, erected to add to the exaltation of His Majesty. Additional tables had been set up and draped with white damask cloths to accommodate the most important members of his entourage: the courtiers and their ladies, his ministers and the nobility from far and wide. Lesser beings, Thurton's servants and guards, were relegated to the back rooms, out of sight of the main guests. There, doubtless, Sarah would eat her meal. No conspiratorial winks could be exchanged between maid and mistress on this occasion.

Thurton and Nancy were waiting inside the Hall. Her uncle looked her over with a delighted expression on his florid face. With pride and triumph he puffed out his chest and squared his shoulders; he seemed to grow in stature as Gervase handed her over. She placed her hand on the crook of Thurton's arm and he patted it with a proprietary air.

'My, but you're a beauty, Meg!' he said. 'No one in

this room comes near you for looks and class. That gown does wonders for you, adds that touch of worldliness you were lacking before.'

More with self-importance than affection he strutted with her to their places at the top table. Gervase followed with Nancy on his arm. Meg had been aware of the leering expressions with which the gentlemen had surveyed her on her arrival at Bixholm. Now their thoughts were even more open, so that she was actually thankful for the protection afforded by her uncle. The effect of that gown was frightening.

Soon after they were seated the trumpeters sounded a fanfare. Everyone rose as the King entered and bowed or curtsied. He progressed slowly to the top table, accompanied by the nobles who were his personal attendants. He sat down heavily as soon as he reached his chair. Meg's natural sympathy was awakened, for undoubtedly his legs were causing him pain.

'Greetings, good friends,' he said. 'Pray, be seated.'

Meg was on His Majesty's left. He turned to her immediately. She was grateful that his eyes did not rove over the gown. Indeed he did not at first seem to notice what she was wearing. He was gazing into her eyes and smiling.

'It is such a pleasure to see your sweet face again, Meg. Did you think of me, my dear, when we were parted?'

'I have thought of you every day,' Meg replied. That was true, though she did not elaborate on the line her thoughts had taken.

'Kindly, I hope?' he enquired.

'How could it be otherwise, sire?' she replied. Again it was not untrue, for he had not been in any way unkind in his dealings with her. It was not in her nature to speak

ill of anyone unless she knew for certain that they deserved censure.

'I missed you when you left so suddenly.' Henry
leaned towards her and whispered the words.

Her instinct was to draw back, for his beard almost
tickled her cheek. Only self-control and instilled good
manners prevented her making the movement. 'I must
apologise, Your Majesty. I had no intention of causing
you any distress. Indeed I did not expect my departure
to be of any importance to you.'

'Ah, there you are wrong. I have hopes that we may
come to know each other a great deal better, little Meg.'

Involuntarily a shudder ran over her. The King noticed. He reached out one hand and lightly touched her
arm, and for the first time his eyes moved from her face,
roving lower.

'It is a wonderful gown,' he said solemnly. 'You look
even more beautiful than before.'

'Thank you, sire.' Her voice was low. His reaction
was exactly as Thurton and Nancy had anticipated. She
trembled. He moved his hand from her arm and caressed
her cheek.

'You are cold, sweetheart,' he said.

It was true, though it was not the only reason she
shivered. Two huge fireplaces blazed with log fires, but
they were placed at each end of the room, far from
where she sat. No other lady in that assembly was ex-
posing so much nakedness.

'I am s-sorry, Your Majesty.'

Henry clapped his hands. One of the pages who stood
behind the royal chair answered immediately. 'Yes,
sire?'

'Send for Lady Margaret's maid. Tell her to bring a
wrap for her mistress. Immediately!'

'Thank you, Your Majesty.' Meg breathed her gratitude.

'I can't have you catching a chill. I hope to enjoy your company whilst we are together.'

Within minutes Sarah appeared. She was not permitted to approach the royal presence, but the wrap was passed from hand to hand, coming finally to Henry himself. He placed it around Meg's shivering shoulders and gave them a little friendly squeeze. She was overcome with gratitude and could think no ill of him after that.

The feast was elaborate, necessitating a constant procession of men and boys who carried in steaming dishes from the kitchens. The King's own food-tasters tested each item against the fear of poison. Four courses were served, each offering to the diners ten or more choices. In pride of place was the head of a boar, with tusks in place, decorated and served with a batter pudding and gravy. In addition there were cygnets, capons and pheasants, sturgeon, baked custard with dried fruits in a pastry case and other dishes too.

The King was served first, then Meg chose sturgeon with vegetables and sauces. Whilst she waited to be served Henry speared a bite-size portion of roast boar on the point of his knife and offered it to her.

'This meat is sweet and tender, Meg. You need more than fish to keep fit and healthy. Try it, my sweet, and see if it isn't as good as any you've ever tasted.'

She could not refuse. She took a deep breath and allowed him to place the meat into her mouth. He watched, smiling his approval as she chewed and swallowed.

'It is indeed excellent, sire, and you are very kind. But please look after yourself. I believe my dish is being brought to me now.'

Throughout the meal he continued to supervise her food, as if he feared she might not be properly served. More than once he insisted on sharing small portions from his own platter with her. Sometimes he passed them to her with his fat greasy fingers. Meg wished with all her heart that it wasn't so, especially as his actions revealed so openly that he had developed a strong affection for her.

All the time at the back of her mind was the harrowing recollection of Richard, held in that abominable dungeon. For his sake she had to pretend an affection for the King, and she was excruciatingly conscious that it did not spring from her heart. It was entirely against her nature to deceive.

When the company had eaten all they wished for from those dishes the residue was cleared away completely and the second course was borne in. Venison cooked in a stew of corn, stuffed suckling pig, peacocks, the white meat of rabbits, bitterns and chickens cooked with saffron and egg yolks. Among items in the third course were curlews, perch and pigeons; quails, snipes, larks and other small birds. Plovers' eggs in aspic. There were more sweetmeats, marzipan and fancy cakes, quince pie, white curd with almonds.

Finally came the soltette. This was the most amazing concoction Meg had ever seen; she found it hard to believe it was edible, made of pastry and sugar. It was shaped like a castle, with turrets and battlements, and brightly coloured flags flew on and around it. To flatter the King his coat of arms had been delicately contrived on the castle roof. Four men from the kitchen staff held it aloft and carried it around the Great Hall, receiving loud applause and exclamations of admiration. On a side-table it was cut into pieces and served by pages on individual dishes. Henry was served first, and at once he picked the most luscious wild strawberry from his portion and insisted upon popping it into Meg's mouth.

Wine had flowed freely throughout the feast, and continued to be served after the tables had been cleared. The musicians had played throughout, and voices rose as at last everyone had eaten their fill, and more. The entertainment began. The King's mood became more and more mellow. He had eaten and drunk well, and he laughed heartily at the antics of the jester and the travelling players. A space was cleared for dancing and some of the company began to step it lightly: pavanes, galliards and the more adventurously performed lavolta.

'Will you not dance, Meg? Where is that young fellow you danced with when we first met? What's his name?'

'Sir Richard de Heigham.' To mention his name was both a pleasure and a sadness. If only he were here! Would she ever dance with him again?

The King turned to Thurton. 'Where's de Heigham? Lady Margaret would like to dance.'

'My apologies, sire, I've had to send him back to my main house at Bixholm. Urgent duties, you'll understand. If you wish my niece to dance for you, Your Majesty, I'm sure another of the gentlemen will be only too happy to oblige.'

Henry turned to Meg. 'Do you wish to dance, my dear?' he asked. 'You may take your pick of the gentlemen to partner you.'

It was not a prospect that held even the slightest appeal to Meg. She made her excuses hastily. 'Thank you, sire, but I have never practised with any other partner and I would not wish to displease you by making a wrong step.'

'Nothing you did could possibly displease me,' the King said. 'But I defer to your wish. If you are content, then let us watch together.'

He lounged back in his big comfortable chair, took hold of her hand and held it lightly. He closed his eyes and Meg sat very, very still. She glanced at him quite often, and was not sure whether he was awake or asleep.

After some minutes he opened his eyes and yawned. 'I am a trifle tired. If you will excuse me, sweet maid, I shall seek my bed.'

The departure of the King awoke a flurry of movement, not always steady. Some of the company had celebrated so well they had difficulty in standing, and wobbled in performing the requisite bow or curtsey as the trumpeters accompanied the royal progression. When the doors closed behind him most of the company resumed their seats and the music, dancing, fun, laughter and ribaldry continued as before. More wine was brought in, and it seemed as if the revelry would go on unabated into the small hours of the morning.

Meg had no wish to stay on, but was uncertain what her uncle's reaction would be if she asked permission to leave. She was pleased, therefore, when her uncle and Nancy approached her.

'You did well, Meg,' Thurton said. 'The King could scarcely take his eyes off you.'

'You shouldn't have put that terrible wrap over your gown,' Nancy complained. 'Spoiled the whole effect.'

'It was His Majesty's suggestion,' Meg defended herself. 'He noticed I was cold.'

'It was a loving gesture,' Thurton said smugly. 'He saw enough to whet his ardour. You go along with Nancy, now; she'll help you get ready for bed.'

'Sarah will help me. There's no need for you—' Meg began.

Nancy took hold of her arm. 'Don't stand there wasting time.'

She hurried her out of the Great Hall and turned in the direction of Meg's chamber. Sarah, always watchful for her mistress, saw them leave and quickly followed.

Inside the room Meg saw, with a sense of surprise and shock, that a flimsy nightgown of a clinging silken material had been laid out on the bed. It was decorated with lace and delicate cutwork, very beautiful—and very revealing. Meg had never yet worn it. She had assumed it was intended as part of a trousseau, for her marriage night. A fearful suspicion leapt into her mind.

'Quick, wench,' Nancy snapped at Sarah. 'Help your mistress out of that gown—and take care, for it cost more than I wish to think about.'

'What—what am I to do?' Meg breathed hoarsely.

'Get changed, of course. And be quick about it. I've told Thurton to stay outside until you're in your nightgown, but he's not the most patient of men. If you keep him waiting too long he'll probably come in anyway.'

Sarah worked as quickly as she could, her fingers less nimble than usual. She was unnerved by Nancy's unfriendly eyes upon her and the horror of why she was having to assist her lady out of the immodest golden gown and into this even more improper garment.

Meg's mind was in turmoil. She was being prepared as if for a wedding night, but no contract had been made, no ceremony performed. Her mouth was dry. She shivered, and this time it was most definitely not because of the temperature.

Even Nancy noticed. 'Put a light woollen shawl around your mistress,' she ordered.

Sarah obeyed. Nancy opened the door and called the Earl in. Meg fell to her knees at his feet.

'I beg you, Uncle—do not make me—'

He was unmoved by her supplication. 'Get up, wench,' he growled. 'It's time you grew up. You know what you have to do.'

'Please, Uncle. I cannot. Truly I cannot—'

'You can and you will. What could be more simple? Just be pleasing to His Majesty; that is all I ask.'

'I beg you, Uncle—not like this—'

'You know what will happen if you continue to cross me in this matter.' He paused significantly. 'They tell me a traitor's death is ugly and painful.'

Again, dramatically, he paused. His words seared Meg's brain. Either the block or—worse—hung, drawn and quartered. She could not allow Richard to be tortured and mutilated! Her own sacrifice would be small by comparison.

'Get up,' her uncle commanded.

She obeyed and stood before him with her head bent. She was defeated. Further protest would be useless.

'That's better,' Thurton commended her. 'You're not the shrinking violet you'd like me to believe. You're a Thurton, as I am, and we are made of tough material.'

Perhaps he was right. Perhaps they were two of a kind. If she had to do—this—this thing—then so be it.

Thurton continued, 'The time is right. Henry is entranced by you. He's dined well, drunk his fill. He'll fall into your arms, if you play your cards right. Now, no more of this squeamish nonsense. You don't need me to repeat what will happen if you disobey. Come.'

They made one concession. Her feet were thrust into sheepskin slippers, for they had to walk along the cold stone corridor to reach the apartments which had been given over to the King. Meg could scarcely make her legs move, she was in such abject misery. Yet she did as she was told. She knew it was no empty threat Thurton had issued; he meant what he said. Richard was already his prisoner. Thurton would trump up some charge of treason, and Henry would order him to be beheaded. If that could not be managed Gervase Gisbon would like nothing better than to thrust a knife deep into his back. Thurton did not give a jot what happened to her—and at that moment nor did she.

One of the King's attendants opened the door when Thurton knocked. There followed a murmured conversation which Meg could not hear.

'Very well. You assure me she carries no knife or other weapon to cause harm to His Majesty?'

'Nothing. See for yourself.' Thurton whipped the shawl off Meg's shoulders; Nancy pulled the woollen slippers from her feet. She was so barely covered the attendant was satisfied. He held the door open.

Thurton gave Meg a shove between her shoulder blades, precipitating her forward. The door was closed behind her. She was in a comfortably furnished parlour. There was no bed, no sign of the King. For a moment her heart lifted.

'This way, mistress,' said the attendant. He led her through to another room, smaller, more personal. There was still no sign of the King.

'His Majesty is already in bed,' said the attendant. 'I will see if he is awake. Wait here. What name is it?'

'Meg,' she answered. 'Just Meg.'

She prayed that the King would be asleep and that the attendant would not wish to waken him. That hope was short-lived. He returned quite quickly.

'You may enter.'

She moved slowly, silent on her bare feet, through the communicating door and into the bed-chamber. The flame of a single candle made a circle of light; all else was lost in shadow. One of the King's attendants was seated beside a big four-poster which dominated the room. She saw an immense hump under the pile of bed-clothes. It moved. Henry's face, topped by a scarlet nightcap with a golden tassel, rose from a pile of pillows.

'Meg?' he asked.

'Yes, Your Majesty.' Her voice was low, but he heard her. She fell to her knees.

Henry spoke to his attendant. 'Leave us.'

The young man stood up. He bowed and left the room with a soundless, gliding movement, as if he was some sort of spectre, adding to her impression that it was all a dream.

'Are you still there, Meg?' the King asked.

There was no doubting the reality, then. He was peering towards her, as if he doubted her existence.

'I can't see you. Give me your hand, my dear.'

She moved towards the bed, still on her knees, and reached up one hand. His soft, plump fingers closed over it.

'Sweetheart,' he said. 'You're still cold. Come into my bed. Let me warm you.'

Chapter Sixteen

There was no escape. The King threw back the bed-
clothes, reached out and fumbled about until he caught
hold of both her hands. Gently he drew her up, towards
him, into his bed and into his arms.

'How lovely you are! My lovely, lovely Meg. How
sweet you smell, so soft and beautiful. But so cold—let
me warm you.'

He cuddled her shivering body against the heat of his
massive bulk. She felt a strange comfort in the home-
liness of his flannelette nightshirt. Solicitously he
tucked the down-filled quilt around her. Then, to her
surprise, he sank back into the deep softness of the
feather bed with a great sigh. She was enclosed tightly
within his embrace, cocooned with him. She listened to
his heavy breathing, felt the rhythmic rise and fall of
his chest and forced herself to stay very still, though
her pulse-rate had quickened. He seemed to be in no
hurry to make any further move.

'There, my dear,' he murmured. 'My new little
sweetheart—it makes me feel young again to hold you
in my arms.'

'But, sire, you are not old. You are in the prime of your life,' she murmured.

'Would that it were so,' he sighed.

His hands moved up and down her back, stroking her through the silken gown, from her buttocks to her neck. He nuzzled his fingers into her hair. Her flesh cringed beneath the gossamer gown. Perhaps if she stayed very still he would fall asleep and she could slip away unnoticed—but the thought was banished even as it came into her mind.

'Lovely. So lovely,' he murmured.

His eyes opened, he gazed at her and his expression was kindly. Could this really be the man who had ordered the deaths of so many people, including that of his own wife? He seemed so ordinary, no different from any other man, and yet he was the one wielding immense power. Richard's face flew into her mind—how different it had been when she had lain in his arms. Powerfully in memory came a vision of him, his touch, his whispered words, the warm muskiness of his body. Tears filled her eyes with longing for what had been and could never be again.

Henry's voice interrupted her racing thoughts. 'Kiss me, sweetheart,' he said, not as an order, but with gentleness. He ran his fingers over her face as he repeated, 'Kiss me.'

She raised herself up, leaned over, took his head between her hands, felt the bristle of his moustache and beard. She sensed rather than saw that there was a smile on his face as she lowered her head, found his lips and brushed hers against them. He responded instantly, his mouth seeming to chew at hers. No response stirred in her, nor indeed did she notice any hot-blooded arousal from Henry. He had an air of lazy pleasure rather than passion.

'Do you love me, Meg?' he asked.

She prevaricated in her answer. 'Am I not kissing you, sire?'

'You are, and it is delicious. I have not been kissed so since my dear Jane died.'

'That was so sad,' she said. 'The whole country wept for you, even though they celebrated the birth of your son and heir, Prince Edward.'

'Aye. A son. I have a son at last!'

'It is no more than you deserve, Your Majesty,' Meg said, ever mindful that she must speak sweetly to the King. Richard's life depended upon it. 'England is fortunate to have such a good King. I believe the little Prince is a fine strong boy and I pray that he may always be worthy of his illustrious father.'

'But it's not enough to secure the succession. I should have more. There have been times when I have thought myself accursed,' said Henry. 'I have put my wives with child so often, and yet I have only one living son.'

'You have two bonny daughters, the little princesses Mary and Elizabeth,' Meg pointed out.

'Girls! A man should have sons to succeed him. I must marry again.'

'I understand your ambassadors have been seeking a bride for you from the courts of Europe,' Meg said softly.

'Aye, but they have found no one to my liking.' He kissed her again. 'I think I should take an English-woman to wife, Meg. What say you to that?'

'It is entirely your decision, Your Majesty.'

The conversation was disturbing, as was his gentle lovemaking. Yet words were staving off the moment she dreaded. For though he showed no urgency she assumed the time would come when he would require more than kisses. Her uncle's words flashed into her mind *'If he gets you with child—he'll marry you immediately.'*

'I understand that you have royal ancestors. Is that so?' he asked.

'On my mother's side,' Meg said. Playing for time, she decided to launch into an explanation. 'Before she married she was Lady Elizabeth Alpington. She was descended from King Edward, but to be truthful I'm never quite sure whether it was from Edward IV or Edward III. Whichever it was, she was his great-great-granddaughter.' She paused thoughtfully. 'Or maybe she was his great-great-great-granddaughter.'

'If your mother was descended from Edward IV, she must also have been descended from Edward III,' said Henry. She detected a dry note in his voice. The candlelight was too dim to read anything from his face. Did he realise she was talking for the sake of it?

'Well, fancy that!' she said. 'How foolish of me. I really should have taken more notice when my dear mother explained the connection. Please accept my apologies, Your Majesty. I mean no disrespect, but you will understand that in those days when I was in the nunnery in Norwich I never expected to come to London, and certainly never dreamed that I would ever meet any members of the royal family.'

'It is of no great moment,' said Henry. 'Kiss me again, sweetheart.'

She complied with his request and permitted her mouth to be locked to his for a minute or two. Then, lifting her head as if suddenly struck with a thought, she continued, 'One thing I do remember was that the

King and his Queen were said to have had a great many sons and also five daughters, one of whom was my ancestress.'

Henry chuckled. 'Both Edward III and Edward IV had five daughters.' His laughter was infectious.

'Really? Isn't that quite amazing, sire?' She laughed with him, for it seemed to her an amusing coincidence!

He spent more time kissing her.

When she could escape she said, as if casually, 'So you see, the connection is rather remote. I could be descended from any one of those ten ladies and I have absolutely no idea which.'

'I shall instruct my archivist to look it up,' Henry said solemnly.

'I believe John of Gaunt came into it somewhere,' Meg said.

'I'm sure he did!' exclaimed Henry, with another burst of laughter. 'The descent of my own family from his is complicated enough.'

'Really?' Meg said again with genuine surprise.

'Yes, really!' the King mimicked her.

Then they both laughed quite merrily, until Henry pulled her head back to his and kissed her.

'John of Gaunt was married three times, as I have been, but his wives were more fruitful than mine; they gave him eight children.' He had become more serious. He lay back, looking up at her. She wished she could read his thoughts.

He caressed her and kissed her. His hands pulled the flimsy silken nightgown from her shoulders. When he started to fondle her breasts she drew in a sharp breath. It took all her will-power to stay still and endure the intimate touch of his large fat hands on those sensitive and tender parts of her body.

She wanted to scream and run from the room, but steeled herself to bear it. She could not, must not allow modesty to rule her. Richard's life as well as her own depended on her acquiescing to the lusts of the King. She racked her brain to find words that might distract his interest, but could think of nothing.

Suddenly he groaned, a long drawn-out, piercing sound.

'Your Majesty—are you all right?' Meg asked anxiously.

'No. It's these accursed legs of mine.'

'Let me look at them,' she said.

'They are not a pretty sight,' he said with unexpected humility.

'I have a little experience of nursing. With your permission, sire, I believe I could make you more comfortable.'

He groaned again. 'Anything. Anything—the pain is tormenting me.'

Without waiting for further consent she carefully lifted the bedclothes. His short, fat legs stuck out from beneath the long nightshirt. They were wrapped around in bandages, through which blood was seeping. If she had come to him from the nunnery she would have brought clean dressings, herbal ointments to apply to the wounds and physic to alleviate the pain.

He moaned again; his face was contorted. She pulled the bell-rope for the attendant.

'His Majesty needs fresh dressings on his legs,' she told the young nobleman who came into the room. 'Bring warm water, clean bandages, comfrey ointment, an infusion of lovage—and more candles so that I can see to work, and sprigs of lavender to freshen the air.'

'Shall I call His Majesty's physician?' asked the attendant. He scarcely glanced at the King; his eyes were fixed on Meg, whose luscious figure was but half concealed by the silken nightgown.

'No,' growled the King. 'I can't bear to have his rough hands on me. Lady Meg will attend to me.'

'Don't stand there!' Meg snapped at the impudent young man. 'Get those things and bring them here immediately.'

Even before the door had closed behind him Meg was unwrapping the heavily soiled wrappings from the suppurating ulcers on the King's legs.

'I fear this may hurt, Your Majesty,' she warned. The dressings had adhered to the wound.

'I know. It always does.' He clenched his fists as she applied water and eased the cloth away.

'You are being very brave, as befits a King of England,' she said. 'I shall be as gentle as I can.'

'Being the King can get wearisome at times,' he murmured. 'I'm a lonely man, sweetheart.'

'But you are surrounded with the cream of society,' she protested, talking as she worked on his leg. 'My life has been so ordinary by comparison. After my father was killed my mother was forced to flee and take refuge in the nunnery, and that is where I grew up. I had lived nowhere else until a short time ago, when my mother died and my uncle sent for me.'

'Your mother was forced to flee?' he questioned. 'What do you mean by that?'

'My poor mother went through a terrible time. My father was killed in battle in France. I believe your army was advancing on Paris—'

'Ah, yes!' said Henry. 'I had hopes of capturing the French crown. We should have gone on. I believe to this day we could have won—I was misled by Wolsey.'

The young nobleman returned, bearing a tray on which were all the medicaments Meg had asked for, and more besides. She checked them over and was satisfied.

'Do you require any assistance, Lady Meg?' he asked.

'Nothing, thank you. You may go.' She spoke sharply and waved him away, embarrassed by his stare. Then immediately turned her attention back to the King.

'You were telling me about the march on Paris, sire,' she said.

'It's as clear to me as if it was yesterday,' he mused. 'Some of my men were caught in a trap, ambushed. Your father was there, you say?'

'I believe so. It was months before my mother received news of him. She was told that he died instantly, without suffering. An arrow pierced his heart. I have thought about him often and wished that I had known him.'

'Your father's name?'

'Lionel, Earl Thurton.' She pronounced it with pride.

'Of Bixholm?'

'Most certainly Bixholm was his. Edmund, my uncle, is his younger brother. The title passed to him on the death of my father, but Edmund was not satisfied with that. He claimed the whole of the estate as well.'

With deft fingers and the lightest of touches she spread a cooling ointment on the wound. The King lay back, more relaxed now—in discomfort, perhaps, but no longer in pain. Their conversation was distracting him.

'My father was with Your Majesty on that magnificent gathering they call the Field of the Cloth of Gold.'

'Of course! I remember him!' exclaimed Henry. 'One of my most honourable and brave commanders in the field. I looked on him as a friend. But how was it that your mother did not continue to live at Bixholm? Surely that was her right?'

'My uncle was determined to take possession of all,' Meg said. 'He threatened her, and she knew him to be utterly ruthless. Whenever my father was absent, Uncle Edmund took charge of the estate. He spent money carelessly and caused problems among the tenantry. He is a cruel man.'

'Very different from his brother,' Henry said. 'It is obvious that you and your mother have been severely wronged. I shall instruct my lawyers to look into the case.'

'That is exceedingly kind, Your Majesty,' said Meg. She paused thoughtfully and looked up into Henry's big, square face as she added, not entirely without guile, 'And he has lied to you.'

'Lied to me? How is that?' His voice was sharp and angry.

'You kindly enquired about Sir Richard de Heigham, the gentleman with whom I danced.'

'Yes?'

'It is not true that he has returned to Bixholm. My uncle has him here, locked in the dungeon in truly appalling conditions.' Her voice shook a little, for Richard's desperate plight haunted her vividly.

'What charges have been made against him?' His searching question reminded her that the King was no fool.

'None. Sir Richard has behaved entirely honourably and he is one of Your Majesty's most loyal subjects.'

She spoke guardedly, mindful that Henry would be angered if he suspected that Richard had already captured her heart. The word 'treason' was bandied about easily. This was no ordinary man who was lying back so trustingly as she practised her medical expertise on his painful legs. He had power over life and death and did not hesitate to use it. She had to attend to her task calmly, as if she had no other thought in her mind.

'There, Your Majesty. That's the worst of it seen to. Does it feel easier?'

'It does, my dear. Much better.'

She began to wind on the clean bandage. He startled her with another probing question.

'What is this man to you, Meg?'

'Sir Richard?' she asked, trying to sound as if she had forgotten what they were talking about.

'Yes. Richard de Heigham,' he said dryly.

'Why, he means nothing to me. Nothing at all. I was only interested because he has suffered in the same way I have. By right this castle, Leet Castle, is his. He too was cheated out of his inheritance by Edmund Thurton.'

'Have you proof of this?'

'He has told me himself.' She went on to explain the circumstances as Richard had told her. 'It is one of the reasons he has been incarcerated in the dungeon.'

'You mean Thurton's had de Heigham falsely arrested?' Henry's voice was angry.

'That is so,' Meg said.

'The devil he has! I need de Heigham to lead the hunting party I've planned for tomorrow. How dare he imprison my loyal subjects and claim ownership of estates he has no right to? He shan't get away with this.'

Henry reached up to pull the bell-rope that hung from the head of the big bed. The young nobleman was back instantly.

'Yes, Your Majesty?'

'Send my Officer of the Guard in to me.'

Within seconds the officer appeared.

'Arrest Edmund Thurton. Take him to the dungeon. And whilst you are there, release Richard de Heigham.'

'Yes, sire. It shall be done.'

'Go, then. See to it.' Henry waved the officer away.

He sank back on to the pillow. The dressings were finished. 'There, sweetheart,' he said. 'Does that please you?'

She dared not express her joy openly. 'I have always been told you are a good and just King,' she said. 'Now I know that to be true.'

Her most cherished wish had been fulfilled: Richard would be freed. It was wonderful to think that she had been able to save him—but at what cost to herself? He had no love for her. He had made that abundantly clear. She had given her heart to him wholly and irrevocably, but he had no real and lasting affection for her. She had provided a pleasant diversion for him, but the magic that was love had not bitten deep into him. For her it was more than life itself.

A great weariness came over her. She cleared away the bowls and soiled dressings, burned sprigs of lavender in the candle flame to sweeten the air. Blood had spilled on to her nightgown. The stain would never wash out, but she would throw the garment away. She mixed a sedative for Henry. He took it as obediently as a child, gave a long drawn-out sigh and lay back on the pillows.

'Sweet Meg, you have been very good to me,' he murmured.

'It was my pleasure to be of assistance, Your Majesty.'

'These accursed legs! They spoil my life,' he grumbled. He reached out for her hand. 'I must apologise to you, sweetheart.'

'But there is nothing for you to apologise for, sire.'

'There is! There is!' He sounded angry and exasperated. 'I should have made love to you properly and I didn't! I couldn't—though I wanted to.'

'Hush,' she said soothingly. ''Tis no matter.' She patted his hand in a friendly fashion. He must never know that she was grateful it was so.

'Now I fear it is too late,' he murmured. 'That sedative is making me sleepy.'

'You must rest, sire.'

'Will you not call me Henry, sweetheart?' he said.

'Most willingly, if it is your wish, Henry.'

'Stay with me,' he murmured. 'Come back into my bed. Give me one more of your sweet kisses.'

She obeyed and kissed him lightly, with gratitude in her heart. It was warm in the bed beside him. She felt safe. Briefly he cuddled her in his arms.

'Goodnight, Henry,' she whispered.

He snored gently and did not reply.

She did not expect to sleep, but it was morning when she awoke.

Taking care not to disturb the King, she slid off the bed, picked up her shawl and wrapped it around her. She wished it was larger as she tried to hide within it. In particular she tried to hold it over the stain of dried blood on her nightgown. She told herself she had done nothing about which she should feel ashamed, yet that feeling was uppermost in her mind as she hurried out of his bed-chamber.

Several gentlemen were gathered in the ante-room. They were grouped along each side of the room, leaving empty a corridor down the centre. She ignored their lascivious and curious stares; pride came to her aid. She would not allow them to demean her, for she knew herself to be as good as any. Lifting her head, she stepped out with determination, her eyes fixed straight ahead, making for the door at the opposite end.

Before she reached it a familiar figure stepped forward in front of her. Tall, broad-shouldered, carrying himself with a swagger, richly clad in a fustian doublet. Dark eyes flecked with gold were focused on her—she knew them so well—

'Richard!' she exclaimed, raising her arms slightly, accidentally moving the shawl.

His lip curled with scorn. 'They told me the King's new mistress was with him.' His gaze dropped to the stain visible on her nightgown. 'I didn't for one moment think it would be you!'

Tears filled her eyes. How could she explain? She had spent the night in bed with the King—she could not deny it. If Richard had been alone, she might have tried to make him understand, but there were too many interested onlookers. Humiliated, defeated, she would not even make the attempt.

'I am pleased you've been released, Richard.'

She longed to tell him she had interceded on his behalf, but could not. His mood suggested that any explanation she made would be misunderstood, even if he believed her. The coldness of his face cut her to the quick.

'It was on the King's orders,' he said. 'I'm waiting here to convey my thanks and reaffirm my loyalty to His Majesty.'

'As indeed you should,' she said.

'I'm told he fancies another day's hunting.'

'I wish you joy of it. Please be so good as to allow me to pass. It is cold and I have no slippers.'

Without another word he stepped aside. She did not look into his face. She could not bear to read the condemnation she was sure must be expressed there. She assumed an appearance of calm as she proceeded through the second ante-room, then ran along the passages until she reached the door of her own bedchamber.

Sarah was huddled in a chair, wide awake, misery pulling down the corners of her mouth. She had been crying; her eyes were puffy and reddened. At the sight of Meg she sprang to her feet and regardless of decorum flung herself into her mistress's arms.

'Oh, my lady. My dear, dear lady!'

'Hush, Sarah. It is all right. I have suffered no harm.'

She broke off. Sarah had noticed the bloodstain on her nightgown. Shock registered on her expressive, open face.

'It's not what you think, Sarah,' Meg said hastily. 'It's the King's blood—'

'The King's blood! Oh, my God! What have you done? If you took a knife to the brute it'd be no more than he deserved. I'll say I did it, to protect you—'

'Hush, Sarah. I haven't harmed His Majesty. He's not a well man. He has the most awful ulcers on his legs. They were painful so I cleaned them and renewed the dressings, and that is the only reason I have blood on my nightgown.'

'He did not use you ill, my lady?' Sarah persisted anxiously.

'Truly, Sarah dear, it was only a matter of a few kisses, and as I was attending to his poor legs I talked about my family and about Richard, and then His Majesty did something wonderful. He sent the Officer of his Guard to arrest my uncle and he has ordered the release of Sir Richard.'

'Well! I never did!' exclaimed Sarah.

'Isn't—isn't it—wonderful?' Meg said, and her voice broke and tears began to run down her face.

It wasn't entirely wonderful. Her uncle would no longer be able to threaten her and force her to marry the King. An enormous burden had been lifted and Bix- holm would be hers again—but she had lost Richard.

'Oh, my lady! You poor sweet thing! Whatever am I thinking about? You must be tired out—won't you lie down?'

'I'm not tired, Sarah. Just a little overwrought, per- haps. I have slept, but it has been such an extraordinary night.'

'Of course it has,' Sarah said soothingly. 'And I know you've conducted yourself bravely, as you always do.' She paused, and a look of joyous wonderment lit her face. 'Is it really true that the King's had the Earl thrown into the dungeon?'

'It is.'

'Whoopee!' The yell of celebration that burst from Sarah's mouth was matched by the beaming grin that spread over her round, red face. 'Oh, I haven't been so happy for years! I hope that Nancy woman's been thrown in along with him!'

'I don't know—' Meg began.

'I'll go and find out,' Sarah volunteered. 'I haven't been out of this room since they took you away, so I've no idea what's been afoot. You sit down there, my lady. I'll have a word with them that work in the kitchen. They'll know! They allus do! An' while I'm there I'll fetch refreshment for you, and maybe hot water—'

'Yes, please, Sarah. I feel much in need of a really good wash.'

Sarah hovered uncertainly, suddenly serious. 'You're sure you'll be all right?'

Meg reassured her with a smile and a nod.

'I'll be quick as I can.' Sarah chuckled. 'I can't stop a-laughin'. Won't it make a change if that old bully's gettin' a bit of his own medicine?' She hurried away in great glee.

Meg sat by the window, but for once she had no interest in looking out. Richard's disapproving face remained etched on her inner eye. His expression had told her so clearly that he had lost all respect for her. He had not loved her when he had believed her to be a good woman; from now on she could expect nothing from him. It would be a waste of breath even to try— and she was far too proud to plead for his understanding. He had no idea of the pressure she had been under to go to Henry's bed-chamber, and she would never tell him.

It was over. Finished. She would start a new life at Bixholm. When she'd left Norwich she had been eager to get away from the religious life. Now she had experienced the hazards, the greed, the superficiality that dominated high society, she felt drawn towards a quieter, more contemplative existence. Not to return to the nunnery; she didn't want that even if it were possible. But perhaps she could use Bixholm for some charitable purpose. Surround herself with other women who had been wronged in some way.

Since the closure of the great ecclesiastical buildings there were hundreds of impoverished people without homes or hope. She would assist ladies like her own dear mother, allow them to live good and useful lives, but without self-denial and with pleasures and companionship.

The idea was only vaguely taking shape in her mind. She had to find something to fill the void where once Richard had been. She would never marry, never have children; she was certain of that. Instead she would fill her days with good works.

Chapter Seventeen

Meg wondered what was being said about her in the kitchens, but thought it best not to ask. What could anyone think? She had no illusions. The whole household must know she had spent the night in the King's bedchamber, and no one would believe in her innocence after that.

When Sarah returned she was accompanied by other serving wenches carrying buckets of water.

'It's true, my lady.' She grinned. 'The Earl's been locked up, just as you said.'

'Best news I've heard all year,' said one of the wenches.

Whatever they thought about Meg, the talk was only of how the Earl had been arrested and frog-marched across the courtyard and thrown into the dungeon. Everyone rejoiced over that, and also over Sir Richard's release.

Sarah supervised the girls as they poured water into a large bowl, then shooed them out of the room.

She assisted Meg to bathe, chatting as she did so. 'There's happiness all over the castle,' she said. 'Even some of the men who came with Thurton say they pre-fer to serve under Sir Richard.'

Sarah talked on as Meg began her breakfast. It was rumoured that Captain Bennington would be returning soon, with a party of loyal men. They had left Leet on Richard's instructions the day that Thurton arrived and had lived rough in the woods, ready to attack when the time was right. The presence of the King had prevented that.

Nancy was staying in her room, refusing to see any-one except Gervase Gisbon. That didn't cause much surprise, and absolutely no concern. They were pow-erless—and likely to drink themselves into an early grave, judging by the quantity of wine they had ordered.

'Is there any word about Alan?' Meg asked hope-fully.

'Nothing at all.' Sarah shook her head sadly. 'I've no idea what's happened to him. There was a rumour that he'd been seen a few days ago. But he's not sent any word to me.'

'He would have if it was possible,' Meg said.

'Aye. There was a time when I believed that,' Sarah said. 'Now I don't know what to think. I don't even know if he's alive or dead.'

'You mustn't give up hope, Sarah,' Meg said.

Tears welled in Sarah's eyes. She turned to the win-dow and wiped them away on her sleeve. Meg's heart was heavy for her, suffering and bravely hiding the pain. At least she knew Richard was alive and well.

'Looks as if they're gettin' ready for a hunt,' Sarah remarked. 'They're bringing out horses an' dogs, an' the verderers are there.'

'The King ordered it,' Meg said.

She remained seated at the table. She pushed the tray

aside and brought out a sheet of writing paper and a quill pen. This was not going to be an easy letter to write, but she must attempt to make peace with the King. She could not bear to go through another night like the last one. Was it possible to make him understand without offending him? She was scared of awakening his wrath, and that would be difficult to contain.

Sarah was still gazing out of the window. 'Your Sir Richard is down there,' she said. 'Looking fine and handsome. Do come and see him, my lady.'

'He means nothing to me.' Meg's voice was hard.

Sarah swung round. Her face expressed concern and disbelief.

'He doesn't love me,' Meg said. 'I've known that for a long time, and this morning he made his feelings absolutely clear.'

'Oh! My lady!'

'I am no longer troubled about it,' Meg lied. 'I've decided to take up residence at Bixholm. There may be a few legalities to be settled, but I won't wait for that. I shall leave here today.'

'Remember what happened last time we rode off,' Sarah said.

'I remember very well,' Meg admitted. 'This time I shall take retainers, armed men to counter any attacks. You say Captain Bennington has returned to the castle?'

'So I was told,' Sarah said. She turned back to the window. 'There's the King comin' out now. They said he woke up this mornin' in the best mood anyone's seen him in for weeks—laughin' an' jokin' with everybody.'

Meg said nothing.

Sarah turned back to the window. 'What a size of a man he is! Can't hardly walk. It's takin' three men to get him up on his horse. You ought to see this.'

Meg had seen enough of the King. She began her letter.

I commend myself to the kind heart of Your Most Gracious Majesty. I beg forgiveness that I shall be unable to speak my farewells to you in person.

'He's up!' Sarah exclaimed. 'Makes you feel sorry for the horse, don't it? Sir Richard's comin' up alongside the King. They'll be off in a minute.'

'Good,' said Meg, without moving. Her refusal to take one final look at Richard was not caused by indifference. It would be like tearing her heart out of her body to watch him ride away and know that would be the last time she would ever see him.

The horns rang out. The sound of hooves and harness, baying hounds, men's voices reached her through the open window.

'They're away,' Sarah said.

Meg turned back to her task.

I am humbly honoured by the interest you have taken in me, and the kindness you have shown. I am also greatly indebted for your intercession on my behalf with regard to the estate at Bixholm.

'Shall I clear away, my lady?' asked Sarah.

'Please do. Oh, and Sarah, if you can find Captain Bennington, will you ask him to come and see me, please?'

'Aye.' Sarah lifted the tray and moved away. She paused in the doorway. 'Do we have to go today, my lady?' she asked.

'I have to go today, Sarah. I'm sorry it has to be so, but I have my own special reasons. You need not accompany me.'

'Don't never learn, do you, my lady? Where you go, I go too.' She flounced out of the room, closing the door behind her with a kick.

Meg gave a wry smile. Dear Sarah! What would she do without her? She dipped her pen into the ink and carried on with her letter.

Now that ownership of this has been restored to me, I feel I have a duty to return there immediately so that I may attend to those duties incumbent upon landowners. Furthermore I have recently felt a strong desire to return to a life more in keeping with that of my early years. Indeed I have a calling to immerse myself in charitable works. I implore Your Majesty to accept my most loyal and affectionate wishes.

I remain, with the profoundest veneration, Your Majesty's most faithful subject and devoted servant. Meg.

She read the letter through and worried over it—could she have put it better? Would the King understand? Was she being too bold in writing at all? But what else could she do? She blessed the fact that she had received a good education at the nunnery, conscious that most women were incapable even of writing their own names. It would have to do. She folded it and tied it with a ribbon.

Sarah returned, escorting Captain Bennington. She stood back, with arms akimbo and a defiant air.

Meg greeted the Captain warmly. 'I trust you are well?'

'In the best of health, thank you, my lady. Greatly heartened by the news of Sir Richard's release and Thurton's arrest.'

'Pleasing events indeed.' Meg smiled. 'Perhaps you also know that ownership of Bixholm has reverted to me?'

'Another welcome piece of news,' he said.

'Since that is so, I wish to return there immediately.'

'Immediately?' he questioned.

'Yes. I wish to set out today, and I shall require protection on the journey. I hope that you will agree to accompany me, Captain, together with such other men as are required.'

'It will be my pleasure, my lady. But would it not be preferable to postpone your departure until tomorrow, when we could set out early in the morning—?'

'No. I have special reasons for leaving today.'

'Does Sir Richard know of your intention, my lady?'

'He does not, and I have no need to inform him. He is not my guardian,' she said. 'I shall leave before the hunting party returns, travel as far as possible, then find accommodation for the night. Are you willing to accompany me?'

'Your wish is my command. How soon can you be ready?'

'There is little I need to take with me. Shall we say in half an hour?'

'Certainly.'

'Sarah will accompany me. Please have two good horses saddled for us.' Meg paused. 'One more thing. I have written a letter to His Majesty—can you arrange to have it safely delivered?'

'It shall be done.' The Captain bowed and withdrew.

The journey to Bixholm was uneventful. In the late afternoon of the second day the two towers of the gatehouse came in sight. Meg heaved a sigh, recalling how Richard had brought her here, and her feelings then, her hopes and her fears. So much had happened. She reined in her horse and sat for a moment, looking over the spread of red-tiled roofs and the tall twisted chimneys. The summer had all but passed; soon it would be time to have fires constantly lit in the rooms—but how lonely it would be!

Would it have been better if she had never left Norwich? If she had never met Richard? She heaved a sigh. The wounds of her loss were fresh and raw. Perhaps, when she was an old, old lady, she would find some pleasure in looking back on this interlude. Now, only empty days lay before her. Her grand talk of opening the house in some charitable manner gave her no glow. She would do it, because she had to do something with her life, but she would never regain her joy in living.

'My lady—are you all right?'

Sarah brought her horse up alongside Meg. Captain Bennington and his men waited, some ahead, others a little behind.

'Yes, I'm all right. Just thinking.'

'I know. I am too,' said Sarah.

They looked at each other. Meg reached out her hand and Sarah put hers into it. There was no need for words. They shared each other's anguish.

'Let's ride on,' said Meg.

A wild yell reached them from behind. Everyone was alerted. Captain Bennington wheeled his horse. Two horsemen were coming at breakneck speed. Surely no one would attack them so close to the castle! The Captain and half a dozen of his men spurred their horses forward, ready to meet whatever trouble was approaching.

Meg strained her eyes, unable to believe what she saw.

'Alan,' cried Sarah. She spurred her horse forward and galloped wildly to meet the riders.

'Richard,' Meg whispered.

Why had he come? She saw Sarah and Alan stop alongside each other. In moments they were off their mounts and clasping each other. Richard rode on. She studied his face as he came nearer, handsome as ever, set in serious lines. He reined in and walked his horse the last few yards.

'Forgive me,' he said.

A shaft of hope lifted her heart, but she said nothing. He dismounted, tossed the reins to one of the men and approached her on foot. Then he reached up both arms to her. 'Please, Meg. I didn't know.'

Those golden flecks seemed to dance in his deep brown eyes. How could she refuse the invitation that was in them, in his outstretched arms? Still she hesitated.

'Meg—I love you,' he pleaded.

She slipped from the saddle and he caught her and held her close, very tenderly. Emotion made tears well up and pour down her cheeks.

'Don't cry, Meg. Please don't cry—I didn't mean to upset you. I'm so sorry for those dreadful things I said; I should have been more understanding.'

'I didn't—didn't—with the King,' she spluttered.

'I know. He told me. He's very fond of you.'

'Did he send you to fetch me?' As the horrific thought came she began to struggle. 'I won't go back to him. Let me go—' She tried to get out of his arms, but he held her tighter.

'Hush, Meg. That's over. The King has been called back to London. They have a portrait of a Dutch lady, called Anne of Cleves. A marriage is being arranged. His Majesty rode off this morning.'

'He didn't ask for me?' She was still fearful.

'He said you wrote him a letter. He asked me to give you this as a token of his esteem.' Richard released his hold on her and took a ring from his pocket. She stepped back as he placed it in her palm. A narrow gold band in which was set one large emerald surrounded by several smaller stones.

'It's beautiful,' she murmured, doubtful whether it was right to accept it.

'He wished to give you something to remember him by. He thinks highly of you.' He paused, then continued, with the familiar authoritative note ringing in his voice. 'Enough of him, Meg. I rode after you, travelling day and night, on my behalf, not the King's.'

Could it really be true—when he said he loved her?

Sarah's voice interrupted. 'Oh, my lady, isn't this a wonderful day?'

Alan brought his horse up alongside them. He was leading Sarah's mare and she was seated gracefully, side-saddle, in front of him. Happiness glowed on both faces.

'I'm very happy to see you safe and well, Alan. Sarah has been so worried—'

'No need to tell him that,' her maid protested. 'Make him big-headed.'

They did not linger long. She envied them; they had never had cause to doubt each other.

Richard said, quite humbly, 'There are things I need to say, Meg. Will you walk with me?'

She regarded him steadily, more in control of herself now.

'If you wish it.'

She remained cautious, uncertain of his motives. The more so as she found his presence irresistible. It was impossible to deny the love she felt for him; it throbbed in the air between them. The sight of him filled her with joy. She could no more resist him than she could stop breathing. But did he really care?

He called to the men to take their horses, to see them rubbed down, fed and stabled. As they trotted away she would have followed, but Richard caught hold of her hand, stopping her. He pulled her round to face him, clasped her again in his arms and kissed her.

'I love you, Meg. I can say it at last. I love you. You must have guessed but I dared not speak aloud. I had a plan to steal you out of their clutches and carry you away.'

Surprised, she drew back. 'You didn't say.'

'I couldn't. If Thurton or Nancy had known what was in my mind, they would have disposed of me within minutes.' He lifted her hand and kissed it, then continued, 'I would have given my life for you, my dearest, but that would have served no purpose. Without me, you would have been even more vulnerable. No one else could have given you any protection. I hired a ship to take you to France. I have friends there who would have taken care of you. The ship was in London, waiting for the right tide, but before I could complete the arrangements you ran away.'

'I thought you didn't care,' Meg whispered.

'Didn't care! Meg, I think I've loved you since that day I first saw you, only then I didn't recognise the strength of my feelings. When I discovered you and Sarah had ridden off I nearly went out of my mind. Alan was no better.'

'Thank goodness you came and rescued us,' Meg said. 'But you gave me no hint—no hope.'

'I knew Thurton wouldn't give up,' Richard said. 'I instructed the skipper of the ship to sail to Harwich and wait there for word from me. I sent Alan ahead.'

'So that's why he disappeared!'

'The ship was held up by bad weather. He only returned yesterday, and by then everything was changed because you'd managed to get me released and Thurton thrown into the dungeon.'

'Now there's no need to run away any more,' Meg said. 'I shall live at Bixholm, and make it into a women's refuge—'

'So you told the King,' said Richard. 'But are you quite sure that's what you want to do?'

'Well—'

He placed one finger lightly on her lips. 'We can talk about that idea later, my darling. First I must ask—did you mean it, that evening in London, when you asked me to marry you?'

'Whatever did you think of me?' she prevaricated.

'I thought then, as I do now, that you are a wonderful woman. May I answer you as I wanted to then? Dearest Meg, I want to marry you more than anything in the world—if you will still have me.'

She gazed into his eyes, and saw anxiety there. She nodded. 'I will, Richard.'

She raised her arms and twined them around his neck, and his mouth swooped down and covered hers in a long, loving kiss. Sarah was right. This was a wonderful day.

Some time later, with their arms around each other, they strolled on and into the castle.

* * *

Two days later a double wedding took place in the little Saxon church within the grounds of Bixholm. Sir Richard de Heigham was married to Lady Margaret Thurton, and Alan Crompton to Sarah Wilgress. The feasting, dancing and singing in the Great Hall went on into the early hours of the next morning, long after the newly wedded couples had slipped away.

Meg delighted in taking charge of the household at Bixholm, and Richard immersed himself in the running of the estate. He appointed Alan as his steward to manage Leet.

'What shall I do about Thurton?' Alan asked, as he and Sarah were about to depart.

Richard consulted Meg. 'I am mindful that but for him, wicked though he is, I should never have met you, my darling. Shall we be generous and set him free?'

'An amnesty to celebrate our nuptials.' She smiled. 'Yes, so long as he never again sets foot on Bixholm or Leet land.'

Sarah and Meg were saddened at being separated, but took comfort that they were only two days' ride apart, and promised to send letters and messages back and forth whenever possible.

Before many months had passed Meg wrote to Sarah that she was with child, and Sarah replied that she also was expecting.

Meg continued to devote some of her time to helping the poor and needy, and became revered over the countryside for her skill with herbs and potions and her generous assistance to the sick. The people spoke of her with reverence as 'the lovely Lady Margaret'. A title with which Richard agreed wholeheartedly.

* * *

On Twelfth Night, 6th January 1540, the marriage took place between Henry VIII and Anne of Cleves. A sad event, for he never loved her. It was said the marriage was never consummated, and six months later it was dissolved, so that he could marry the young and lively Catherine Howard.

* * * * *

MILLS & BOON®

*M*akes any time special

Enjoy a romantic novel from
Mills & Boon®

Presents...™   *Enchanted*™   TEMPTATION.

Historical Romance™   **MEDICAL ROMANCE**™

MILLS & BOON®
Historical Romance™

THE SILVER SQUIRE
by Mary Brendan
A Regency delight! No. 2 of 4

Miss Emma Worthington was on the shelf, but even that
couldn't make her enter a bad marriage. It was bad
luck that her escape to Bath was thwarted by
Richard Du Quesne.

SATAN'S MARK
by Anne Herries
Restoration

Puritan Annelise Woodward is baffled by Justin Rochefort,
Marquis Saintjohn, but living with his mother brings them
into close contact—and a deepening attraction.

On sale from 3rd March 2000

*Available at most branches of WH Smith, Tesco,
Martins, Borders, Easons, Volume One/James Thin
and most good paperback bookshops*

0002/04

The Drifter

SUSAN WIGGS

"Susan Wiggs turns an able and sensual hand
to the...story of the capable, strait-laced
spinster and sensual roving rogue."
—Publishers Weekly

Available Now

M139

FREE!

2 Books
and a surprise gift!

We would like to take this opportunity to thank you for reading this Mills & Boon® book by offering you the chance to take TWO more specially selected titles from the Historical Romance™ series absolutely FREE! We're also making this offer to introduce you to the benefits of the Reader Service™—

- ★ FREE home delivery
- ★ FREE gifts and competitions
- ★ FREE monthly Newsletter
- ★ Books available before they're in the shops
- ★ Exclusive Reader Service discounts

Accepting these FREE books and gift places you under no obligation to buy; you may cancel at any time, even after receiving your free shipment. Simply complete your details below and return the entire page to the address below. *You don't even need a stamp!*

YES! Please send me 2 free Historical Romance books and a surprise gift. I understand that unless you hear from me, I will receive 4 superb new titles every month for just £2.99 each, postage and packing free. I am under no obligation to purchase any books and may cancel my subscription at any time. The free books and gift will be mine to keep in any case.

HOEB

Ms/Mrs/Miss/Mr ....Initials...............................
BLOCK CAPITALS PLEASE

Surname..

Address...

....

....Postcode ....

Send this whole page to:
UK: The Reader Service, FREEPOST CN81, Croydon, CR9 3WZ
EIRE: The Reader Service, PO Box 4546, Kilcock, County Kildare (stamp required)

Offer not valid to current Reader Service subscribers to this series. We reserve the right to refuse an application and applicants must be aged 18 years or over. Only one application per household. Terms and prices subject to change without notice. Offer expires 31st August 2000. As a result of this application, you may receive further offers from Harlequin Mills & Boon Limited and other carefully selected companies. If you would prefer not to share in this opportunity please write to The Data Manager at the address above.

Mills & Boon is a registered trademark owned by Harlequin Mills & Boon Limited.
Historical Romance is being used as a trademark.